HIS FORBIDDEN PRINCESS

VIVIAN WOOD

AUTHOR'S COPYRIGHT

Cover Design: *Veritas Covers*

Proofreader: *Jenn Allen*

I would just like to say a HUGE thank you to all my beta readers and my proofreaders.

Patrica, Kathy, Kym. *You ladies KILLED it this time around! You are essential. Thank you so, so much — for this and for listening to my neuroses.*

Jenn, Rachael, Antje, Belinda, Zsa Zsa. *You guys are so generous with your time! I owe you big time. Thank you!*

To my readers... thank you for reading! It means a lot to me.

HIS FORBIDDEN PRINCESS

1

ERIK

"For fuck's sake," I grumble to myself. "Tonight will never end."

My eyes travel over the crowd and to the ceiling of the event space; for the King's engagement announcement party, the ballroom has been decorated lavishly. The walls are adorned with trailing ivy and beautiful cascades of white blooms. Every table has a cluster of white flowers as the centerpiece. Waiters swish by me with trays of colorful cocktails named after Stellan and Margot. And overhead, a thousand glass orbs hang, each flickering with a white candle.

Everyone Stellan has ever known is packed into the large space, milling about and talking in little clumps. I notice a few waiters discreetly pulling discarded plates off tables. The time for eating has long since come and gone; soon Stellan and Margot will leave the party and then I can depart too.

Running a finger underneath my bowtie, I sigh. I can't wait for this royal party to be over so I can be anywhere but here.

I keep my eyes on Stellan's dark head, trying to gauge how much longer he will remain here. This party is to celebrate the announcement of his engagement to his beautiful pink-haired fiancée Margot. Right now, they stand in the middle of an adoring crowd looking like nothing so much as a wedding cake topper. Even now, I can see Stellan and Margot as they move through the crowd.

He's tall, dark, and handsome in his tuxedo. She's a tiny fairy of a person, pink-haired and wearing a pink dress. Her hand rests on his arm, his hand curls protectively around her waist. They keep looking at each other with these sneaky little grins. They are the center of their own blissful little universe.

And the way they gaze at each other and smile as they trade touches...

It makes me sort of wistful and a little bit jealous. I want someone to look at me the way that Margot looks at Stellan. I see hope and excitement and jubilance on her face.

It would be disgusting if it weren't so damn wholesome.

I'm over it. And this party... Everyone who is anyone here in Denmark turned out dressed to the nines, all to kiss the rings of the King and his future Queen.

Standing in the corner of the ballroom, I lean against the wall and clutch a tumbler of scotch. The expansive room is packed, everyone milling around, waiting for a chance to shake the new King Stellan's hand. Everywhere I look, symbols of opulent wealth are practically shoved down my throat.

The swish of expensive fabric. Men in their bespoke tuxedos, women in glittering ballgowns. Towering high heels, glittering jewelry, the floral scent of incredibly expensive perfume. The flush of young women when their randy husbands lean in to tell them just what's planned for their private afterparties.

There is unimaginable privilege is in this room tonight. Almost everyone present was just born into the lap of luxury. They've never had to struggle for a damn thing.

After so many years, it still makes me silently seethe.

I wasn't born to this life. I've lived it secondhand, mostly because King Stellan needed a confidante and I was deemed *good enough.*

As the newly crowned King's best friend and private secretary, I'm watching the crowd as they mix and mingle. Stellan has had his head in the clouds lately, living in an alternate reality from the rest of the world. One where his new fiancée Margot is his sun and stars… and everything else is just not worthy of his attention.

Stellan looks back at Margot, his expression enraptured. He isn't worried about anything else going on around him. But just because Stellan is on semi-permanent vacation from being the new king doesn't mean I get to slack off.

I drain the last of my glass and try not to look as bored as I feel.

Lars Løve comes ambling over to me, looking like a crooked photocopy of Stellan. He's Stellan's brother, one of the five Løve siblings. His dark hair is messy and a little too long. The collar of his tux is open at the throat, his bowtie nowhere to be seen. "There you are. We missed you at dinner."

Leaning over to a table, I set down my empty glass. "We?"

He squints. "You know. Me, Pippa… other people."

Pippa is his beautiful, elegant *will-they-or-won't-they* girl. It's always been that way, ever since he and the gorgeous redhead met in eighth grade.

I cast an eye over him. "I was in here, being lectured by Sarah from the royal press office. She didn't like it when I told her that Stellan was going to have to cut down his daily engagements."

Lars makes a face. "That sounds wretched."

I nod. "It was, mostly." Glancing around, my brow furrows. "Where's Pippa?"

He grunts. "Damned if I know. The last time I saw her, she was flirting with some loser in an overpriced tux."

I narrow my eyes at his comment. "Are you talking about yourself? Because you wear easily twenty thousand pounds more than anybody else in the room. You and all your siblings have that in common, my friend."

"Shut up. You act like you're not wearing a bespoke tux yourself." Lars snags a glass of champagne off a tray, sipping it coolly. He nods across the room to a group of people surrounding Stellan and Margot. "They seem very happy."

I look at Stellan, who keeps grinning at Margot like a total fool. It makes me happy for him, even as it turns my stomach.

That kind of love is not for me, just like so many aspects of Stellan's life. I'm the dutiful best friend, not actual royalty. That has been made crystal clear to me time and time again, ever since we were children.

"They do look happy," I say.

Lars's lips twitch. "So, do you think they will last?"

I look at him with a surprised expression. "Why would it not?"

He shrugs, pursing his lips. "It's just fast, that's all."

I roll my eyes. "Says the man that met the perfect girl before he was even in high school."

Lars frowns. "Pippa and I are friends. Nothing more than that."

I chuckle. "*Ja*, okay. Whatever you have to tell yourself. I've seen you two together, Lars."

He shoots me a glare. "My love life is private. I don't see you parading any new relationships around either, my friend."

My lips curve up. "No. I'm not Stellan. I'm the stable hand's son. I can't break the rules about class and date whoever I want. I can't just think that everything will be fine. I'm not royalty." My lips curl. "But I spend all my time with you lot, so I don't meet a ton of girls that are actually attainable."

His brows rise as he looks at me. "What does class have to do with anything? You're practically one of the royal family. I bet there are a dozen girls here tonight that would kill to get into your bed."

I press my lips together to avoid frowning. Instead of responding to that, I just look away. His comment was well-meant… but it was also naive. It just goes to show that he is definitely privileged in a way that few others could ever be.

A flash of movement catches my eye. A beautiful young blonde in an extravagant red ballgown storms into the room, her light blue eyes fixed on something out of my line of sight.

Annika.

I stare at her for a second, taking in her haughty posture and bright red lips. She's obscenely beautiful, with her waif-like figure and her elegantly pinned up hair.

The tiniest shudder runs through me.

It's important to remind myself that she's also Stellan's little sister, just nineteen years old. She makes me feel old and decrepit at twenty six. But my body and my brain are not on the same page here. They're not even reading the same book.

My body finds every little thing that Princess Annika does to be *extremely* attractive.

"Are you fucking serious?" Lars asks, interrupting my train of thought.

I tear my eyes away from Annika. "What?"

He slowly shakes his head and rakes his fingers through his messy dark hair. "You can't really think that ogling Annika openly is a good idea."

My neck heats. "What? No. I wasn't ogling her. I was just trying to see what she's throwing a fit about." I squint. "Probably some dramatic nonsense, knowing your sister."

Lars snorts. "I see your mouth moving, but I don't trust anything you're saying right now."

I roll my eyes. "Even if I found Annika the slightest bit attractive — which I don't — there are a thousand reasons why I would never, ever touch her. Not the least of which is Stellan." I squint into the distance.

He laughs. "No fucking kidding. That's pretty much the only reason I can think of, aside from you being way too old to date her."

I slide him a look. "There's also a great deal of income disparity between us."

Leaning against the wall, he sips his champagne. "She would find that with almost anyone she tries to date. And besides, aren't you some kind of secret day trading wizard? Last time we talked about it, you were making the stock market your bitch."

My lips twitch. "I shouldn't have told you that. I was drunk, as I remember."

Annika materializes, eyeing both of us as she stalks over. I push off the wall, straightening.

Lars gives me a look out of the corner of his eye. I button my tuxedo jacket as Annika arrives, looking flushed.

"Ugh!" she declares, looking around. She flags down a waiter and grabs a glass of champagne. "Momse is such a piece of work."

I clear my throat, looking over at Lars. He seems unconcerned by Annika's complaint, sipping his drink. So, I step in.

"What happened now?"

Annika flaps her hand impatiently. "Nothing. I just had an argument with Momse. It's so ridiculous."

She's referring to the Queen Mother, or Momse for short. The Queen Mother is the one that pulls all the strings in this royal Danish puppet show. Her son, the former king, and her daughter-in-law are...

What's a polite way to say that they've never shown much aptitude for parenting their five children? Maybe... disinclined to be in the state of Denmark, much less spend any time with Stellan and his siblings?

That still sounds harsh but it's true.

"What did the old girl do now?" Lars asks.

Annika's mouth turns down. "She says that I have to figure out what I'm doing with my life. And I'm like..." She makes a strangled gesture. "I'm *trying*. Momse is always in such a hurry to make decisions. God."

She finishes her statement by swallowing half her glass of wine.

"Easy with the champagne, Nika," Lars says, surveying her critically. "You're toeing the line with Momse as it is. The last thing you need is to get drunk and misbehave while at an event like this. The place is packed with the press. And we both know that the press already has you pegged as a troublemaker."

She makes a wounded sound, scrunching up her face. "I thought you would be on my side, Lars."

He pushes off the wall with a shrug. "I'm on my own side. Always have been, always will be."

With that, he strolls off toward the door. I catch a glimpse of bright red hair moving out of the ballroom; he must be going after Pippa.

Annika puts her hand on her hip and shakes her head at him. Then she makes a moue of displeasure as she looks me up and down. "Isn't it past your bedtime, old man?"

I glare at her, checking my watch. "I'm here for as long as your brother is here, little girl. I go wherever he goes. I'm hoping that he'll leave soon… but I've already heard whispers of an afterparty."

She looks at Stellan, tilting her head thoughtfully. "Stellan is pretty damn victorious tonight. I can't believe my big brother is engaged."

I slide her a glance. "No?"

She shrugs. "I mean, it's not like Stellan and I are very close. I've only been back from Swiss boarding school for a year. Stellan always looks surprised to see me, like he forgot that I was here or something. But still." She scrunches up her face. "I have to say, I do like Margot."

I tug on my tie. "Yes. She's very… American. Very brash. But she's a good egg anyway."

She makes a face at me. "What will you do once my brother gets married? Huh? That's sure to open up a lot of free time."

My neck heats. I cock my head. "Oh, Annika. The things you say. You have truly been a shining gem since you've returned from boarding school."

Her lips twitch, her eyes on me. "I'm so glad I can perform that service for you. Really fill a niche. You must love me for that."

My lips curve upwards even as my eyes narrow on her face. "You are a brat, Annika."

She runs her fingers around the rim of her champagne flute, her eyes sparkling and sparking. "So, I've been told. I wonder, will you take me over your knee and spank me?"

My expression goes from shocked to disapproving almost instantly. "Annika, what the fuck!"

She dips her fingertip into her wine, then pops it in her mouth, sucking off the remnants. "What? You can admit it to me right now. There is no one listening."

Shaking my head, I give her a baffled face. "Admit what?"

She arches a brow. "That you totally want to sleep with me."

"What?!" I ask, my voice choked. "Annika, I could never… *That's unthinkable*. And I don't want you to go around telling people that, either."

She gives me a pout. "Ouch. It's lucky that I realize that you're full of shit." She grins. "Everyone wants me. Or a facsimile of who they think that I am." She rolls her eyes. "Haven't you heard? I'm the only princess and I'm almost old enough to marry. The boys flock around me like bees swarm around a rose."

My fists clench. "You are so full of yourself, Annika. Christ."

She blushes but keeps grinning. "Nah, not really. I just like to goad you because it gets you all tongue tied. Nobody else sees my wicked side."

Shaking my head, I adjust my stance. "Lucky me."

"I know, right?" Annika winks and then looks over her shoulder. "I don't see Stellan… I think I'm going to leave."

Arching a brow, I cross my arms. "What, you have somewhere better to be?"

She turns, pinning me with her gaze. "Wouldn't you like to know." She lifts up her voluminous skirts and tosses her head. "Goodnight, Erik."

And with that, she heads out of the ballroom, strutting like she's on a runway. I stare at her retreating figure, wondering why I find her so compelling.

She's too young, too wealthy, too privileged… and that's not even counting the fact that her brother is my best friend. She is the very definition of taboo and off-limits.

I heave a sigh and start searching the crowd for Stellan.

2

———

ANNIKA

I LOOK OUT THE REAR WINDOW OF THE CHAUFFEURED CAR, pressing a hand to the cool glass of the window. The sun has slunk behind the horizon now and the last rays of light are slowly disappearing on this June night. I stare at the bright flashes of Copenhagen's stately skyline as we drive.

As the manor comes into view, I gaze at it out the window. My eyes widen as the car swings around the long, perfectly landscaped driveway. Every light is on in the house, every door thrown open. There are people spilling out of the house and across the lawn.

Straining to look out the window, I can hear the techno being pumped through the unseen sound system. I start laughing, looking over at my best friend Kalindi. She glances at the looming mansion, tucking a few strands of her long, shiny, black-brown hair behind her ear. A blush creeps into her cheeks, pink tinging her tawny skin just in the apples of her cheeks.

"I can't believe that Stellan sent us here," she mutters. Her accent is a melting pot of cultures: a little Indian, overlaid with British and Swiss, and finally finished off with just a dash of Danish. She turns her head to look at me. "Annika, are you listening to me?"

I wiggle my eyebrows at her. "Yes. You were saying that you are surprised that my big brother is supporting this enormous party. And my response is that it's a whole new world out there. Stellan and Margot just told us as much by announcing their engagement tonight."

She frowns just a bit. "Surely you support their marriage. Even though Margot is an American and a *commoner*." She makes a sound of distaste. "I actually hate that term. It's rather colonial, isn't it?"

I sigh. "I have no problem with them. Margot is nicer than most of the girls who tried to date Stellan. And I have to love her fire." I smooth out my skirt. "I'm just apprehensive about the press. They've been following me absolutely everywhere lately. If the paparazzi get one more photo of me that they can splash across the headlines of their papers, the royal press office may have a collective heart attack."

She wrinkles her nose daintily. "We don't have to go to this party, Nika. I mean… it is totally okay to tap out after… you know…"

My cheeks go pink and I look down into my lap. "My latest and greatest brush with being admitted to a psychiatric ward?"

"Well… yes," she admits. "The doctors said that you just had a panic attack but…" She grabs my hand, looking at me with serious eyes. "I was there, Nika. And it was scary. You never had panic attacks before we came back to Copenhagen.

Playing the royal princess and having the spotlight on you isn't doing you any favors."

I sigh, squeezing her hand. "Kal, you are sweet to worry. But I feel fine. I just…" I look out the window again, biting my lower lip. "I need to stay out of the newspapers. Stellan asked me to 'cool it' until the wedding so…"

She nods. "Got it. We should be able to stay off their radar." She turns to look out the window, eyeing the scene with some skepticism. "I mean, this mansion looks like someone's house."

I lean forward, excited. "This afterparty is going to be wild. I doubt if Stellan even knew that, because he's such a fun vampire. This night just got interesting."

Kalindi looks at me, scrunching her nose as the driver pulls the car to a halt. "I hate it when you say that. It inevitably turns out insane rather than interesting."

I grin, opening my door. Loud music pours into the car, thudding so hard that I can feel it in my bones. "Come on!"

I scoot out, straightening my white linen dress. It's super short and strappy, showing a rather daring amount of cleavage.

Well, what little I have, anyway.

"Princess Annika!" A couple of giggling teenaged girls call to me. "Can we have your autograph? Please?"

They wave a piece of paper and a pen in front of my face. I take a deep breath, then give them my most dazzling smile. "Of course. Tell me your names!"

One girl squeals. The other tells me their names.

"Sofia and Agnes," she says. "I don't have the words to tell you how much this means to me. God, I have to call my mother and tell her. She'll be so jealous that I got to meet you!"

I shift from foot to foot, my perfect princess smile unwavering. "*Tak*, ladies. It is awfully nice to meet you as well."

I spend a full minute chatting with them and signing their piece of paper. When we're done, they run off into the deepening darkness, excited beyond words.

Kalindi favors me with a look. "You are so nice to everyone you meet. If I were you and I were accosted here, I would tell them to take a hike."

I roll my eyes. "It's a part of my job, Kal."

"Is it?" she asks. "Have you figured out what you're doing with your life, other than being an actual princess?"

My mouth pulls down. "No. I haven't, thank you very much. Now if you don't mind… there's all kinds of excitement waiting right here."

I squint out at the party raging in front of us. The mansion itself is quaint, red brick and covered in ivy. There are probably nearly a hundred party guests on the lawn alone, drinking and talking, tapping a keg in the far corner. The front door is open like a hungry mouth, inviting us in.

I grab Kalindi by the hand and halfway drag her up across the manicured lawn. She allows it too, her free hand fluttering over her conservative, preppy outfit. Her white blouse is tucked into a light blue skirt, topped off with a herringbone tweed jacket.

I slide her a look as we climb the steps of the front porch. "Expecting to see someone?"

She looks at me, blushing. "No." I narrow my gaze at her, and she lifts her chin. "I'm not. I'm just… being prepared. You should try it some time."

I grin, pulling her deeper inside the house.

Taking a deep breath, I reach in my purse for a piece of hard candy wrapped in a shiny gold colored wrapper. I pop it in my mouth and let it start to melt onto my tongue. The creamy toffee flavor instantly brightens my mood.

I can admit it; I'm more than a little addicted to these hard candies. And because they are low in sugar, I pop four or five of them in my mouth a day. Just whenever I need a little boost.

Once we get past the doorway everything is harder to make out. If there are any lights on in here, I don't see them; I continue straight down the main hallway, bumping into at least a dozen people, squeezing past a whole clump of girls gathered at the foot of the grand staircase.

Once we are past them, we make it into the kitchen. There I find Stellan and Margot, holding court in one corner, leaning against the kitchen counter. A dozen people I don't recognize are gathered around them. The music is a fraction quieter in here, so when Stellan sees me, he raises a plastic cup.

"Annika is here!" he calls.

My lips twitch. He and Margot are clearly drunk; poor little Margot doesn't look like she can stand on her own. It's a little cute how she leans on Stellan. She looks at my ridiculously hardheaded brother like he's the reason for her very existence. He slips his arm around her and pulls her closer.

I roll my eyes and ignore their handsy, drunken PDA. "Kalindi is here too. Where can we get something to drink?"

Margot hiccups. "Can someone please give them some punch?"

Just like that, we are each handed a plastic cup filled with a dark red punch. Kalindi looks into her cup with a frown. But I'm not put off by the alcohol and fruit scents floating up off of the cup's contents.

"To Stellan and Margot!" I cry, lifting my cup.

Everyone cheers. I take a sip, wincing a little bit. It tastes just like it smells, a ton of fruit flavors layered with a lot of aquavit.

Kalindi tries some and coughs a little, her free hand moving up to cover her mouth. "What is in this?!"

I grin at her. "Bottoms up?"

She wrinkles her nose. "Fine. But only because I'm just catching up…"

I'm already tipping the cup up and letting the alcohol pour down my throat. After a couple more drinks, I'm loose and warm and ready to dance. I lead the way to the dance floor, which was at some earlier point a dining room slash living room.

The hardwood table and matching chairs have been pushed against one wall; the other walls have the white plush couches and chairs seated by them. People are dancing and making out on the couches as I tug Kalindi into the dark space.

We start to dance, feeling the beat of the baseline. I shoot Kalindi a grin. "Keep your eyes peeled for hot guys, okay?"

She laughs. "Hot guys for you. I'm not kissing a stranger tonight."

"Oh, we'll see about that!" I yell.

She pulls a face. "I have to find the bathroom. Will you be okay here by yourself?"

I stick my tongue out at her. "I'm obviously completely fine."

She heads off the dance floor, weaving around a group of particularly exuberant dancers. I watch her go, realizing only after she's been gone for a minute that I don't feel like dancing without a partner.

Swiveling my head around, I look for a replacement. What I find though…

A tall, broadly shaped man in the corner is looking right at me. I take a step closer and a grin spreads across my face.

Blond hair, green-brown eyes, tanned skin, and more muscles than he even knows what to do with. It's none other than Erik, my brother's stoic best friend. He is still wearing his tux, but he's ditched the jacket and rolled up his sleeves to reveal his hot as fuck forearms. His gaze is fixed on me, his expression unreadable.

In the nine months that I have been back in Copenhagen, being able to torment Erik is really one of the only bright spots. I mean, I'm glad to have Kal, but she's so busy with university stuff.

Erik is always around, perpetually insanely handsome, and always so freaking stiff when I talk to him. It's impossible not to rib him a little.

Or a lot, as the case may be.

I sway my hips as I saunter right up to him. "I didn't expect to see you here. How have you not turned into a pumpkin, Cinderella?"

His handsome face twitches for just a moment, then he sighs. "I was just about to ask you the same thing, little girl."

My mouth makes a moue of displeasure. "Don't hate me for my youth and beauty, you joy kill."

He scans the room casually, shrugging. "One man's joy kill is another man's savior from the brink."

I roll my eyes. He's so starched and polished, even here in this room full of drunk idiots making out. "Do you tell yourself that when you go to bed alone every night?"

His greenish-brown eyes rake over me. "Don't you have a boy your age to torture?"

A sharp laugh is pulled from my lips. "Why would I do that when you're so much more fun? Taking the starch out of you is so much more… pleasurable."

He shakes his head at me, turning to move away. It's instinct to reach out and catch his wrist.

But when he rounds on me, his eyes snapping and crackling with an unexpectedly fierce energy, I gulp. He shakes off my touch like one would a burning brand, glaring at me.

I see his hand flex, tightening to a fist and then relaxing. How he had such an emotional reaction to something so simple as a touch astounds me.

He growls at me. "What are you doing, Annika?"

I pout. "I wasn't done talking to you."

He steps up to me, leaning down and getting in my face. "I don't think that I left it up to you, princess."

My eyes widen. I'm pretty tall for a girl, almost five foot eight. But he dwarfs my size, his muscular body much more immense than mine could ever be. It's kind of nice to feel like the fragile one for just a second, even though I'm definitely playing with fire.

My heart starts pounding. If Erik could wound me with those fiery eyes of his, I'd be skewered through.

When I finally find the words, they leave me in a mere whisper. "Now who's the killer of joy?"

He snorts angrily, turning and storming off. I am left with a frantically beating heart and trembling hands. A few moments later Kalindi returns, looking over her shoulder.

"The bathroom line is so long that I can't stand in it anymore." She looks back, then senses my mood. "What? Did I miss something?"

My lips twist sourly. "Not really, no. You just missed The Ghost of Christmas Past, stirring up trouble."

Kalindi looks puzzled. "I'm sorry, what?"

I pull a face. "I'm talking about Erik."

"Erik… Erik Moen?"

"The very one."

Kalindi cocks her head. "Why isn't he in bed already?"

I burst out laughing. "I said as much to him and he did not take it very well."

She shrugs. "He is tall and blond and unbelievably hand-some... but he has a steel beam lodged up his you know what."

I grin, rolling my eyes. "Kalindi, you are old enough to say ass."

I hear a shrill scream from a nearby room. Everybody seems to freeze up, turning toward the sound. Then a loud male voice booms out.

"*Politibetjente!*"

"Shit," I mutter. I'm drunk, too drunk to deal with any police.

Without really thinking it through, I grab Kalindi's hand and start running. Everybody else has the same idea, running out of the house and into the manicured back yard.

What I did not anticipate was the flash of cameras as soon as I step out onto the lawn. I'm blind for a moment as I throw up an arm to guard my eyes.

"What the fuck?" I say, blinking rapidly. When I can see again, I see several paparazzi there about twenty yards away, going crazy taking pictures of me while I'm disoriented. "Fuck!" I shout, trying to shield my face from the paparazzi as best as I can. Kalindi is right there, shielding my face from their view with her tweed jacket.

"Come on," she cries, tugging me toward the front yard. "Let's get out of here."

We run across the spongey green grass to the smoothly paved driveway. My mind is all over the place, mostly focusing on what just happened.

I don't see any police cars... which means that this was just a paparazzi ploy.

Oh, god. They must have gotten some good pictures of me, standing there with my mouth hanging open, looking totally dazed.

As we climb into the first car we see, I sink down in my seat. Because already, I can hear Stellan's voice.

Can you just cool it until the wedding?

I close my eyes. "Take me to the palace, please."

Back to my upcoming punishment…

3

ERIK

MY OFFICE IS A CRAMPED SPACE IN THE BASEMENT OF Amalienborg palace. It's really confined, the space no bigger than one of Stellan's walk-in closets.

Not that I'm exactly jealous of my best friend, the King of Denmark. He has some big fish to fry, especially with his upcoming nuptials to his American journalist Margot.

But my office is really rather ridiculous. It's musty. It's dark. It's always freezing. It's only large enough to hold a desk and three chairs. It has a single window placed far above my head through which sunlight only streams in during the earliest hours of the day.

It's a little depressing, frankly.

I'm rarely in it anyway, preferring to always be on the go. But just now, it serves its purpose. It is cool and quiet, exactly what I need today.

My head pounds. Why did I drink so much last night?

I stretch out and kick my feet up on my desk, upset that I still have to wear my suit. Stellan is still in bed with Margot, but me… I am working.

I am always working. I squint and then unbutton the top button of my shirt. Loosening my tie a little bit brings an unimaginable kind of relief.

I think it also summons *her*.

When the Queen Mother sweeps into the drab little room that I call an office, I shoot to my feet and shut down my iPad screen. I'm still extremely hungover and trying to cover it up with an astounding volume of coffee and breakfast pastries. The leftovers of my breakfast are still on my desk but there's nothing to be done about it now.

I clear my throat, trying to appear presentable. I bow, wishing that I hadn't just loosened my tie. "Your Royal Highness."

The Queen Mother looks me up and down, as if examining me for flaws. She's a tiny person, probably only five feet tall. But what she lacks in physicality she more than makes up for in formidability.

She tucks a strand of her iron-gray hair back, looking above reproach in her modestly chic white dress. I stare at her blankly.

God, she makes me so nervous. No one else has this effect on me.

"Did we have a meeting that I forgot about?" I blurt out.

Her eyes narrow on my face. "No, Erik." She glances behind herself at the doorway, then looks back at me. She smiles tightly. "Do you mind if I sit down?"

I look down at my desk and the couple of chairs that have been crammed into this tiny space, intended for theoretical guests. "Of course. Make yourself comfortable."

As she squeezes herself into the chair furthest from the door, I find my seat again. A second after she sits down, I hear the clatter of high heels approaching very quickly.

Annika pokes her head into the room, making a face. "This is where your office is? God, could they make it any harder to find?"

"Annika!" the Queen Mother scolds. "You are late. Come in here."

Annika steps into my office. My eyes widen at the lavender minidress she's wearing, her long wavy hair covering a full third of the dress's skimpy length. Her long, tanned legs are bare and dazzling; they make my brain short circuit for a second.

The Queen Mother's expression turns thunderous. "You cannot wear that dress, Annika! If anyone sees you dressed like a street walker it'll shame the entire royal family."

Annika rolls her eyes, putting her hands on her hips. She purses her lips, looking at me.

"I'm too hungover for this. Are you feeling the same way?"

I favor her with a glower. "No."

I'm lying; I absolutely am hungover as fuck, but I'll be damned if I'm going to let Annika embarrass me in front of the Queen Mother.

The Queen Mother frowns. "Erik wasn't stupid enough to let a bunch of paparazzi snap his picture, Annika. That was you.

And you did it after I specifically told you not to cause any commotion."

Annika scrunches up her face, pulling the remaining chair out and plopping down. "It wasn't my fault. The photographers used trickery to force us to run out of the house."

The Queen Mother arches a brow. "So? How can you not expect something terrible to happen when there is such an easy opportunity?"

Annika looks offended, her button nose wrinkling up. "I'm sorry, what? Are you saying that you expect me to suspect everyone at all times?"

The Queen Mother's expression grows pinched. She turns to me, smiling coolly. "I've decided that until Stellan's wedding, you should be pulled off of your duties as Stellan's private secretary. Instead, you will be in charge of making sure that Annika stays out of the newspapers."

Annika makes an outraged noise. "No way!"

My heart thumps hard against the wall of my chest. My eyes widen slightly. I must've heard her wrong. "I'm sorry. Say that again?"

The Queen Mother shoots me a glare. "The royal family needs you to help make sure she stays below the radar." Her lips thin. "If it makes it any more appealing, we could perhaps attach a title to it. Let's say... if you are able to successfully keep her out of the papers for three months, you'll get..." She pauses, thinking. "A duchy or something like that. Doesn't that sound good?"

I'm stunned. It's a generous offer, to be sure. My neck grows hot when I think about never working for Stellan again...

We wouldn't be equals, but we would both be titled gentry. My hands form fists as I think it over.

"Umm, excuse me!" Annika waves her hands. "You can't be serious right now. I do not need a babysitter. And I especially don't need… him."

Her whiny tone would hurt, if I actually gave a fuck about her feelings. Lucky for me, I don't.

I scoot forward in my chair. "Tell me more about what you are asking. I would only have to keep the princess under control until the wedding?"

The Queen Mother shifts her position. "Yes. For three months. Keep her from creating any new drama of any sort. Let the media focus their attentions where they should be, on the King and Margot."

I consider her words for a moment. "I see."

Annika shoots to her feet. "You can't really be thinking about taking Momse up on her offer, Erik."

I cock a brow at her, frowning. "You don't control what I do or say, Annika."

She makes a frustrated noise, throwing herself back into her chair. "For fuck's sake."

"Annika!" the Queen Mother scolds.

I sigh. "She's not wrong though, Your Royal Highness. I know I don't have a lot of say in the matter, but if I have any sway at all… I don't want this assignment."

Annika's brow pulls down. She huffs.

The Queen Mother levels me with an icy glare. "I don't care what you want, Mr. Moen. You might have been raised as

Stellan's equal, but you are not. You are, at best, a step above the maid that cleans my rooms."

Annika goes silent, her brows rising. For a moment, I'm stunned too.

I glower at the Queen Mother. "If you don't mind me saying, that is a very simplistic view of the world you have."

That earns me a nasty glare from her. "It's honest. And it's not as though I was asking you to do it for free. I'll pay you quite handsomely, if that is indeed your issue."

I grind my teeth. "It's not."

Annika looks between us. "Momse, you have to realize that this is a bad idea. I mean, Erik is just… so stuffy and boring! He's a control freak. You can't expect me to just go along with this scheme."

The Queen Mother stands, running a hand down the skirt of her white dress. "Annika, my dear. You have been disappointing my expectations for most of your life. You would do best to sit down, keep your mouth closed, and be a little more demure. That's good life advice for you generally, but in the next few months? It's not an option." She slides a glance at me. "For either of you."

Annika crosses her arms, wearing a pout on her glossy pink lips. "I think you're being ridiculous, Momse."

The Queen Mother scoots past Annika, heading for the door. "I don't care." She pauses in the doorway, looking back. "This is what the royal family needs right now. It has given you both so much… so try not to disappoint my expectations."

With that, the Queen Mother exits, her head thrown back regally. I raise my brows, unsure how to respond to that.

Sure, the royal family has done a lot for me. They fed me, put me through the finest schools. I served as a major in the military because that was the rank assigned to Stellan. And for the past three years, it has allowed me to slowly amass my personal wealth while acting as Stellan's right hand.

But also… fuck that.

Annika looks at me, scrunching up her face. "She is such a bitch. Momse acts like Stellan walks on frigging water… meanwhile, she is so high-handed when she deals with literally anybody else. I can't stand it."

Leaning my elbows on my desk, I rub my temples. My headache has only intensified since Annika and the Queen Mother stepped into my office, that's for sure.

"I have a very bad feeling about how the next three months are going to go," I murmur.

Annika stands up, surveying my desk. She picks up my coffee cup and takes a sip out of it. Then she wrinkles her nose.

"Ugh! That coffee has turned to ice."

I stand up, pissed off, and pluck the coffee cup from her grip. "Jesus, Annika. Learn some fucking boundaries."

She heaves a sigh. "You're just going to have to accept me for who I am. Get used to it."

Glaring at her, I put my feet back up on my desk. "You know what? I've been treating you like a princess. But I think from now on I'll treat you like the brat that you are."

Her eye roll is unmistakable. "Great, then join the club. The rest of my family treats me like either I'm impossible to control or I don't exist at all. So… welcome. Get cozy.

Because no matter what happens in the next few months, I'll still be the only princess of Denmark."

Then she turns on her sky-high heels, strutting like a model on the runway. I watch her walk away, biting my bottom lip.

I can't help but look at her legs and ass as she goes, which I know is exactly what she intended. But the fact that I grow hard at the sight of her tanned inner thighs…

That definitely makes me feel like a fucking pervert. I'm too old, too common-born, and too sensible for this… this *attraction* that I feel.

I close my eyes and sit back in my desk chair, sighing.

The next three months are going to be dark. I'm as sure of that fact as I've ever been of anything, ever.

4

ANNIKA

I MEASURE MOST DAYS BY THE NUMBER OF TOFFEE HARD candies I need to get through the day. Some days are good; they only register as a four-candy day. That's the sweet spot, no pun intended.

But today? Today is definitely a ten-candy day. I unwrap another piece and pop it in my mouth, savoring the sweet caramel flavor of the toffee. I try not to focus on the fact that every piece of candy is a few extra carbohydrates as well as surplus calories.

I have bigger issues today.

"I can't believe this is happening," I mutter, glaring out the window of the SUV. The city has long since fallen away; now I look out at the coastline, little bits of scrub brush clinging to the sandy ground. Below that I get glimpses of a seemingly endless beach and restless ocean waves.

Erik looks at me from the driver's side seat. "This beach vacation has been on the books for three months. Stellan has been going on and on about it. Were we supposed to stay in Copenhagen just because you can't behave yourself?"

I glance back at Kalindi, who is asleep in the back seat, sprawled out with her mouth open. Lucky her; she doesn't have a frigging babysitter on this trip.

I scowl, scrunching down in my leather seat. "Lower your voice," I whisper. "Kalindi is asleep. And for your information, this is not about me behaving myself. I think you know that, though."

He snorts. "*Ja*, okay."

I scrunch my face up. "Aside from being an uptight stuffed shirt, you are also a total jerk. Just in case you were wondering how I feel about you."

He gives his head a slow shake. "I wasn't... and now that I know, I still don't care."

I glare at him, crossing my arms. "Fine."

He looks unimpressed. "We are almost to the beach house. Can you just shut up until we arrive?"

I direct my glare out the window. "Sure thing, oh Benevolent and Great Dictator."

He just shakes his head but doesn't comment. I stare out my window and watch the massive mansion that we are heading to appear over the horizon. It is extremely Scandinavian in design, appearing as a sleek black block. When I can make out the details, I see a lot of chrome and glass, with almost a third of the house taken up by soaring windows and skylights.

Most importantly, there is a whole huge patio set between the house and the beach. It's an outdoor barbecue, a number of wicker chairs, and picnic tables. All surrounded by tall posts, from which twinkly lights and colorful lanterns are strung.

It actually makes me smile and lifts my mood a little. We have been coming to this particular beach house since I can remember. I will have a good time here, hell or high water.

Kalindi stirs just as Erik pulls up to the front of the beach house. She yawns. "How did we get here so fast?"

I glance and her, wrinkling my nose. "You slept through most of the drive. That's how."

Her cheeks glow pink. "Ah. I guess I needed to catch up on my sleep. Being on the medical track at university is slowly but surely draining my life force. I pulled four all-nighters this week alone."

I scrunch my face up sympathetically. "I'm glad you got some rest, then."

Erik gets out of the SUV, stretching his big arms out over his head. I get out too, my gaze taking in the mansion again. Three stories and excitedly modern looking, I see the brick fireplace running through the entire house. Erik is unloading the bags from the back of the SUV and piling them on the ground.

Kalindi yawns again and takes a few steps toward the dark wood front porch. I take a step toward the house.

"Hey!" Erik calls out.

Kalinda and I both look back at him, surprised.

"I'm not your manservant," he says in an irritable voice. "Get your own bags."

Shoving a hand through his sandy hair, he picks up his duffel and stalks past me.

Rolling my eyes, I head to grab my own bag. Kalindi trails after me as I follow Erik up to the front door and inside.

Everything is hushed inside the neatly decorated house. The clean, modern lines of the main living room are to my right. To my left is the formal dining room, it's light oak furniture somehow still looking right.

Erik disappears down the hall and I can hear him clattering up the stairs. I follow him, hoping that a room that overlooks the ocean is still available.

"Are we the first ones here?" Kalindi asks as we climb the stairs.

"No. I think we are the last, actually. Stellan and Margot got here yesterday. The rest of my brothers and their guests came in earlier today."

I sprint all the way upstairs and down the hall, pleased to find the room I wanted still open. I call down the hallway. "Come in here! There are two beds."

Tossing my suitcase on an empty double bed, I go over to the floor to ceiling window and push the heavy privacy drapes aside.

The whole beach is right there below me, the patio the only thing separating me from the beach.

I see a clump of Løve boys down on the beach. Stellan stands and stretches. Margot's bright pink hair bobs around next to him as she sits on a beach blanket.

"Whoa," Kalindi says.

I turn to her with a frown. "You've been here before, Kal."

She tosses her suitcase on the second bed, admiring the view. "That doesn't make the view any less spectacular though, does it?"

A smile tugs at my lips. "No. You're right about that."

She tilts her head at me, an empath to her very core. "Are you still trying to figure out what cause to champion?"

I give her a rueful smile. "Yes. Everybody just expects me to know what charity to back. But none of them really make sense to me. Not even the fashion-based charities. Like… okay, your whole marketing thing is about how everything you make is made out of recycled plastic bottles. Good for you. But I'm not your shill."

Her brow wrinkles. "I can point you in the direction of some great medical causes."

Heaving a sigh, I turn back to the beach. "Maybe later. You know, it's too bad we came down so late. The sun is already beginning to set."

"Yeah. Wait… did you take your little green pill?"

I shoot Kal a look. "Yes, mother. I took my crazy pills this morning. No burgeoning mental breakdown on the horizon today. Besides, I'm at a lower risk for having panic attacks way out here. The press isn't around."

She smiles. "I'm just checking up on you. You know me. I'm a mother hen until my last breath."

I shoot her a rueful smile. "Thanks. I mean it. But you can hang up your stethoscope for the weekend, Dr. Kal. It's time to have fun and kick back."

She wiggles her arched brows at me. "There is a hot tub, if I remember correctly. We should definitely get in that thing as soon as we possibly can."

"Umm… we should definitely go do that, right now." I change into my barely-there bright pink bikini and head downstairs. The hot tub is on the tiny back porch and currently unoccupied.

I lean down and turn on the levers controlling the hot tub. As I do, Erik strolls by on his way out to the beach.

Our gazes catch. His eyes widen a fraction as they slide down my body. He stumbles for a second, taking me in. Then he yanks his gaze away from me, scowls, and trots off.

My mouth opens. Of course, Kalindi wasn't here to see what just happened, so there isn't an easy way to know… but I'm pretty sure that Erik was just attracted to me. He may not like my personality, but my body appeals to him on some level.

I look after him, watching his tautly muscled frame. He's wearing a sleeveless gray t-shirt and swim trunks that are clearly designed for men with normal proportions. His tanned knees and hairy, toned thighs are on full display.

I cock my head, thinking about it. I guess I feel the same way about him, now that sexual attraction bubbles to the surface. I know I like to tease him about it… but I think there might be a real spark between us, somehow.

I get the distinct feeling that he would rather die than admit it to me, though.

Kalindi comes out onto the back porch, two flutes of sparkling rosé clasped in one hand, a bag of snack chips in the other.

I take one of the glasses from her, taking a grateful sip. "Mm. Oh, this is just what I needed."

She dips a toe in the now bubble-filled jacuzzi, letting out a loud sigh of pleasure. "Oh, that's nice. I'm getting in."

I climb in too, taking another sip of my wine. Copying Kalindi, I sit down facing the beach. My gaze slides over to the figures on the beach, finding Erik again without even really meaning to.

He stands away from the crowd, watching Stellan and Margot with a blank expression. I can't help but wonder what is going on behind that placid mask he always puts on.

I lean back, enjoying the heat and the bubbles that surround me.

"What do you think of Erik?" I ask. It just sort of pops out of my mouth, unheeded.

Kalindi frowns as she opens the bag of chips. "What?"

I feel myself redden slightly. "I mean… you know. Do you think he's attractive?"

She arches a slim eyebrow. "Do I? Of course. I'm not blind. He's a true Scandinavian. That fetching hair of his. Well, he doesn't have blue eyes. But his eyes are certainly interesting. They're piercing. He has Viking blood, I'm sure of it."

I push my cheek out with my tongue, setting my glass of wine on the deck. "I always wonder what he is thinking about."

Kal looks thoughtful, turning her gaze to the beach. "Yeah, he is definitely hard to read. But that's part of what makes him attractive, I think. He's handsome and mysterious."

She munches on a chip. I reach for one, crunching down on it. It's salty and tangy and delicious, dissolving on my tongue.

"Hey, remember what we were talking about last weekend?" I ask.

She squints. "You're going to have to be more specific."

I bite my lower lip. "About... my... issue? I've been so coddled and protected my whole life that..."

Kalindi's brows rise. "Are you talking about how you are still a virgin?"

I blush to the roots of my hair. "*Ja.*"

She sighs. "I've told you this a dozen times. I'm a virgin too. There is literally nothing wrong with it. I'm... saving myself."

I pull a face. "For whom?"

She rolls her eyes. "I don't know. For marriage, I guess. Anyway, that is not the point. The point is obviously that you shouldn't be in a hurry to lose your virginity."

I roll my shoulders, loosening some knots. "I wouldn't say that I'm in a hurry... but don't you think Erik would be sort of perfect? He's hot. And I get the feeling that he's been with enough women to do it right. Omigod, and can you imagine the look on Momse's face if she found out?"

Just picturing how sour she would look fills me with glee. My mouth curls up at the corners. "She would die. After all, it would be because of her meddling. Sort of, anyway. And she secretly like... can't stand him. It would be so funny."

"You are terrible!" Kalindi says, wrinkling her nose. She laughs though.

On the beach, Erik strips off his shirt. I nudge Kal, nodding. "Just look. That man is literally a hundred and forty percent muscles. Abs… delta… triceps…" I squint. "Okay, I'm not sure why I started naming actual muscle groups, because I don't have any idea of what the rest of them are."

Kalindi lights up. "Ooh! Call on me. You just tell me what area of the body you're trying to compliment, and I'll try to fill in the blanks. We just learned all the muscles in human biology."

My lips lift. "Umm, pass. That's work. We're here to play."

She shakes her head and drinks the rest of her wine in a couple of swallows. "I'm going to bring the bottle out here."

She gets out of the hot tub, dripping wet, and runs inside. I'm left to sip my wine and watch as Erik disappears into the water down on the beach.

5

ANNIKA

Dusk has just fallen over the beach, coating everything in sight in a dusting of shadow. The ocean looks dark and intense as the last rays of light disappear over the horizon. Our enormous beach house is the only structure around for miles and its back patio spills right out onto the dunes of sand that lead down to the water.

Other than the twinkle of fairy lights on the patio, it's quickly growing dark. I open my arms to the unbelievable spread of the night sky. The stars wink down at me.

Maybe tonight is the night.

My best friend Kalindi looks over at me from her beach blanket, looking beautiful as ever. She has light brown skin and dark eyes, with hair as thick and lustrous as a raven's wing. She leans back, adjusting her pink bikini.

"What would you think about me snogging your brother?" she asks. Her accent is a mix of British and Indian influences, and her voice is melodic. But her words make me pull a face.

"Which one?" I ask. "Don't say Stellan. All my life, my friends have been asking me whether he is single."

She shakes her head with a soft smile. "No, Annika. I'm talking about Finn."

My eyebrows rise. "Finn?" I glance back toward the house, at the picnic tables where the older guys and their friends are sitting, Finn included. "Are you sure you mean him and not Anders?"

Kalindi cocks her head. "What's wrong with Finn?"

I scrunch my face up. "Nothing. He's just… odd. Remote. You are a beautiful ray of sunlight and I wouldn't want him to dim your vibrancy, that's all."

She rolls her eyes. "I just mean a casual make out, nothing serious." She turns and looks at the group again, wrinkling her nose as they get up and head for the house. "I think I'm going to go inside and take a shower. This bathing suit is cute but itchy."

"Okay." I sit back, noticing that a lone figure walks by us out toward where the water laps at the beach. With his ruggedly good looks and his pushed-back hair, I can spot Erik easily though it's dark. "I'm going to stay for a while."

Kalindi shakes her head. "You shouldn't like him, Nika. He's almost ten years older than us."

Pouting, I look down at my sun-kissed skin in my tiny black bikini. "Erik is only seven years older than me, first of all. And second of all…" I look up at her. "It's just snogging, as you say."

She shakes her head. "You are crazy. He doesn't even know you're alive."

That stings. I make a face. "I know."

She smiles. "Okay. As long as you realize. I'll be inside, cleaning all this sandy goodness off of my limbs."

I nod, not watching her leave. My eyes find Erik again, silhouetted against the darkened beach. He wears jeans and a plain white button-up, his sleeves rolled up in a way that shows his bulging biceps. He bends over and rolls his jeans up to mid-calf. He keeps walking down a little further, submerging his bare feet in the foam left by the lapping sea. Without realizing it, I stand up, brushing myself off. It's only when I've pulled my shorts and black t-shirt on that I realize that I'm going to go talk to him.

I shiver. I have a half-hearted plan. A plan that involves me, Erik, and a hell of a lot of writhing and heavy breathing. If I can just talk to Erik about taking my virginity, I feel like a weight will be lifted from my shoulders.

The subject of my innocence, of being the perfect and pure princess that Denmark expects... it has caused almost as many panic attacks as seeing my face in the tabloids ever has. I can't hope to live up to the sterling standard that has been set out for me.

So I will shed my virtue. Make it less of an issue. I just need someone to take my virginity.

Someone who I find attractive. But more important, I need someone *kind*. Erik may be stuffy... but the last thing that I think when I look at him is that he is cruel.

It just doesn't exist in him. I can tell.

Shoving my fingers through my hair, I take a deep breath. As I pad barefoot through the sand, I give myself a mini-pep talk.

Just be casual.

Don't be an awkward weirdo.

Play it cool!

A few feet away, Erik turns and notices me. His expression hardens for a split second and then he turns away.

"What do you want, Annika?"

I freeze. This is not the reception I anticipated. Far from it, actually.

Walking forward to pull even with him, I take a deep breath. But when I speak, my tone is pouty.

"I didn't realize that you had the whole entire beach booked up," I say, gesturing to the vast darkness surrounding us.

He looks at me sharply but doesn't respond right away. I take a moment to drink him in. He's extremely tall, taller even than my older brother Stellan's massive height. His body is perfect and muscular without being too bulky. He has a face that is made for movies, with high cheekbones and long eyelashes, and these deep green-brown eyes that make me melt.

Erik grunts. Half a minute goes by, with me looking at his gorgeous face and him gazing out at the horizon. He finally says, "Stellan is a fucking asshole."

I squint, crinkling my whole face. "It must be so *hard* to be best friends with the king of Denmark. Especially when it means you basically get a free ride wherever you go."

As soon as I say it, I wish I could take it back. There is something about Erik that makes me mean and petty when I really want to be sweet.

He lets out a bark of laughter. "You are a brat, Annika. A spoiled little brat. You know that?"

My face heats. Of course, I know that.

"No," I say, sticking my tongue out at him.

He scans me head to toe and then shakes his head. "Yes. You are."

He turns around, walking back toward the house. My heart wrenches; this was my chance to sweet talk Erik a little. Maybe tell him that I think he's dreamy. Ask him to take my virginity. If all else fails, I can probably seduce him.

Now that chance is ruined.

I curse my mouth, which operates on its own sometimes. When Erik stops a few feet away and picks up a bottle of liquor, I raise my brows.

He uncaps it and takes a long pull, letting out a gasping sound when he's done. He turns back to me, holding the bottle out to me.

"Whiskey?"

A breeze blows, making me shiver as I jog the couple of steps toward him, taking the bottle from his hand. He casts another glance at me as I uncork the bottle.

"You should be inside," he murmurs. "Where it's warm and safe."

I take a sip of the whiskey and wince as it burns its way down my esophagus. It's half a minute before I can speak. "Safe? Safe from what?"

Erik looks at me, smirking a little and shrugging. "I don't know. Give me the bottle back, little girl."

I narrow my eyes at him, handing it over. Our fingers brush, our gazes collide. His serious eyes are shadowed so I can't read his expression exactly, but for a split-second I swear there is a carnal interest there.

That, or I'm just imagining what I want to see.

Erik's eyes dart away. He takes another long slug from the bottle. Then he pulls a face. "This whiskey is bullshit."

I wipe a couple of drops from the corner of my mouth, not really knowing how to respond. I'm nineteen; it's not like I have a ton of whiskey tasting experience.

"It's better than some," I come up with at last.

He eyes me skeptically. "*Ja*. It will get you drunk, which I guess is what counts."

I study him. "Are you? Drunk, I mean."

He turns to stare stonily out at the waves. "Maybe." He squints. "I'm on vacation. I almost never get to relax."

He sounds defensive. I shrug my shoulders.

"I'm not judging. I was just curious. I don't think I've ever seen you drunk."

He looks at me again, screwing his handsome face up. "*Ja*, okay."

When he offers me the bottle again, I shake my head. "No. I like champagne, not whiskey."

He lifts a shoulder. "Suit yourself." Tipping his head back, he drinks.

I watch his neck as he gulps the liquor down. I notice his lips then, looking plump and perfectly kissable. Licking my own lips, I let my gaze wander down his body. His arms are both bare and impressively muscular. I can see a hint of the definition of his abs in his tight white t-shirt.

Before I realize it, words are leaving my mouth. "I changed my mind. I want some."

Erik raises his brow. "All right."

He takes a step toward me, handing me the bottle. I let the bottle drop to the ground, putting my arms around his neck. He gives me a startled look.

"Wait— "

I am too close to finding out what his lips taste like to stop now. I push up on my tiptoes and press my mouth against his, hesitating once my lips touch his. He seems frozen for a second, his brain taking a moment to catch up to reality. His eyes sink closed.

Then his hands find my lower back, drawing me against the firmness of his body. At the same time Erik deepens the kiss. No more peck on the mouth; his kiss is rough and dominant, his lips working against mine.

I open my mouth to him, and he takes every inch I give him, sweeping his tongue inside my mouth like a man staking his claim on unchartered territory for the very first time.

A rugged rumble leaves his chest. If I weren't kissing him, I would have missed it. But it spurs me on, makes me spear my hands into the back of his short flaxen hair.

That's all it takes to make him push me back a step. His eyes fly open, shocked.

"Fuck," he grits out. "Oh, fuck. That… that should not have happened."

My cheeks go pink. "Erik— "

He shakes his head, cutting me off. "No, no, no. That... I mean, you're barely nineteen! You're my best friend's baby sister."

I shrug. "So?"

He looks horrified. "So? So, your brother will kill me if he ever finds out. It doesn't matter that I'm drunk..."

I bite my lower lip, looking at him. "I won't tell. It'll be just between us."

Erik shakes his head. "This is bad. This... this can't happen again."

And with that, he picks up the whiskey bottle and starts a slow jog back to our beach house. I stare after him, touching my still-warm lips with my fingers.

Despite everything that Erik just said, my lips still curve upward.

I stand amongst the sand dunes, as the moon comes out to light the night with its soft glow. It's my only comfort as I watch Erik's figure walk away.

6

ERIK

ANNIKA IS THE DEVIL. THAT'S THE SIMPLEST EXPLANATION FOR the torture that she's been inflicting on me.

That kiss... that brief moment where I lost control and just took what I wanted from her. Her soft lips hot against mine, a little hesitant once they brushed my suddenly sensitive skin.

Fuck.

My hands clenched as they slid around her waist. My cock instantly hardened. She made this sound... this soft moan... And she tasted like cotton candy with whiskey overlaid, somehow at the same time.

It doesn't get much more erotic than that. I guess I can't let my guard down around Annika... although she found me at the beach while I was drinking.

She kissed *me*.

I just shouldn't have liked it so fucking much. What in the hell is wrong with me?

Two days later when I'm stonily staring at my little desk in my bleak little office, I'm still thinking about it. I can still feel the weight of her in my hands.

This… this insanity… has to stop. A young brunette from the royal press office pokes her head into my office and I sit up straight as an arrow.

"*Haj*," she says. "I have your altered schedule here."

She holds a sheaf of paper out toward me and I beckon her forward. "I'll take it now. Thanks."

She hands me the schedule. I leaf through it, a sigh on my lips. Every single engagement that I set up for Stellan is now wiped clean from my schedule. Even the things that I personally lobbied for, like a meeting with the local high school students interested in technology.

Gone.

What a bunch of bullshit. Instead my schedule now contains more galas and soirees, plus luncheons for Annika's preferred charities. It looks like she has a lot of art museums and a ton of meetings with fashion designers on her upcoming schedule. Great, two things I couldn't give a quarter of a fuck about.

Rereading the first page, I check my watch. Shit, if I don't hurry, I'm going to be late. I don't even know where I should meet Annika to leave for this luncheon.

Grabbing my dark wool suit jacket, I put it on as I rush upstairs to Annika's quarters. When she returned from boarding school last year, it was decided that Annika was too young to live on her own. So, she's still on the top floor of the palace, in a suite of rooms that would be otherwise unoccupied.

I head up the staircase and down a hallway which is a perfect replica of Stellan's hallway, except done in hushed royal navy tones. Dark blue carpet, soft blue drapes, demure blue upholstered chairs at ten-foot intervals. The walls are hung with the same gilded mirrors and paintings of long-past relatives.

When I knock on Annika's door, her response is immediate, as though she were waiting for me. "Enter!"

I open the heavy dark wood door suspiciously. When I step in, I find Annika in the sitting room. The room looks totally unlike any other in the palace, though… it's like she emptied the room of all its furniture and replaced it with an eclectic blend of expensive, modern pieces.

In the corner, I see that she's set up an area dedicated to a three-way mirror and several lights. All the lights are turned on and focused on a single spot before the mirror.

What a waste of resources.

Annika herself is seated on a low gray tweed couch near the window. A blond male hairdresser is standing behind her, holding a can of hairspray and a comb, pursing his lips. Her hair is long and lustrous as per usual; I'm not sure what if anything he is even here for.

"It's done," he announces.

Annika turns, taking me in. She looks amazing in a stylish light pink dress, but then again, she always looks like that. Her lips twitch and her eyes shine with something akin to mischief.

"Thank you," she tells the hairdresser. "I'll see you again in the morning."

He walks out, casting a dour look over me as he goes. I look at my watch again.

"We're already late to your first appointment," I say, adjusting my cuff. "We should leave immediately."

She stands up, rolling her eyes. "Oh, that's a little trick that the royal press office tries to pull. They write down everything two hours earlier on my schedule in a blatant attempt to manipulate me into showing up early for events. I just ignore it and show up later."

I hunch my brow at that. "I see."

She walks over to a full-length mirror, stepping into the first of four pairs of heels that are laid out for her. She looks at her reflection and then kicks the shoes off, leaving them haphazardly on the floor. Then she slips on another pair, looks in the mirror, and poses.

I stand near the doorway, wondering if I should bring up what happened over the weekend. She doesn't seem troubled by the incident… but maybe I should be worried about that.

After all, the kiss felt earth shattering when it happened. For me, anyway…

Annika turns, pursing her lips. "Which pair of shoes makes me look the most fuckable?"

She sticks out her leg, modeling a shoe for me. I stare at her for a second.

Yeah, we definitely need to talk.

"I don't know," I say, adjusting the knot in my tie. "But I think we need to lay down some boundaries, Annika."

She looks up at me, her eyes dancing with merriment. "Like safe words? Mine will be *forage*. Or do you mean a list of sex acts that are labeled red, yellow, and green?"

I shoot her a look. "That kind of humor is not allowed, for one thing."

She rolls her eyes. "You really are a drag, you know that?"

I fold my arms across my chest and narrow my eyes at her. "I think it's important that we talk candidly to prevent any confusion between us. What happened at the beach the other day— "

She grins, interrupting me. "Are you trying to tell me that it was super hot?"

I flush. Did I fantasize about that moment later when I was drunk and alone? Yes. Did I think about her when I was stroking my cock? Definitely.

But I'm not proud of it… and she doesn't need to know about it, either.

"It was out of line. It's the reason that we need boundaries. A very firm set of rules of engagement, so that nothing untoward ever happens again."

Annika pulls a face. "Untoward? What are you, my grandmother?"

I glower at her. "I'm serious, Annika."

She favors me with a long look. "Things happen, Erik. We're both pretty people. We were both in the same place at the same time. So what? So, we kissed. Big deal."

She turns away, kicking off her heels and slipping her feet into another pair. I take a moment to absorb her words.

"I think we should have some rules, just in case."

She rolls her eyes, turning sideways to look at her slight frame in the mirror. When she doesn't disagree, I clear my throat and continue.

"No touching," I say, ticking items off on my fingers. "No talking about sensitive topics. No questions about my private life. And no discussion of anything that you wouldn't talk to the Queen Mother about."

Annika turns to me with a glare. "Don't tell me what I can or cannot do, Erik. I'm a part of the royal family. Like it or not, you technically work for me."

I huff out a laugh. "I work for your brother, not you. And if you have a problem with any of my conditions, you can go tell someone about it. Anyone, really. I'd love to see the look on your grandmother's face when you tell her that you're upset because you can't ask me about who I've fucked lately."

Her brows rise at that. "Who have you slept with? It must've been a while ago. Because you were so needy back there on the beach…"

"I was drunk!" I thunder. The words burst forth, so vehement and sudden and loud that Annika widens her eyes and goes still.

My words aren't a good excuse; alcohol is never a decent reason for anything. If anyone should know that, it's me. But I think I've wanted to shout at her for a good long while now.

Sadly, it's not very satisfying. Especially not when I can see that she's a little shaken by my tone.

"Annika," I say, shaking my head and looking off toward the window. "Jesus. You bring out the worst in me, you know that?"

She bites her lip and shrugs a single shoulder, looking very young all the sudden. "No."

I can't stand her sudden vulnerability, how it lurks behind her fullness and bratty attitude. It's a sword sharp enough to shred me into a million tiny ribbons.

"Stop it," I grit out.

She looks at me sharply. "Stop what?"

"That little innocent, wide-eyed ingenue thing you're doing. It's not working on me."

Her brow furrows. "What? I'm not doing anything."

"Maybe you're not trying, but you definitely are," I grate. My fists clench. "And it's not playing fair, okay? Just... behave yourself."

Her eyes narrow. Her expression cools. "So, you are just like everyone else, then. You make assumptions about my behavior. And then when my actions don't line up perfectly, you shake your finger at me and scold me." She lifts her head, tossing her hair back. "I'm done with that. I've had plenty of that in my life already. So, if you don't mind, get the hell out of my rooms. I'll meet you by the limousine in two hours."

She turns and marches to the doorway that leads to her bedroom. She opens it and slams it after herself hard enough that a painting shifts on the wall, skewing slightly.

I glare after her, shaking my head as I exit the room into the hallway.

Annika is a mess. One minute she's joking, the next she's on the verge of tears. Defiant, then charming, and then vulnerable. How am I supposed to handle someone like that?

I won't be drawn into her insane world of high drama and petty bullshit, that's for sure. With that reaffirmed in my mind, I head downstairs to my office to brood in peace.

7

ANNIKA

As I sit down in the very front row of the Greta von Grissel fashion show, I smile wanly at the big names that are present to support the show. I suck on my hard candy discreetly and try not to wonder how some of the people around me get so *thin*. A couple of actresses, a celebrity blogger, a fairly famous rocker... they're all stuffed around me, arranged like dolls for the cameras.

One of the actresses shyly asks me for a selfie. I smile and comply, not because I'm particularly in the mood. But because it's expected of the princess of Denmark.

I'm playing the part, being the perfect Danish princess. Short black velvet dress, sky high black heels, and a tiara to top it all off.

Normally I would relish a Grissel fashion show. After all, being here is paying tribute to my primary hobby. Change the world through using fashion to raise money for charitable causes. But the reason I'm in a sour mood is heading my way... and he looks like he just walked off the pages of a fashion magazine.

Tall, elegant, with sandy-colored hair and those cutting green-brown eyes. He's dressed simply but stylishly in a slim cut navy wool suit, a pristine white shirt, a crisp black tie, and spit-shined black leather Oxford shoes.

I watch the crowd notice him as he approaches me. The gorgeous women attending this fashion show arch their eyebrows and aim their pouts at him. The handsome men cock their heads and wonder who he is.

And Erik doesn't even know that he's being measured. His gaze locks on to me and narrows a little. Even from a distance, he appears brooding.

The lights start to dim. Behind Erik, the runway is lit while the area given over to the guests darkens. He walks right up to me, looking at the people carefully arranged around me on the white marble bench.

"Do you mind if I move you down?" he asks the young actress seated beside me.

She flushes prettily. "*Ja, ja*. Let's see…"

My mouth thins. She stands up and motions to everybody to move down. My gaze slides to the event planner, who is staring at us as though we've just ruined her life.

Erik sits down beside me. "Your highness," he says, nodding to me.

I narrow my eyes at him and adjust my dress. I continue to smile as there are camera flashes about every five seconds. But inside, I'm seriously pissed off at Erik. He is definitely high up on my shit list for the things he said yesterday.

I freeze him out, turning ever so slightly away from him. He casts a skeptical glance over me.

Then I hear the actress on his other side introduce herself in a whisper. I force myself to continue smiling and lean forward so that I can see her around Erik.

"He's in trouble," I say, smiling brightly. "Please don't talk to him."

The starlet's eyes go wide but she just nods. Erik shoots me a glare. But before he can say anything, the music starts blaring.

He shifts in his seat, watching as the models begin to work their way down the runway. I keep up my end of the bargain, applauding politely at every single model.

Privately, I'm not paying a single bit of attention to what's going down the runway in front of my face. But Grissel doesn't need to know that. And I still want her to make me ten designer dresses for next season…

A few minutes into the fashion show, Erik shifts his weight, pressing his thigh up against mine. My eyes widen just a bit.

It's probably an unknowing move on his part, but holy hell. The warmth of his big body radiates, heating my exposed skin.

I look down at where our bodies are pressed together, distracted beyond reason. Why is this the most erotic thing that's happened to me all week?

I stare at the spot where we touch. For some odd reason, all I can think of just now is Erik moving his hand to my thigh and inching up my dress.

I lick my suddenly parched lips, a rush of memory hitting me. Now I can remember exactly why I wanted him to be the one to take my virginity.

Suddenly the house lights go up. Everyone around my is rising and applauding Greta von Grissel, who traipses down the runway looking like a mythical goddess in a flowing dress of her own design.

I rise and clap too, wondering where the last twenty minutes went. Did I really spend them fixating on how good Erik's thigh felt when it was pressed against mine?

The designer bows. The paparazzi swoop in, shooting photos of us famous people.

"Can we get a shot with you and Greta, your highness?" one man calls.

"Who is your escort, your highness?" a woman asks.

I blanch. "Thank you, everyone! I have to go, unfortunately." I lock eyes with the designer, gesturing to mimic a phone. "Greta, I'll call you!"

And with that, I turn, raise my head, and sweep out of the room. Bodyguards fall in around me once I step outside of the ballroom.

Another of Erik's decisions, I bet.

By the time I climb into the back seat of the limousine, I'm furious. I pluck the tiara from my hair and run my hands through my strands, pulling out bobby pins and wrecking an entire morning's worth of effort.

Erik climbs into the backseat beside me, glancing at me as I irritably pull bobby pins from my sinuous mane.

I avoid his green-brown gaze, my brow hunched as I glare at the seat in front of me.

"What is wrong with you?" he asks.

I snort. "Believe it or not, I'm still pretty damn mad at you."

He exhales loudly. "Is this about yesterday?"

I glare at him. "Yes."

I gather all the bobby pins into a fat bundle, toying with them.

Erik grunts. "I'm sorry I said... whatever is making you upset."

"Agh!" I moan, sinking down in my seat. "The fact that you don't even know what made me mad, but you apologized anyway... that makes me angrier."

He laughs, a humorless sound. "This is insane. I can't keep up with you." He shakes his head. "You know what? I think this is still about how I rejected you on the beach."

I roll my eyes. "Oh, please. Like I can't have whatever or whoever I want, whenever it pleases me. I am the only fucking princess of Denmark, you know."

He glares at me. "Maybe that isn't good enough for you. Maybe you have some... some fixation on me. Forbidden fruit and all that."

I look at him, shaking my head. "Actually, you aren't explicitly taboo to me. This whole forbidden fruit thing only really works from your perspective."

He narrows his gaze on me, eyeing me up and down. "No. I think you are infatuated with me."

I open my mouth, hitting him on the arm repeatedly. "I am not, you pompous… arrogant… jerk! I could never be interested in somebody so self-righteous and buttoned up! Ugh!"

His lips curve upward. "You seemed to think differently on the beach last week."

I turn straight ahead, blushing deeply. "That was just a physical thing. I was there, you were there…" The lie feels a little forced, but I just keep on anyway. "I could never, ever, ever actually feel romantically attracted to you." I laugh at the very idea of it. "Like… no. Ew."

Erik frowns, crossing his arms and adjusting his position against the seat. "It's nice of you to lay it out there so that even I can understand it, princess."

I shoot him an annoyed glance. "I'm just expression my feelings, Erik. You may be hot, but you are essentially a walking suit. Just… there's no substance to you except doing what you're told and minding your p's and q's."

He rolls his eyes, looking at his watch. "I suppose you dream of falling in love with a man every bit as dramatic and shallow as you are. Maybe an actor, hmm?"

I scoff. "You don't get to tell me who to date, thank you very much."

He smiles and stretches out, dominating the space in the back of the limo. "We should talk about your next engagement, shouldn't we?"

I scrunch up my face, still annoyed with him. "The press office lies about how soon I need to be there, remember? It's so hopelessly stupid. How long of a gap is there on the schedule for today?"

He gives me a measured look then pulls his phone out and scrolls for a second. "Three hours."

Throwing my hands up, I pull a face. "There's no telling how long of a gap there actually is between events. Everything gets very distorted very quickly."

He considers that for a moment. "I can try to talk to someone in the press office about it, if that would please her highness."

I look at him sharply. What he said sounded sarcastic, but his words were meant to be helpful… at least, I think so.

"I thought you told Momse that the press office has blacklisted you."

He looks startled for a second. "Oh. Well… I did, but I can still see if I have any pull." His eyes narrow. "How did you know that?"

Blushing, I turn my head away and look out the window. "You mentioned it in passing two months ago. I remember everything. It's…" I think for a moment. "It's just something that I do."

I notice and memorize insignificant details of everyone else's lives. Well, actually… only the people who really matter to me.

Does my subconscious believe that Erik is somehow important?

"I see," Erik says. He seems to get lost in thought.

Sinking down a couple more inches, I shade my eyes and pray for our car ride to end.

8

ERIK

"Is this a rare glimpse into the master working in his studio?"

I glance up from a stack of tedious papers to find Stellan leaning in the doorway. Throwing my pen down, I lean back in my chair with a grin.

"You surfaced for air! Tell me, how is it being suctioned to Margot's side?"

His lips twitch. He strolls over and plops down in one of my chairs, running a hand through his dark hair. "Not as tough as being king, it turns out. Especially when my best friend and right-hand man vanishes on some mundane task."

I roll my eyes and fold my hands behind my head. "Hey, don't complain to me about it. Complain to your grandmother. She's the one that thought that Annika needed such close supervision."

Stellan sighs, looking around my tiny office. "We should really get you a better place to work, Erik. This place is too dark and too small for someone of your stature."

He's referring to the fact that I'm taller than everyone I meet, himself included. I shrug.

"It works for me. I don't need anything grand. It's sort of apt, don't you think?" I glance around my cramped office.

Stellan squints. "It's okay for now. But you are going to be titled gentry soon. Isn't that what my grandmother offered you for dealing with Annika?"

I stare at Stellan for few moments, studying his face for a hint at what he could possibly mean. He gives me nothing, his face a perfectly blank slate. Finally, I just shrug.

"Yes, she did offer that. But that's not the reason I'm minding Annika. Or at least not the only reason. I consider it to be a personal favor to you, Stellan."

His brows rise. "Oh?"

"Your royal highness! There you are." A red headed young man appears in the doorway, flustered and overexcited. "I've been looking for you everywhere!"

Stellan gives me a look. "Erik, this is Thor. He's your replacement until after my wedding."

Thor raises his head a little. "Your royal highness, you are going to be quite late— "

"Oh, god. Do calm down, Thor." Stellan rises, giving me another look. "I'd best be on my way. I just wanted to make sure you weren't just languishing down here."

I give him a tight smile. "Not too much, no."

Stellan smirks. "All right, then. I'll see you soon. Next week, I think we have some sort of family dinner or something?"

I nod. "You know where to find me in the meantime."

Stellan looks around my office once more. "That I do."

He heads out of my office, his footsteps echoing down the hall as he rushes off toward his next engagement. After he's gone, I try to focus on the papers in front of me again.

But it's no use. Glancing at my watch, I wonder what my father is doing. It's been almost a month since I've seen him. And Annika is locked in her rooms with her friend Kalindi, whispering and giggling like a couple of little girls.

With a sigh, I rise. If there is a better time to go visit my father, I don't know of it.

It's the work of a couple of minutes to exit the palace through the gardens. I roll up my sleeves and shove my hands through my hair as I walk. It feels silly but if I walk into my father's house looking like I have my shit together, my father will lose his temper.

And he will undoubtedly aim his anger at me.

The stables are only a few minutes further travel down a narrow, paved path. The birds are chirping in the trees, the sun is high in a perpetually blue sky, it's about as nice as Denmark can get.

But as I skirt the stables and head to my father's cottage, my mood darkens with every step. Bracing myself, I knock on the door of the charming, well-maintained little cottage.

I hear my father cough first, long and ragged. "Who is it?" he calls out.

I close my eyes briefly. "It's Erik."

The door swings open and I look into a very real image of my future. My father is my height, thin as a whip, with his hair gone completely gray. He's dressed in a pair of fresh khaki overalls and a button up shirt with the cuffs rolled and shot up as far as they will go.

He doesn't look happy to see me. "Haj, son."

He backs up and lumbers back into the kitchen, taking a seat at the heavy old table. Before him are a bunch of horse bits, a bucket of soapy water, and a rag. And the ever-present schnapps bottle, of course.

Blanking my expression, I close the door and circle the table, taking a seat at the long bench.

My father takes a quick nip from the bottle of schnapps, wincing. Then he picks up a bit and the rag and starts cleaning.

I try not to look around too much; there are memories in this cottage, and not pleasant ones. Memories of my beautiful blonde mom. Memories of my father, drunkenly screaming at her. A memory of her crying and wishing me goodbye, then slamming the front door one last time.

"Well?" my father demands. "What are you here for, Erik?"

Blowing out a breath, I eye him. "How are you?"

He glowers down at the bit in his hands. "Does it really matter to you? *Herre* High and Mighty." He makes a sour face and looks at my shirt. Then he shakes his head, setting the bit aside and picking up the bottle again. "You look like a poor man masquerading as one of them royals."

My neck heats. I want to fuss with my shirt, but I don't. Instead I paste on a smile. "You made that choice for me, *far*. I was barely out of diapers. You'd driven *mor* away…"

My father grinds his teeth. "It's not my fault that your mother left, okay? And I was just trying to scrape by."

I level a look at him. "You made enough money. That's never been the issue between us."

My father takes a swig from the bottle and narrows his eyes at me. "I'm not saying you was at fault then. You was little. But when I told my troubles to King Goran… and he offered to take you off me hands… well, I never expected him to turn you into that little prince's shadow. I thought…"

He trails off, wiping his chin with the rag. I fold my arms across my chest. "I didn't come here for this."

My father looks up at me, his hazel eyes pinning me in place. "What did you deign to come all the way down here for? The royal palace is only five minutes away, but it must be too comfortable to leave. Even to visit your own flesh and blood…"

Taking a deep breath, I brace my fingers around the bridge of my nose. "And why would I not visit more? I can never get enough of your gruffness."

My father narrows his eyes at me. "I'm just telling the truth."

My hands form fists. I want to hiss with rage and turn this fucking table over on its side. But I don't.

Instead I school my expression into a bland mask. "Let's change the subject, *dar*."

He shakes his head, looking down at the bit in his hands. "I imagine when you find a girl and settle down, you two will just move away and leave me here. Won't you? Better to start over, without an old man weighing you down."

His tone is self-pitying, an abrupt switch from his accusations just moments ago. I am ready for it, though. He usually vacillates between the two the entire time I visit.

I turn my head, stretching my neck. "I don't know, *dar*. That's years down the road, if ever."

What I don't say is that I'm absolutely certain that he screwed me up so badly that I'll never be able to love another person. At least not anyone other than Stellan, who I feel a bittersweet mix of love and envy toward.

He grunts. "Is this when you tell you're a fairy, boy? I'll tell you this right now, there's no use in you pining away over that prince of yours."

My muscles tense. "We've had this conversation. I'm not gay. I am not in love with Stellan. End of story."

My father throws down the bit and the rag with a *thunk*. "Then why haven't you got a girl? Hmm? When I was your age, I was already married. Come to think of it, you had already arrived."

I notice that he just avoids talking about my mother altogether, as though I simply appeared on his doorstep one morning.

I force a hard smile. "Romantic love just seems... messy. You should understand. You and *mor* couldn't make it work— "

He shoots to his feet. "Her leaving was your fault, Erik. Before you came along, she was happy. It wasn't until you were born that she... she..."

I stand up. "What? She couldn't stand to be in this house, belittled by you day and night. I'm not surprised that she left, *dar.*"

He turns red. "Get out of here, Erik. You don't want to be here anyway. According to you, I treat you and everybody else so terrible. So, I'll say it again, get the fuck out of here."

Shaking my head, I walk toward the door. "Gladly, old man."

He sits down, picking up the horse bit and resuming polishing. "No son of mine would treat me so bad, I'll tell you that much."

I shake my head, pushing out the door of the cottage with a bang. This. This feeling right here, this ball of black hate right where my heart should be?

This is why I don't visit my father, even though he's so close. Even though he's the only family that I have left.

As I storm up the little lane, the birds chirp and the sun still shines. But I'm far too wrapped up in my angst for them to make me feel any better.

9

ANNIKA

I STARE AT THE TABLOID NEWSPAPERS SPREAD OUT ON THE table before me, horrified. The headlines are a variation on the same theme.

PRINCESS ANNIKA PIGS OUT (AGAIN)!

Followed by pictures of me in an unflattering royal blue dress, about to take a bite of dessert. My eyes gleam like that bite of dessert is the apple of my eye. In the insets are half a dozen other photos from the same event, with me trying different desserts.

What they don't mention, of course, is that I was the royal assigned to attend a dessert competition. They also neglected to mention the fact that I went hungry for two days leading up to that to save up a bank of calories just for that event.

All I had for forty-eight hours was unlimited water and a handful of my favorite hard candies. I wish I could scream that fact at the paparazzi that snap my photos... but they don't really care.

No one cares about the work that I put into being perfect except *me*.

I tilt my head, surveying the photo closest to me. I'm wearing a shapeless dress with bell shaped sleeves in the picture, which isn't really even that unflattering. I just look like a person who's eaten thirty bites of cake, which is exactly what I was at that moment.

Standing up, I grab a waste bin and sweep all the papers into it. Then I stomp to the door of my parlor, putting the waste bin outside of it.

I breathe, trying to get the image of me and the words PRINCESS PIGGIE out of my head. But I just can't. Later when I'm done getting dressed in my room, I still hear the words to a particularly cruel song in my head.

A small choir of children happily croon: Princess Piggie, Princess Piggie. Eats her weight in toast smeared with figgie...

Kids used to sing that old nursery rhyme when I was in earshot, knowing full well that it would make me die inside. Like everyone else in the world, I went through an awkward stage from age ten to fourteen. But unlike the rest of humanity, my awkward stage was caught on film and celebrated throughout Denmark.

I can picture myself now, being twelve and trying not to eat in front of anyone, because I would feel judged later. My expression hardens as I march out to the huge three-way mirror in the corner of the parlor.

Standing as straight as I can, lifting my ribcage and posing just so, I look at myself. The girl that looks back at me isn't fat. If anything, she's a little bit too skinny to really be what anyone would call beautiful. I turn and angle my body this way and that, reposing my arms dozens of times.

If only I could control what people saw when they looked at me… but I've long since learned that I can't.

It doesn't matter that I have a designer white lace dress on. It doesn't matter when the last time was that I actually ate a full meal. It doesn't matter to the paparazzi that I'm a real person with tender feelings.

I take a deep breath in, my eyes filling with tears.

A knock on the door sounds. I whirl, cursing my emotions for running wild. Carefully swiping at my eyes, I call out.

"Just a moment!"

I check the mirror, telling myself to lock those damn emotions away for now. After making sure that I look okay, I call out again. "Come in!"

The door opens and Erik enters, his expression stormier than usual. He is wearing a dark suit that fits him like a glove. as though he was just called down off of a runway. He shoots his cuffs, running a hand through his neatly combed hair.

"What is this?" he asks, waving a tabloid paper at me. He tosses the newspaper onto the table, pinning me with a glare. "When did this happen?"

I flush but raise my head a little, running my hands down the front of my dress. "Months ago. It must've been a slow news day."

He folds his arms across his chest, starting to prowl the room. "This isn't good, Annika. You aren't supposed to be covering any papers. What did you do to get the attention of the paparazzi?"

I give his words a little huff of disbelief. "I was born into the royal family, for starters. Do you know that when I was only two years old, a paper published photos of me and called me chunky?"

He stills. "No."

I shake my head, turning back to the mirror to put my earrings in. "I have had a contentious relationship with the press since I had the gall to draw breath. The Danish people claim to love me. But they also buy every single paper that says nasty things about me so…"

I shrug helplessly.

Erik's tawny green-brown gaze spears me when I turn around. He's closer than I thought he was… almost close enough to touch.

My gaze dips down from his face to his impressive physique, exceptionally showcased in that tight white button-up and his tautly fitted black wool jacket. He's dreamy, I'll give him that.

"You can't be doing anything to capture the attention of the paparazzi," he says solemnly.

I roll my eyes. "Like you know anything about it. You just got here. Give yourself a minute to settle in and see how insane it all is."

I walk past him, bumping his shoulder intentionally. But I don't expect his reflexes to be so good that he catches me just as I brush against him.

Erik's hands clamp around my arms. Eyes widening, I look up into his elegant face with its savage expression. His body presses against mine tightly. His hands control my every movement.

This close, he could kiss me. He could ravage me. He could even really hurt me. When he speaks, his deep voice slides down my spine like a chill.

"I don't think you understand the implications of what we're dealing with," he grates out.

My gaze drops to his mouth. I bite my lip. "Oh, no?" I ask. My mouth curves upward, unbidden.

He gives me a little shake. "Be serious, Annika."

I look him in the eye, raising a brow. "And if I am not?" I ask quietly. "What will you do with me then?"

He bristles. His hands press into the flesh of my arms so hard that they may leave me bruised. It's obvious from this close that Erik is so much bigger than I am, that his height and weight mean he can haul me around with ease or even genuinely hurt me if he really wants to.

And though I don't want to admit it, I think that's what really turns me on about him. Lurking underneath that calm surface is something sleek and dangerous and calculating. It's a little like going for a swim in a placid sea, knowing that just under the surface, a shark waits for his next meal.

"You should be punished." His voice is gone to gravel. The anger in his expression and the volatility in his eyes is nearly frenetic; there is something *almost* violent mirrored in his eyes.

I open my mouth, my core clenching. "What will you do, Erik?" I look him square in the eye and toss off a haughty laugh. "What *can* you even do?"

If my goal is to goad him into action, to push him to a breaking point, I get exactly what I wish for. He glares down at me, sliding a hand into my mane of fair-colored hair. Fisting my hair, he tugs my head back, exposing my throat to him. My eyes widen and I stop breathing for several seconds.

"Someone should have taught you a lesson years ago," he rasps, a cruel smile on his perfect lips. Then Erik bends his head down, placing a searing kiss on my throat.

I gasp at the feeling of his lips against my skin. But when he moves up an inch and bites my neck hard, I just shudder. I'm turned on, confused, and a little scared all at once.

Yes. Do it as hard as you want, I think.

But I don't say that. I find myself strangely tongue tied around this furious, sexual version of Erik. He's so uptight and controlled that seeing this side of him is fascinating and frightening and arousing all at once.

My hands come up to clutch at his arms, but he knocks them away. "Uh uh."

His lips touch shoulder, my collarbone. Flexing his hips into me, he leaves me with no doubt that his cock is rigid. Pressed against my belly, every time he moves his hips, his cock thrusts against me *hard*.

I shiver as he trails hot, rough, wet kisses inward toward my breasts. He releases one of my arms and tweaks my nipple through my dress, pulling another gasp from my lips. It hurts... but there is a corresponding throb low in my body after he releases my flesh.

My body wants his. Between my tightly pressed thighs I can feel a slither of moisture slipping from my core, preparing me for him.

Erik lifts my head up, his eyes glittering. "It's what you deserve, princess."

I bite my lower lip, swallowing heavily. "Erik…" I manage.

His hazel eyes lock on mine. "Let's see."

Maintaining his brutal grip on my hair, he uses his free hand to begin rucking up my skirt. My eyes widen and I start struggling. Erik just lifts his fist clutching my hair and I wince, stilling.

"Stop resisting, Annika."

His hand touches the inside of my thighs which is a shock to me. I feel burned, scorched by his touch. How dare he touch me like this? I push at his torso uselessly, my mouth twisting with bitter bile.

Then he looks down at my body, my white lace thong bared to his gaze. He brushes the apex of my thighs, his fingers arching in toward my core. He delves into the folds of my pussy and finds a pool of sticky moisture there. I stiffen, feeling both aroused and like I've been caught doing something naughty.

An involuntary shudder and a huff of breath leaves my lips. "Erik!"

He looks me in the eye, lifting a single brow. He wiggles the fingers he has pressed against me so intimately. "Don't try to lie to me, princess. Your mouth says no, but your body says yes."

I shake my head, trying to argue with him. "No, you don't— "

Erik pulls my head toward his face for a brutal, devastating kiss. It leaves my lips feeling bruised and my pride feeling dimmed. At the same time, a part of me wants… more.

It makes my body *ache*.

He releases me suddenly, stepping back. "Before you try to fucking rattle my cage again, you'll remember what happened here."

Then he whirls and stalks out of the room, slamming the door behind him so loudly that it actually makes me jump. One of my hands runs across my lips. The other one is already pulling down my skirt, returning things to normal.

But things aren't normal... things may never be normal again.

Shivering and trembling, I sink onto the couch and try to stop my thoughts from spinning out of control.

10

———

ERIK

Clearing my throat, I stand ramrod straight as I hold the door to the ballroom open for a crowd of ladies. My face creases as I peer inside the ballroom. The walls are draped in a light pink velvet. The many tables are each covered in spring green or off white or baby pink. The tables are set with gleaming silver tiered trays of macaroons and sandwiches, polished water glasses, and white porcelain teacups.

Looking at how intricately decorated the room is for high tea makes me tense.

Doubly so when my glance trips over Annika. She's breathtaking just now in her baby blue dress, her blonde hair swept off her neck in a fashionable knot.

I escorted her here of course, because apparently, I'm a very expensive and very glorified babysitter. But she didn't so much as speak a word to me in the car on the way here. Instead I just stewed in the icy tension brewing between us.

And tried not to relive every second of the evening before, when I grabbed her. When I pulled her close, dug a hand into her hair, and kissed her neck. When I ran my hand up the soft skin of her inner thigh.

When I touched her pussy, finding it hot and wet and ready for me.

A fine shudder runs through me, remembering the sensation. I know that I misbehaved. The fact that I completely lost my mind for a moment and laid my hands on Stellan's little sister makes me so deeply ashamed.

I just don't know what to do about it. And it's clear that Annika doesn't either.

I move inside the ballroom, smoothing a hand down my navy tie and black suit jacket. Everywhere I look there are fancy ladies in sleek light pink or white dresses, gathering at tables to sit down. I see that Annika is standing awkwardly by her mother the former queen and her grandmother, waiting. for them to take their seats. She looks like she's about to drown in this sea of older women.

My attentions aren't needed there. Like many times in my life, I think that it would be best if I were to just wait downstairs near the cars.

I turn around and am brought up short when I almost knock over a young brunette in a skintight pink lace dress. Her upturned nose and severely plucked eyebrows look familiar but I can't immediately place her. She grins and latches onto my arm.

"Erik!" she crows. Her voice is loud and high-pitched, and it brings me back to last summer. She's a royal hanger-on, one of those girls that used to flutter around Stellan, hoping he would look their way.

"Dalia," I summon her name out of my memory. "Right?"

She beams at me, leaning close and hanging on my arm. "Of course, you remembered my name. How gentlemanly."

My eyes narrow. "I was just leaving."

Dalia widens her eyes. "But why? When I heard that you were going to be at our table, I got all starry eyed. You can't leave me all alone at the Queen Mother's table!"

I blanch, glancing behind me. The Queen Mother and Annika are just now taking their seats, Annika with a scowl on her face.

"Yeah, I don't think—" I start.

"Shh. Come on," Dalia says sternly. She starts towing me toward the table in question,

I resist. "Seriously, Dalia— "

But Dalia is already making a scene, waving to the Queen Mother. "We're coming!"

I release a sigh, allowing myself to be pulled over to the table of honor. There are six women already seated and just two seats left on opposite sides of the table. One is next to Annika; I can see from the place cards that it's intended for me.

I shake off Dalia's grip. "This is my spot."

Dalia pouts as she slinks to the other side. I slide into my seat, trying not to call too much attention to myself. Annika gives me the cold shoulder, tossing her hair and turning away.

Just as well and fine with me, honestly.

"Dalia! Who have you found?" an older brunette asks, indicating me.

Dalia smirks and makes the introduction. "*Mor*, this is Erik. He's one of Stellan's friends. Erik, this is my mother, Lady Shane." She pauses, eyeing me. "As you can see, the Shanes and the royal family are very close."

I repress an eye roll, bowing my head briefly. "It's a pleasure, Lady Shane."

The Queen, who is usually noticeably absent, clears her throat politely. It's obvious that Annika and her mother share the same gene pool; they have the exact same aristocratic nose, the same impossibly high cheekbones, the same pouty lips. I can tell exactly what Annika will look like in twenty years' time just by glancing at her mother.

And I have to say, she will still be undeniably beautiful.

"Erik, it's so nice to see you here," the Queen says.

I incline my head again, deeper this time. "Thank you, your highness. His Royal Highness is feeling well, I hope?"

Without even thinking about it, I just casually mentioned her husband the former king. Until a recent Alzheimer's diagnosis, he reigned as king for my entire life.

A flush comes to the Queen's cheeks. Annika kicks me under the table, shooting me a frown.

The Queen recovers gracefully though. "He is very well. Thank you for asking. And thank you for taking care of Annika." She smiles at her daughter, patting her hand. "She does need a little extra attention. Right, darling?"

Annika's cheeks turn scarlet. I expect her to say something sarcastic. But to my surprise, she doesn't. She just looks down at her lap and mumbles, "Yes, mar."

My eyebrows rise a fraction. Looking back and forth between the Queen and her very unhappy daughter, I think that I'm missing some important info. I have no idea what, just that there is something about the Queen that makes proud, reckless Annika… submissive.

What is that, exactly? I wonder about it while several waiters come around our table, filling our teacups with dark, fragrant tea. The Queen looks at me. "How have you been, Erik?"

I raise my gaze from my teacup, feeling a little put on the spot. "Very well, your royal highness."

She smiles. "Please, call me Thora. We are practically family, after all. And besides, I feel like Margot and Stellan have really shaken things up in the royal family. I stepped down as Queen, Margot will take my place later this year…"

Annika gives her mother a small smile. "That's a good view to take."

Her mother tilts her head and sighs. "I was just talking to Stellan yesterday, and he said the same thing. Which of course meant the world to me…"

Annika flinches at Stellan's name, looking back down at her lap. The Queen doesn't notice her daughter's distress; she goes on to tell a long, rather uninteresting story about how as a child, Stellan would bring her flowers and brighten up her day.

Dalia narrows her eyes at Annika, smirking just a bit. "That's so wonderful. I'm glad one of your children only brings you joy. What do the others bring, I wonder?" She pretends to think about it for a second. "Nothing but news headlines, I suppose?"

The Queen smiles and reaches out her hand to Annika's. "My other children bring me joy. And occasionally, they are the thorns in my bouquet of roses. But they still make me proud."

Lady Shane clears her throat, sensing tension bubbling between Dalia and the Queen. "Of course. I am certain that Dalia only meant to tease. Didn't you, dear?"

Dalia beams. "Oh yes. Certainly. I didn't mean to bring up those ugly headlines about Annika stuffing herself— "

Annika shoots to her feet, her face contorting with rage. "That's enough from you, Dalia. And FYI? You'll never be a member of the royal family. My brothers all hate you— "

"Okay!" I jump up, cutting her off. I laugh a little as I slip my arm around Annika. "You know, I think Annika is tired. Poor girl, we had a late event last night…"

I see Annika's chin start to wobble; a telltale sign of tears sure to come. The Queen folds her arms across her chest and looks displeased.

"I see," is all she has to say.

"Ladies, if you'll excuse us," I say, bowing my head.

Annika wrenches herself out of my grasp and storms off, leaving me to chase after her. It's a little dicey because there are still waitstaff circling and serving the many other tables. Annika manages to slip through the crowd, something someone of my stature can't do nearly as easily. But after dodging several tea-wielding servers, I catch up with Annika outside the ballroom.

"Annika," I try.

"Don't," she warns, barely repressed fury in her tone. She dashes away a welling of tears from her eyes.

She looks angry as she stalks down the hotel's grand white marble hallway.

"Annika—" I say, trying to grab her.

She suddenly stops, squaring off with me. Her head tips back, her face is flushed, and she glares at me utterly defiantly.

"I won't…" Her eyes suddenly shine with unshed tears, her voice growing strained. "I won't… apologize."

I step closer, my hands coming up to brace her arms. Not a hug, exactly. But I can't very well stand here and be a stone wall.

"I wouldn't ask you to," I say, searching her face. She peers up at me, guileless, her blue eyes shimmering.

"I know that you don't want to be here," she says, her voice breaking. "I know that you're just doing as you're told. The good little soldier. God, what must you think of me?"

I grip her arms, frowning down at her. "I don't know, Annika. I can't seem to decide what to think."

Annika hangs her head. "If you read the newspapers, you'd have an opinion. Did you know they call me Princess Piggie?"

A muscle ticks in my jaw. "That's not how I see you."

"No?" She flexes her hands, looking down at them. "My hands feel weird." She wheezes the next few breaths, looking back up at me with a distinct note of worry. "I… I can't breathe. My chest is…" She shakes off my touch, clawing at her chest. She continues to struggle for breath. "I think… I feel like I'm dying."

My brow hunches. I glance around the hallway, feeling like a fish out of water. When Annika grips my arm hard, I glance back at her, feeling helpless.

Fuck. Is she going to be okay? Do I need to get a doctor?

"Get me…" she pauses, wheezing. "Get me somewhere quiet."

I can hear her struggle to breathe. I can feel the waves of anxiety coming off of her.

"Okay." I look around, spotting a door only a few paces away. "Come on."

I guide her to the door, opening it to find that it's just an empty closet. I hesitate for a moment. But Annika breaks out of my hold, going straight inside and huddling in a corner.

Leaving the door open a sliver, I get down on the floor beside her and try to offer some kind of comfort. She sits down and puts her head between her knees, leaning against my body.

"It's okay," I say, looking down at the top of her golden head. "Everything is okay."

She wheezes, pulling oxygen into her lungs. She's trembling, clenching and unclenching her fists. And I am just sitting here beside her, completely out of my depth.

"Should I do something? Should I get someone to help?" I ask.

Annika just shakes her head. She reaches out a hand to me. After a moment of staring at it, I take her hand and grip it in both of mine.

I feel like a fucking idiot. Putting my arm around her shoulders, I wait for a few minutes. Her breathing relaxes a little.

Her trembling subsides. She finally sits up, leaning her head back against the wall.

"Fuck," she says. "For a good ten minutes, I really felt like I was going to die."

I frown. "You should go to a doctor, Annika."

She chuckles humorlessly and glances at me out of the corner of her eye. "Believe me, I did. It was just a panic attack. I've had them for years."

She tugs at her hand, which I have forgotten that I'm still holding onto. I let go, my neck heating.

"I see," is all I can manage.

Annika gives her head a little shake. "I think that I'll call it a day. Surely the royal press office can't say anything if I'm sick. Help me up?"

Narrowing my eyes, I climb to my feet. I offer her a hand, which she takes. As I hoist her up, she squeezes my hand. She pins me with her powder blue gaze and cocks her head.

"Thanks," she says softly. There is a moment, just a few beats of my heart, where something shimmers in the air between us.

A sensation of emotional openness.

Then she drops my hand, whirls toward the closet door, and bolts away. I'm left to follow her, my heart squeezing in my chest, a million questions crowding into my brain.

11

ERIK

Our chauffeur pulls the limousine around the entrance of Amalienborg castle. I take a moment to look at the majesty of the place. Made of light-colored brick, the four massive tan brick buildings all huddle in a circle, all saluting a rather large statue of a man on a horse. With their white-trimmed windows, dark roofs, and guards dressed in scarlet, the palaces definitely proudly exude *money*. It's truly a sight to behold.

I glance over at Annika. Her expensive black designer heels are on the seat between us. She has hiked up her floor length blue velvet dress to mid-thigh. The delicate silver tiara that adorned her upswept hair is tossed carelessly next to the shoes, and she's run her fingers through her wavy mane. She is slumped against her door, scrolling through her phone with a glazed expression.

For a second, my lips curl. She reminds me of nothing more than a big cat right now. Resting, yes, but still monitoring what is going on with a jaundiced eye.

The second the limo pulls to a stop, she is in motion. She flings the door open and vaults herself out of the cool leather seats. She doesn't wait for anyone to open the doors for her… and she completely ignores the tiara and shoes that she's discarded.

I frown and scoop them up, following her out of the car. Annika is already disappearing inside the palace, the tail of her long blue dress carelessly crumpled in one hand.

I follow her inside and up the grand staircase with a sigh. "Annika!"

She doesn't even pause. She's been acting oddly all night, as if she isn't wasn't aware of my presence. We went from a school opening in the morning to an afternoon at a water polo match and ended the evening at some charity gala or another.

And the whole time, I never once saw her smile in my direction or even acknowledge my existence. So, when I enter her private living area, I am not really in any mood for her drama and hysterics.

"Annika!" I call again, trying to project my voice into the open doorway across the room. She has disappeared into her bedroom but left the door ajar. "You forgot your fucking tiara and your goddamn shoes!"

Her golden head appears in the doorway, her guileless eyes piercing me through and through. "Could you help me with the zipper to this dress? It's stuck."

Squinting at her, I nod. "Yes, your highness. Whatever my mistress desires."

Arching a brow, Annika steps back through the doorway, a smirk on her lips. "You're very salty tonight, Erik. My grandmother would hate that you're talking to me in such an insubordinate manner."

My eyes travel down the length of her body. Midnight blue velvet clings to all the right places. Her tits look amazing. The curve of her hips is alluring. And her tight little ass in that dress?

It looks more expensive than all the money and jewels in this house, combined.

Annika walks over to me, turning around. She holds her long platinum hair up and flashes me the back of her neck and her sleek upper back.

My heart starts to pound. How Annika always does that to me, I have no idea. All I know is that being so close to her, reaching out to touch her... it's definitely filling my head with perverted thoughts.

I move closer, seeking the hidden zipper that runs along the column of her spine. As my fingers brush the back of her dress, all I can think about is the feel of her lips pressed against mine and the little sounds she made when I kissed her.

Swallowing, I manage to unzip her dress, baring her sun kissed bare skin to my eyes. I blink, forcing myself to step back. "I'm done," I say, averting my eyes.

I feel like such a fucking predator right now, preying on someone so much younger and more inexperienced than I am. Yet Annika turns around, a mischievous glint in her eye.

"Thanks. Pour me a drink, will you? I have to change out of this dress." She points to the bar cart near the floor to ceiling window.

I narrow my eyes at her as she vanishes through the doorway leading to her bedroom once more. "Annika…" I husk out, shaking my head.

She has no answer for that, it seems. I turn toward the door but can't seem to make myself walk out of this room.

What is it with this girl? Why do I feel so much… lighter when I'm around her?

Heaving a sigh, I walk over to the bar cart. There are only those funny-looking prohibition-era coupe glasses on top. It pairs well with the little fridge filled with several bottles of expensive champagne.

Shaking my head, I pop one of the bottles of champagne and fill two glasses with the aromatic bubbles.

When I find a seat on the gray tweed couch, sipping the champagne, Annika reappears. I almost do a spit take at the slinky little white silk robe she's wearing.

"Ah, thanks," she says, tossing her hair and taking the coupe glass from my hand. She sits down beside me.

I swallow and stare. Just six inches of couch sit between me and her silky-looking, bare knees and thighs. She sips at her champagne.

"That hits the spot."

I drag my eyes back to my glass and make a noncommittal noise. "Mm."

She leans back on the couch and scrunches up her face. "That charity event was boring with a capital b."

I swirl the contents of my glass and glance at her. "I wasn't even sure what it was to raise money for, actually. But it seemed to be in poor taste to ask."

She throws back her head and laughs. The sound is low and throaty. "Hah! It was for school lunches or something."

"Yeah. I mean… there were ladies that stood in front of the whole audience and talked. But I'll be damned if I can remember what they talked about. My mind definitely wandered."

Annika tilts her head to the side, sizing me up. "What did you think about? You're always so mysterious. Just a huge, brooding question mark to me at all times."

My neck heats. I definitely spent no less than thirty percent of that time wondering what exactly Annika had on beneath her slinky dress. And fantasizing about what I would do with her if she were anyone else in the world…

I clear my throat. "I was plotting my next move on the stock market."

Her eyes widen; her expression turns questioning. "What do you mean?"

I give her an odd look, a teasing smile on my lips. "Do you need me to speak more slowly? How can I be clearer about what I just said?"

She bats my shoulder. "I meant… like… are you trading stocks or something?"

I roll my eyes a little. "Yes, princess."

A little line of worry forms in her brow. "Are you any good at it? Like… do you make money doing it?"

I shrug. "I do all right."

She nods slowly. "I had no idea."

"No one does." I chuckle, sipping my drink. The bubbles burst on my tongue, almost too sweet to even drink. I roll the wine around my mouth.

"This is really terrible champagne." I set my glass on the floor.

Annika glance at her coupe, shrugging. "I don't know. It's whatever the sommelier buys for the palace."

"So, it's fancy and terrible. Good to know." I sigh, sitting back against the rough tweed of the couch. "Buying that wine was a decision… but that isn't the worst advice I've ever received. Actually, it's not even the worst thing that has been pitched to me today."

Annika's lips turn upwards. "No?"

"Nope. This morning, a professor cornered me at the event and told me all about how solar cells are really going to power everything in two years' time."

She wrinkles her nose. "If it makes you feel any better, some woman at the gala caught me in the line for the bathroom. She told me about how she feels for me every time she sees me in the newspapers. And then she started talking about some kind of radical self-love movement…" She shudders. "She was one of those ladies that doesn't wear a bra but needs to."

I roll my eyes. "Did she have a pamphlet? I hate when they have pamphlets to show me."

She flashes me a dimple. "No. She did tell me to look up radical self-love on Instagram, though."

I laugh. "You'll have to report back when you've learned what that is. Unless it's just… you know, masturbating a lot."

She crows with laughter, batting me on the arm again. "Shut up. You think it could be?"

I lean closer to her, lured by her laugh. "I think the probability is high."

She grins, wrinkling her nose. "Ah, I needed to laugh. This… this is nice."

"What?"

It's only then that I realize how close we are sitting. I kept moving closer, charmed by her smile. But I see now that we are probably too close.

Okay, definitely too close.

I clear my throat, moving back a few inches. "Sorry. I forgot that."

I trail off, not really wanting to finish that sentence.

That we need way more space between us?

That I'm just here to babysit you?

That if there weren't a title on the line I wouldn't even be here right now?

She scrunches up her face. "Don't be so weird. You were just starting to be a normal person, Erik."

I shoot her a glare. "And what was I before, Annika?"

She puts a hand on my arm. I freeze.

Her casual touch shouldn't feel like a burning brand… but it does. It's the simplest thing and yet… I would do almost anything to find out what it feels like when she grips me, pulls me closer.

My eyes widen at the thought and I dart my gaze over to the window, feeling guilty.

She's not for you.

She's a literal princess.

And she's your best friend's little sister.

I bite my lip.

She just smiles and crinkles her face. "Call me Nika. Okay? We can be friends while you keep an eye on me. But only if you stop calling me Annika. You sound so matronly when you say my name like that."

I stand up, shaking off her touch. Awkward is my middle name right now. "Sure. Whatever you want."

She arches a brow. "Are you going to be okay, Erik?"

My neck heats. "Yeah. I just realized that I'm late. For... a date."

That's a lie. I'm not late for anything but lying in my bed alone, touching myself and fantasizing about the beautiful girl right before me.

Her eyes narrow on my face. "Oh. Well... don't let me keep you."

Committing fully to my escape plan, I start stalking toward the hallway. "Goodnight, Annika."

As I get to the doorway, she calls after me. "It's Nika!"

I give her a backwards wave and flee the room, feeling like a complete ass.

12

———

ANNIKA

WHAT DO THE TERMS RADICAL SELF-LOVE AND SELF-ACCEPTANCE even mean, anyway?

I furrow my gaze, rocking back on the flimsy plastic chair I'm sitting in. I scroll down the screen of my phone, trying to figure that exact question out for myself. The ballroom I'm sitting in is dank and musty with disuse, the overhead lights flipped off and the floor to ceiling green velvet curtains pulled shut.

Faintly I hear laughter coming from the other ballroom of this hotel. Someone has obviously said something funny at the gala. But I couldn't suffer through another minute of smiling and laughing politely so I snuck in here to do a little reading.

Plucking at my white chenille dress, I screw up my face.

Radical self-acceptance is a philosophy that means that you are enough. More than that, you are doing fine...

A door creaks open, the lights overhead flicker on. Erik is illuminated, looking mouthwatering as ever in his dark blue suit and black tie. He cuts quite a figure, tall and light-haired and muscular.

He crosses his arms, pushing out his cheek with his tongue. When he speaks, he doesn't sound happy. "Why are you hiding in here?"

Sighing, I turn off the screen to my phone. "If I have to hear one more old rich man tell one more story about the good old days before the immigrant problem, I'm going to snap. I'm not here to make rich guys feel like they are winning the war against progressivism or whatever."

Erik cocks his head. "We can't leave. We just got here. And we were two hours late for this event because you had a hair emergency."

I stand up, brushing at my skirts. Strolling toward him casually, I come to a halt less than a foot away from where he stands. "If I have learned anything from my grandmother, it is that a princess's beauty is far more important than whether she is always precisely on time."

He gives me a dubious look. "I doubt that very much, An—," He catches himself. "Nika."

I smile at him slyly. "If you really believe that, you don't know Momse at all."

He scowls. "Let's go. All you a required to do is smile and nod for the next..." He extends his arm, checking his watch. "Thirty minutes."

A light bulb goes off in my head. My smile widens. "Orrr... we could be bad and sneak off to do something fun. No one will probably even notice that we're gone. It's not as if either of us is as important as Stellan, right?"

His eyes narrow on my face. "We're still required to do our jobs, Nika."

Biting my lower lip, I scrunch my face up. And then I grab his hand, giving it a tug. "Please? Come on, you know that you're dying of boredom out there. Have a little fun for once in your life, Erik."

For a moment, I can almost feel his critical gaze as he looks me up and down. I expect him to say no. I expect him to give me a stern talking-to about how we're here to represent the royal family.

But to my surprise and delight, he glances behind him and then shrugs. "Where do you want to go, princess?"

My eyes widen. I beam at him, pulling on his hand. "I actually have a place in mind. Come on."

Erik gives me a funny look and pulls his hand from my grip, looking like he might already regret saying yes. But when I run across the ballroom, kicking up little dusty whirlwinds in my wake, he trudges after me. I open a door that lets out into a quiet, brightly lit corridor. Hiking up my white skirts feels natural. Sneaking down the corridor and down a back staircase is less so, but still fun as hell. When I finally push my way out into a breezy Copenhagen evening, I grin back at Erik. The block we're on has giant buildings everywhere I can see. There are a ton of lit up signs and a lot of foot traffic.

I make a sweeping gesture. "What did I tell you? Freedom."

Erik rolls his eyes a little bit, but his lips tug upward too. I count that a victory. "Lead the way," he says, stuffing his hands into his pants pockets.

I shake my head at that and lead him down the block, trying to blend in. People passing by do double takes when I scurry past them. I'm more than used to it by now.

Looking at the signs on the tall buildings, I spot exactly what I want.

A faded light up sign, white with yellow lettering that says, "The King's Ransom Games".

"Here we are," I say, pushing inside the steel double doors. As soon I step in, I'm transported to somewhere else entirely.

The room is dark and warm, the lights and noises from the old school arcade machines instantly comforting. At the far end of the single room shop, a bored looking teenage boy scrolls through his cell phone.

"Oh my god," Erik says, suddenly beside me. I notice Erik's height because he's only an inch or two shorter than the ceiling. I hadn't actually thought about it, but I guess the ceilings are pretty low in here.

Erik grins. "I… I thought you were going to take me to another bar or something. This is…" He looks around with wide eyes. "This is awesome!"

He heads into the lion's den with no fear at all. I follow him, grinning at his reaction. There are machines with joysticks and names like Ultimate Fighter Four. There are a few racer games, a Ms. Packman game, and an air hockey table. The arcade has a few customers who don't pay us the least bit of attention.

That's one of the reasons my father would bring us all here when we were little kids.

I bite my lip, wiggling my eyebrows. "This is my top-secret place. No one ever hassles me here. Everyone is absorbed in their games. I can just... kick back and play some Skee-Ball." I lean in and whisper the last bit. "If I had a choice in the matter, I would never leave this place."

Erik nods, looking me up and down. "That makes sense. This arcade is a weird place that I would never expect to find you in."

He is already pulling out his wallet and approaching the prize counter. He waves at the oblivious teenage boy. "How do we play?"

Without even looking up from his screen, the gawky teen points to a row of vending machines. "Right there."

Erik smirks a little at me, making change. He ends up with a big handful of silver tokens. He glances at me.

"I don't actually know how games are priced," he says, looking around the crowded room. "What should we try first?"

I glance at the Dance Dance Revolution game where two players are challenged to see who dances better to Japanese music. "Maybe that?"

Erik pulls a face. "Something easier."

I crinkle my nose and look around. My gaze lands on two decrepit Skee-Ball machines. The object of the game is to roll a heavy wooden ball up a sloping incline, managing to sink the ball in one of the holes cut in a slanted wall.

I wiggle my eyebrows at him, heading over to the game. "I used to be so good at this game. I bet I can kick your ass."

He follows me over, slapping down a few tokens on my machine. "I'm willing to take that bet, princess."

I grin. "You should probably take your tie off because this competition is about to get serious."

He takes his tie off, stuffs it in his jacket pocket, then unbuttons the very top button of his shirt. I kick my impractical heels off even though the floor is cheap, old, sticky carpet.

"It's on," I say, grinning. A game behind me beeps triumphantly, a sign that someone has won.

But I hardly notice the sticky floor or the noises going on around me… because Erik laughs, looking like an overgrown kid.

He puts two of his tokens in the machine and balls roll down a slot, making a noise that I've never heard anywhere else.

Shaking my head, I do the same. Then I face the inclined ramp and pick up a ball. The *thunk* of the wooden ball when I wind up and release it underhanded is so satisfying.

So is the way that the ball climbs the ramp effortlessly, dropping into the nearest hole.

"Yes!" I cheer.

Erik rolls his eyes. "Calm down, that was a twenty-point shot. Watch this."

Thunk. I watch his ball sail up the ramp and up the wall, coming close to the upper left hole. That one is worth a hundred points… but it doesn't matter, because the ball rolls down into the gutter.

"Hah!" I say, pointing at Erik's machine. "Take that."

"Whatever," he says, rolling and stretching his neck. "That was only the first one. Let's see you land one of the top holes, Nika."

I wiggle my eyebrows, grabbing another ball and rolling it up the incline. We both do it over and over again, twelve times total, until we are out of balls. The machines start beeping and trilling, pushing out some tickets.

I end up winning by twenty five points, which I rub in Erik's face. "I told you I was the master of Skee-Ball, didn't I?"

He takes off his jacket. "Let's go again. I'm sure that the jacket was just holding me back."

I throw my head back, laughing so hard I'm honestly afraid for the seams of this expressive dress. "You must be dreaming!"

A throat clears behind me. I whirl, expecting an adult. But I find a red-cheeked little boy, probably about ten years old. He clutches a pen and a piece of paper.

"Princess Annika?" he says, blushing. "Would you mind if I got your autograph, please?"

I beam at him. "Of course not. What is your name?"

"Paul," he says, turning an even brighter red. I take the pen and piece of paper, chatting with him for a second and then signing it.

And then I end by offering him a hug. He agrees and hugs me surprisingly hard around the middle, for so long that Erik clears his throat and steps toward us.

Paul squeals and takes his autograph with him as he flees back into the wall of beeping and ringing machines. Erik's lips twitch.

"You just earned yourself a fan for life." He screws up his face. "He's too young to be creepy, right?"

I laugh. "I think so."

He leads me back toward the Skee-Ball machines. "That was the first time I've ever seen you being the princess of Denmark. I mean, I'm sure you do it plenty. But that was the first time I've ever been around when it happened." He puts two tokens in his machine, making the balls roll down. "You were very natural with him."

I put my tokens in, eyeing the machine before me. "I should be. I've had nineteen years worth of practice."

He chuckles. "I just meant that you were good with kids. That surprises me for some reason."

I pick up a ball, rolling it up the incline. "I don't know why. I love children. I plan to have at least four when I get older."

The ball sinks into the gutter, causing me to pout. "Damn it."

He's looking at me. I can feel his eyes on my figure. I frown, trying to concentrate.

"What?" I ask.

Erik shrugs a shoulder. "Nothing. It's just... I didn't realize you were so..." He pauses. "Complicated, I guess."

I roll another ball, which also goes straight into the gutter. "Damn it!"

I whirl to him, frowning. "Everyone is much more complicated than they seem, Erik. Even the most seemingly boring person has multiple facets to their personality."

He reaches out and grabs my arm, giving me a squeeze. "Okay, okay. I'll make a mental note."

For a second, the breath leaves my lungs. Our gazes connect. The warmth of his fingers against my skin makes me shiver.

I swear, I see some forbidden emotion lurking there in his eyes.

Desire, maybe. Or is it just lust?

I lick my lower lip, my mouth opening.

And then he gives himself a shake, dropping my arm and stepping back. When he smiles at me again, it seems faded and plasticine.

"Throw another ball," he says, jerking his head toward my machine. "See if you can beat me again."

Then he looks down at his own machine, concentrating on his first ball. When he rolls the ball again, he hits the top right hole. The Skee-Ball machine goes nuts, ringing and announcing that he is a winner.

He grins and pulls a long strand of tickets from the machine. "Come on. Help me choose what prize to take home."

"Here." I giggle, handing him all the tickets from my machine. As he leads me over to the prize counter, I scrunch my face up. There is a whole wall of prizes, everything from stuffed animals and remote-controlled helicopters to smaller prizes in bins behind a glass counter.

Cellophane wrapped candies. Tiny, brightly colored cars. Shiny silver stars. Fake mustaches in different colors. Bouncy balls that look like little planets.

Erik looks at the tickets in his hand thoughtfully. "I don't think we have enough tickets for any of the stuffed animals. It looks like we are stuck picking a couple of these trinkets."

Looking at the goods behind the counter, I grin. "Well, you need that one."

I point to a pair of Groucho Marx-style glasses that have a fake nose and moustache attached. Erik rolls his eyes, handing his tickets to the disinterested teenaged boy. The guy doesn't even count them. He just grabs the glasses and hands them over silently.

"Hmm," Erik says, bending down to see a second shelf of plastic jewelry. "Oh! Can I get that one too?"

The boy looks bored as he fishes the piece of plastic out.

"No, no. The ring. It's for her," Erik corrects.

The attendant pulls it from the case and slaps it on top of the counter. It's gaudy, looking like a solid pink piece of bubblegum made into a ring with a multifaceted surface.

"Oh yes," Erik says, picking it up. "That's the one."

I laugh as he slides the ring on my finger, just like a wedding ring. "Oh darling, it is so thoughtful. You must have put so much thought into picking this out."

"Hold on." He picks up the glasses, fitting the fake nose and frames on his face. "There! Now we are perfect for each other in every conceivable way." He sticks out his elbow. "Come on, Ms. Potato Head. Let's go back to the Barbie Dream Mansion and race our Hot Wheels against each other."

I can't hold back a grin. "You know, you kind of look like Ken."

He shakes his head, leading me to the exit. And I look up at him adoringly, wishing that we could always be the people we were tonight.

13

ERIK

ANNIKA CROSSES HER ARMS AS WE WALK UP TO ST. MARK'S preparatory school. It's the sister school to the boarding school all of the younger Løve siblings were sent to and it is right in the middle of downtown Copenhagen.

Annika raises her head and schools her expression. I glance at her stylish wide legged black trousers and white top with an oversized pale blue flower on the shoulder. With her hair pulled back into a crisp bun and her understated makeup, she looks every bit the princess she is supposed to be.

But that in itself makes me worried. It's like Nika is making herself smaller somehow, less noticeable. I should be glad…

But all I feel in the pit of my stomach is acid.

She's been quiet this morning on the way here. Too quiet, in my opinion.

Just before we climb the steps to enter, I cast my gaze over Nika. "What's going on with you?"

She glances at me, arching a brow. "What do you mean?"

I glance around, then grab her elbow and pull her aside. "We're here to promote your boarding school to prospective new students. I assume that you agreed to this… so why are you so…" I squint at her face. "Subdued?"

She lifts her chin an inch, her cool blue eyes expressionless. "I am only trying to be who they expect me to be today. That's all."

She fingers the pearls strung around her neck, her gaze flitting to the ornate door that leads inside.

I grip her elbow harder, drawing her gaze back to my face. "Do you want to leave?"

She arches a brow. "No. My grandmother expects me to show up here and wow the applicants with my presence. So, I'm here. Let the wowing commence."

I stare down at her for a few more seconds. The heavy doors behind us open, a priest sticking his head out. "Ah! You're here! Come in…"

Annika gives me a strange look, twisting her lips and rolling her eyes. But then she pushes past me, heading toward the black-frocked priest.

"It's lovely to be here," she murmurs.

The priest absolutely beams, offering her his elbow. "It is so nice to meet you, princess Annika. I'm Father Jean. Come, meet some of the parents and potential future St. Xavier's students…"

I follow them through the set of doors, into a long hallway that is lined with beige lockers that match the tan floors. The air here smells slightly astringent, like someone has only just wiped down everything in the hallway.

I look around, wondering where everyone is. It is, after all, a school day.

Father Jean steers Nika through a set of wooden double doors to the left. I am right behind them, my eyes opening as I step into the huge room.

WELCOME FUTURE ST. XAVIER'S STUDENTS AND PARENTS is hung on bunting at one end of the room. In between, there are a number of priests speaking with several dozen pleased-looking parents and their bored or nervous looking children. A table is set up by the window offering coffee, tea, croissants, and fruit.

They all turn to look at Nika when we walk in, bursting into a light smattering of applause. I notice that Nika's free hand makes a fist, clenching. But when I move around to her side, she is smiling pleasantly.

There is obviously some cognitive dissonance going on here.

Father Jean raises his voice. "Everyone, if you would gather around. Princess Annika is here today to talk to you all about how important her education at St. Xavier's was. Annika, if you would just say a few words? Why did you decide to go all the way to a Swiss boarding school?"

Her fist clenches again. "Thank you, everyone. If you don't mind, I have written down some of my thoughts…"

I step forward, handing her a piece of paper straight from the royal press office. She clears her throat and begins to read it aloud.

"My time at St. Xavier's was the most fulfilling experience…" she reads.

I move to the other side of the room, trying to figure out just what is going on with her. She smiles on cue. She laughs at the father's jokes. She answers a few questions from the audience.

She even signs some autographs.

But her vibrancy, her almost catty sense of humor… it's just missing. It's almost like she's been sedated or something.

I frown, keeping a close eye on her. And as soon as the questions have been wrapped up and the autographs signed, I get her the fuck out of there.

I tuck her into the backseat of the limousine myself, feeling strangely protective. When the limo pulls out, I look at her.

"What is going on?" I demand to know.

Nika looks at me with a little yawn. "Nothing. My psychiatrist gave me something to calm my nerves in situations like this. I think it worked well, don't you?"

"What situation? Will you please just tell me why the hell you hated St. Xavier's so much? Because it's obvious to me that you did."

She closes her eyes, leaning back into the cream-colored leather of her seat. "I did hate it. You are right about that much. But my grandmother made it clear to me that I shouldn't talk about my feelings. It's bad for the royal brand."

A strange feeling blooms in my chest. "Did… did somebody at the school hurt you?"

She opens her eyes and chuckles. "No. Nothing like that, Erik."

I sigh, letting out a breath I didn't know I held. "What's your issue, then?"

She rolls her eyes over to me, then turns her body toward me, shifting her knees up onto the seat. "Being Princess Annika is great. Except for rare instances... like being trapped at a Swiss boarding school with seventy other twelve-year-old girls. Almost everyone had pedigrees, lineage, and all of them had already decided before they even met me what I was like. They read the tabloids and they decided that I was cold and aloof. So, they treated me like an outsider." She crinkles her upturned nose. "Except Kal, of course. If there is a god, I seriously have to thank him for assigning us to live together. She was my refuge."

I tilt my head. "But everyone else... didn't warm up to you?"

A bubble of laughter escapes Nika's lips. "That would be putting it mildly. The whole time I was there was wretched. My locker and gym clothes were trashed once a week. I would find huge blown up pictures of myself eating pasted all over the school, with and without pig ears and a pig snout. I've lost count of how many times I was intentionally locked out of my dorm building or came back to my room find that all of my clothes were gone."

I give my head a soft shake. "So, you are saying... your class-mates bullied you? You're the princess of Denmark, Nika. You should've been able to snap your fingers and put them all in their place."

She sighs, looking away from me. "The girls at St. Xavier's were cruel. And no amount of adult attention or intervention did anything to put a stop to it. I figured out quickly that when I went crying to the house mother or even the dean, that just told everyone that their tactics worked."

Her hands close into fists. I look at her, at how angry she still is. And that anger echoes around inside of me, finding the darkness in my heart.

I know what being told that you're not good enough is. I have been told that practically my whole life, although it was more subtle than what Nika is describing.

I want very badly to touch her. Embrace her, tell her I'm sorry. Tell her that it's over.

But I don't know that I can do that and still maintain the distance between us.

"I'm sorry," I grit out. "That shouldn't have happened to you. And you shouldn't have to sell the school after the experience you had."

She gives me a humorless smile. "I couldn't get out of there fast enough. But I did get out. And now I'm just trying to look forward."

Her eyes sink closed. It's just as well, because I'm not sure what to say.

Annika being bullied for simply existing? That doesn't sit right with me. It makes me wish that I could draw her close and protect her.

That's not my job, of course. But it has to be someone's duty to look out for her... doesn't it?

I look at Annika as she falls asleep. Her wavy hair is coiled like a mass of snakes. Her long, dark lashes rest on her cheeks, her skin looking as smooth and clear as skimmed cream. Her button nose is sprinkled with a few freckles. Her lush lips are just below, begging to be touched.

Not by me. I know that. We are from two different worlds, just by virtue of being born. But someone will come along someday...

Someone worthy of her.

Someone that's not me.

I try not to think about the vague unsettled feeling that stirs within me at that notion.

Annika's head falls down, gravity doing what it does best. And I can't help but catch her as she slides toward me, cradling her like I've just been handed a delicate bird.

Nika's eyes open for the merest second, their innocence pinning me in place. Then she stretches out in my lap, closing her eyes once more. She murmurs something.

It might be, "I hoped it was you."

I go stiff and frozen, feeling very much like the new owner of a kitten who has fallen asleep in their owner's hands. I shouldn't be touching her like this, nor should she be touching me. And yet... I can't wake her up.

Not just yet.

Even though her body is warm and pliant, pressed against mine. And it's giving me ideas.

Very, very bad ideas. Flashbacks to the afternoon that she sassed me, and I lashed out at her. I kissed her and touched her hot, wet pussy...

For that moment, she belonged to me. She was mine to do with as I wanted.

She murmurs again, snuggling against my lap. I have an erection the size of the Eiffel fucking tower that she presses against, causing me pleasure and pain all at once.

That can't be comfortable to lean against. But she doesn't seem to notice or mind. I lean my head back, blowing out a breath and blanking my mind.

Still, it's a long ride back to the palace... and Nika being curled up on top of my cock doesn't make it any shorter.

14

ANNIKA

Friday morning, I am stuck inside while outside, the weather is glorious. I am listening to a much older man with a purple striped bowtie tell me that there are important things that his generation can pass to mine.

"You see, it's just a matter of you young people paying attention." He tuts, winding up for what seems like a long diatribe. "If you would put down your phones and your internet for just a few minutes, you would really be able to learn."

I smile, not quite understanding how I became this man's unwilling prey.

More than anything, I wish I had brought the entire bag of hard candies with me. I feel no shame in front of this old man, who is lecturing me rather than trying to engage me in conversation. My attention wanders to the other people that are milling around at this charity luncheon. I am the youngest person that's here by a mile, although Erik is a close second. My gaze trips over him.

Tall, fair haired, and handsome as all get out. I can just make out the shape of his muscles beneath his tightly fitted sleeves. That light gray tweed suit he's wearing ought to be outlawed. It's unfair to me, especially when his green-brown gaze wanders over my way.

His eyes lock on me. I feel my cheeks growing warm. He cocks a brow, as if to ask if I need to be rescued.

God yes. I nod subtly, then refocus my attention on the man in front of me. "You know, when I was a young man, we had principles!" he wheezes.

Erik cuts in, taking my elbow. "I'm sorry. May I borrow the princess for just a moment?"

The older man's face darkens. "Bring her back when you've finished, young man. I could tell you both a thing or two about common decency— "

Erik just pulls me away from the older man, tucking me beneath his arm and escorting me out of yet another bland gymnasium. My heart beats a little faster at Erik's touch.

As soon as we escape into the hallway, I look around. Spotting an exit door, I take his hand and tug him toward it.

"Nika," he warns. "We have only been at this engagement for half an hour..."

But there is a distinct lack of concern in his voice. I look up at him, wrinkling my nose. "You know you want to come outside with me. Just do it for once, rather than putting up a front."

His gaze tightens on my face and his lips turn down a fraction, but he just shrugs. "Whatever you say, princess."

Grinning wickedly, I push out of the doors. I exit into sunshine and immediately start beaming. I raise my hands up high toward the sun, not caring that the hem of my short white silk dress might show off more than I had planned.

"Yesss," I say. "This is already so much better than inside the gymnasium, don't you think?"

His gaze is heavy on me as he smirks. "I can't disagree with you there."

I grin over my shoulder at him, wiggling my eyebrows. "Where should we go?"

His lips quirk. As he scans the fields just outside the doors, he tilts his head. "There is a playground over there, way to the left." He points it out. "It probably has benches. Or we can just walk…"

My eyes widen. "Umm, or we can swing." I grin at him, unrepentant. "That's my vote."

He rolls his eyes, but he can't stifle the smallest smile that appears ever so briefly on his lips. "Okay. Lead the way."

I take a moment, leaning against Erik's muscular form, to take off my six inch heels. Standing next to him barefoot is a little funny; without my heels, I'm basically tiny compared to him.

Holding my stilettos in one hand, I skip along toward the little park that Erik pointed out. It turns out to be pretty nice. There are several big, shady trees. Underneath those is an oversized swing set, a seesaw, and a large dark wooden jungle gym complete with a bright blue plastic slide. All of it is enclosed in a giant sandbox, well-tended yet vacant.

I jog over to the swings, dropping my shoes behind me in the sand. I perch on one of the swings, giving Erik a huge grin. He hangs back, watching me.

It's a little frustrating sometimes, seeing Erik not just dive into things. He's so careful about everything. Then again, I could learn a little restraint, I guess.

"Come on!" I urge him. "At least come over here and push me."

His eyes tighten on mine. For a second, I think that he's going to say no. But eventually he shrugs and comes into the swings area.

I smile as he awkwardly makes his way around me. "Hey." I stop him. "Here."

I stand up, reaching to ease the knot of his tie. He goes still and expressionless under my hands. But his eyes study me intently, the green brown standing out to me just now.

I smile up at him. "What are you thinking?"

He shakes his head. "Nothing."

I unknot his tie, slipping it off. I scoff. "Seriously? I'm willing to bet that isn't true."

He tilts his head. "Maybe it's just private. Ever think of that?"

My expression turns teasing. My fingers undo the top button of his shirt. "I definitely have thought about that. It only makes me more curious. What does Erik Moen think about that is private? Hm?"

He stills my fingers by grabbing my hand. "Most of my thoughts are private, Nika."

My lips quirk. "Even from me?"

He releases me, letting out a bark of laughter. "Especially from you."

I shoot him a pouty face. He just rolls his eyes and walks around the swings. "Sit down."

I seat myself against the black rubber of the swing, gripping the silver chains that rise all the way up to meet the top of the swings. Erik grips the chains too, just a little below where my hands are. He pulls me back gently and lets go of the chains.

I glide forward gently.

I send Erik a look over my shoulder. "You're terrible at this. Push me harder!"

He smirks at me. "That's your response to everything."

I laugh, leaning my head back. He does push me harder though, making me glide a little higher each time his warm hands touch my back.

I beam at him. "Admit it. This is way better than talking to people about serious issues back there at the school."

"I will never concede to it," he says, feigning seriousness. "You know that's my motto. Never admit to anything so that no one can be mad at me."

I put down a foot, slowing my swing by dragging it along the ground. "And how would you say that's going, Erik?"

He flashes a smile. "Perfectly okay. Absolutely bland."

I stop the swing, leaning back to look at him. "Want to sit on the jungle gym for a little while?"

He offers me a small smile. "Your wish is my command, princess."

Rolling my eyes, I stand up and bite my lip. "Race you there."

I take off at a sprint, not waiting for him to catch up. I head for the solid wood structure only thirty yards away.

"No fair!" he cries.

As it turns out, I don't need to wait for him. He's so tall and has such long legs that he has no problem catching up to me.

I give him a glinting look as I climb up to the top of the jungle gym. The floor beneath me is made of sturdy slabs of wood and there is a view of the school from here that is actually quite charming.

Erik climbs right up beside me. I sprawl out on the slab, patting an invisible seat. He sits down more carefully than I did; he's all knees and elbows for a second before he settles down beside me.

He heaves a sigh. I arch a brow.

"What?" I ask.

He shrugs. "I don't know. Don't you ever get tired of being a princess on parade? I'm sick of it and it's only been a few weeks."

My lips lift at the corners. "Of course."

His eyebrows lift. "Really?"

I nod. "Yeah, definitely. I just don't know how else I am expected to behave. If I just went by Momse's set of moral codes, I would just do this cheerfully. Every single day for a couple of years. Then I'd marry some suitable boy, pop out a couple of great-grandchildren, and sort of fade away."

Erik frowns. "That's what you think is expected of you?"

Shrugging a single shoulder, I pull a face. "I know that it is. It's what my dad's sisters did. And the generation before that… and the generation before that…"

"But you don't want that, I'm guessing."

I smile a little ruefully. "No. I mean… do I want kids someday? Yes, absolutely. And I don't want to sacrifice my life for theirs. But I also don't want to be…" I pause, hesitating. "I don't mean to sound selfish. I just don't want to repeat either my mother or my grandmother's mistakes."

His eyes narrow. "What do you mean by that?"

"I just mean I don't want to raise children that are complete strangers to me. But I also have no desire to control every single aspect of my unborn children's lives. I'd like to find a balance, I guess."

"Ah." He nods, looking off. "Yeah. It's hard to even think about being a parent right now. Like… how do you know for sure that you're not completely screwing them up?"

I try to think of the best way to phrase my question. "Is that what you think your father did? Screwed you up?"

He scrunches up his face ever so briefly. "It's hard to say," he says, avoiding the subject neatly. When he looks back at me, he smiles. "It's time for a change of topics."

I look at him, at his golden hair and bewitchingly fiery eyes, at his cheekbones and jawline carved of rock. Raising a hand to his face, I gently trace my fingers along the length of his jaw, up the side of his face to feather along his temple.

He allows my light touches, closing his eyes briefly. God, he is insanely gorgeous just now.

"You're not at all what I imagined," I murmur.

He opens his hazel eyes, smiling a little. God, I would do anything for him to keep looking at me with that expression on his face.

"Is that so?" he asks.

I trace my touch back down to his jaw, trailing it along the skin outside his mouth. Shaking my head, I smile. "No."

He bites his lower lip for just a second. "Nika," he rasps. "What are you doing to me right now?"

I move closer to him, pressing the gentlest of kisses against the very corner of his mouth. He stiffens, going still.

I grab his hand and put it around my waist. "Kiss me, Erik," I beg him softly.

I can feel his fingers flex against my back. "Nika…"

When I close my eyes and lift my mouth to his once more, a hungry little growl escapes his lips. He pulls me closer and sets his too-hot lips against mine. I draw him in, running my hand up into his short hair.

Erik nips my lower lip hard, making me gasp. Then he bends me back, spearing his free hand in my hair. He kisses me again, so deeply and with so much passion that it takes my breath away. I curl my fist in the collar of his suit jacket.

He closes his hand in my hair into a fist and draws my head back, making me gasp more loudly.

He could do anything with me. He holds all the power now and we both know it. His lips traverse down the narrow column of my neck and leave fire in their wake.

But when he kisses his way down between my breasts, that's when I actually lose my breath. He buries his face in my cleavage, then turns his face and places a hot, stinging, hard hickey on my left breast. It hurts… but it also makes me want more.

My eyes widen. My hand tightens in his hair.

Erik breaks away to kiss my lips again, as brutal and as punishing and as real as anything I've ever experienced. I moan and open my mouth to him, making a soft sound as he sweeps the sweetness of his tongue against mine. My hand clutches at his suit, trying to pull him closer. I would bring him inside of me just now if that were physically possible.

I want him. My breasts ache. My pussy drips. I'm as ready as I have ever been.

If only we weren't out here in the open, where anybody at all could see us. I don't have much self-control, but I don't want my first time to be so… exposed.

Or do I? Because the longer he touches me, the quieter the voice of reason is in my head.

When Erik finally pulls away, we are both struggling for breath. He looks deep into my eyes, passion and anger and frustration all playing across his face.

And I understand him perfectly, for once in my life.

He gives his head the tiniest shake. When he speaks, his voice is gone to gravel.

"Annika… we can't," he says. He doesn't move away, but I can feel him begin to withdraw. "We just can't. We shouldn't have ever even touched."

I bite my lower lip, dropping my gaze from his. "I know."

He raises my head with a finger underneath my chin. "It's my fault. Okay? It's… god, it's not fucking you. You're perfect."

And just like that, my eyes fill with tears. I pull out of his grasp, standing up suddenly. "I think we should go back. Don't you think?"

Erik blows out a breath. "Sure, Nika."

I jump down off the jungle gym, running to scoop up my heels from where they lie in the sand. Then I take off at jog, heading back to the school.

Tears prick my eyes, but I refuse to let them fall.

"Annika!" Erik calls.

I wave behind me, not interested in whatever he has to say. After all, he's already said everything I'm meant to hear.

"See you at the school!" I call out, picking up my pace.

And gentleman that he is, Erik lets me go.

15

ERIK

STRIDING INTO NIKA'S LIVING ROOM, I FIND HER CURLED UP on the couch in high-waisted jeans and a white crop top. When I enter, she looks up, flushing when she sees me. Her eyes are the same fiery color that goes right through me.

This is the third day since I kissed her on the playground. And it's the third day that she's been avoiding me.

But no more.

"Come on," I say. "Grab some riding boots and meet me in the stables in five minutes."

Her brow rises delicately. "Why?"

I cross my arms, favoring her with a serious look. "Because we still have to work together for another two and a half months. So, this thing where we don't talk? It won't work." I give her a sharp stare. "Five minutes. Hurry up."

I turn, leaving her rooms. I just have to hope that she actually follows me. Heading down to the stables is a short enough walk through the bright mid-morning sun.

It's just starting to get hot. I eye the verdant landscape as I trot toward the stables. All I can see is the fresh green pasture lands and the soaring blue sky overhead. There is nothing for several miles here. It's just untamed wilderness owned by the royal family.

I straighten the cuff of my hooded sweatshirt. It feels odd to be dressed down in a black hoodie and dark gray sweatpants. It's as if I'm going to work out, but I don't own any clothes just for this purpose.

Why would I?

I stalk into the stables, smelling the unique mix of clean horses, sweet horse feed, and the tang of horse shit. It smells incredibly nostalgic to me, harkening back to my earliest days.

Spotting a groom, I order two horses to be saddled. I know my father has the day off. I made sure of that before I hatched this plan.

It's unlikely that I'll see him. He's surely already drunk.

But there is still a vague unease in the pit of my stomach. It stays with me as I watch the groom saddle a black gelding for me and a smaller dappled gray mare for Annika.

When Nika actually shows up, looking uncertain about why she is here, that feeling grows even stronger. The groom leads our horses outside, holding them as we mount up.

"You know how to ride, right?" I ask, getting settled in the saddle.

Her gaze narrows on me as she adjusts her seat, petting her mount's neck. "Yes. I'm surprised that you do."

I take my reins from the groom, thanking him. "It's been a while since I've had to ride," I admit. "But I grew up in these stables. My father used to be in charge around here."

She looks down at her horse, nudging her into a slow walk. "I think I knew that. Your father is not here now though, is he?"

I squint against the sunlight. "No. He still works here though. I think he's off today."

I use my heels to urge my horse forward, breaking into a trot. Annika keeps pace with me but doesn't say another word.

I look over at her. She's pulled her hair back into a messy bun and there are two blotches of color on her cheeks. Her bare-faced beauty is especially stunning against the ruggedness of the landscape.

We turn down a wide dusty path that cuts through the greenery. I know that I shouldn't even be thinking about her in this way. But I can't help it.

What I can help is how I act.

I clear my throat, slowing my horse to a walk again. "Do we need to talk about the other day?"

A hint of a smile ghosts over her lips. "What is there to talk about? You've made your level of interest quite clear."

I grit my teeth, adjusting in the saddle. "I told you. It's not personal. I'm... I... find you... pretty." My neck heats. "But there are reasons why we shouldn't... be close."

She tosses her head. "Stellan isn't a good enough reason. He's defying the rules to marry Margot."

"He's my best fucking friend!" I bark.

Nika looks at me, pausing. I'm pinned by her ice blue stare, so intense just now that it's almost electric. Then she returns her gaze back to the path in front of us.

"I appreciate your loyalty to Stellan," she says softly. "But does he even notice? From what I can see, you follow him around and he just expects you to do his bidding."

I glower at the reins clutched in my hands. "I can't help it if you don't like my friendship with Stellan. Like it or not, he is the king. So, what he says goes."

She arches a brow. "And he said that I'm off limits?" She slides me a sour look. "I bet you haven't even tried to discuss it with him."

I shoot her my blackest of looks. Nika is perfectly right in that regard, of course. But that's not entirely the point.

I roll my shoulders back. "Even if Stellan was okay with it, which he is very much not, other people wouldn't smile upon it."

She cocks her head at me. "Why do you care so much what other people think?" she asks, frustrated.

I squint at her. "Why do you?"

She flushes. "I don't."

"You do. You care very much about how everyone perceives you. Don't try to hide it from me."

"Ugh!" she declares. She urges her horse forward all the sudden, quickly shooting out and leaving me to try to catch up.

I spur my horse onward, knowing that I messed up. The plan was to come out of this on better terms than before but now I'm worried about Nika even talking to me.

"Nika!" I call. I nudge my horse more urgently, until I'm riding hard. We thunder down the little path, the dusty road disappearing beneath the horse's hooves.

I close the distance eventually. "Annika!" I try again when I know she can hear me.

She throws a look over her shoulder, slowing down once more. Lifting her chin, she says, "It's always Annika when you're angry with me. But this time, I haven't done anything wrong."

I school my expression. "No. You haven't."

Nika makes a face. "What if we just… did what we wanted to do and kept it hush hush?"

My neck heats. I've thought about this very subject at great length for the last few nights. I look down, toying with the reins.

"That wouldn't be fair. One of us might… develop feelings. Only to have them dashed the very first time that we had to attend a function with a date."

She tilts her head, her eyes narrowing. "You're expecting me to be the one with feelings, then?"

I glance away with a shrug. "I didn't say that."

Her lips twist and she rolls her eyes. "You thought it, though."

I give her a small smile. "Not even once."

She eyes me with a sigh. "So, what do you propose? Hm?"

I lift my shoulders. "It's just a summer. Surely, we can both just… resist. It'll just call for a little willpower."

Nika looks at me very frankly. "I'm a virgin, Erik. No one has ever accused me of not being able to keep my hormones under control. I just… I'm ready to lose it. How will you feel if I give my virginity away to some other guy?"

I grip my reins tightly and try not to scowl. Of course I want to be the one she chooses. If I had my way, we would stop right now and fuck right here, in the middle of the goddamned road.

But that's not the way that Nika needs it to be. She deserves a hell of a lot more than a quick fuck on a dirty path behind the palace. She's worth so much more than I can ever give her.

It's time to lie my ass off.

"It would be better than the alternative," I bluff. "We couldn't keep it quiet forever. Eventually someone would find out. And I don't want there to be any consequences over what is essentially just a very bad crush."

I can see her open her mouth to argue. I hold me hand up to stop her. "Can you not just believe me when I tell that that's what this is?"

Her lips twist again. "I'm just supposed to listen to you, huh?"

I slide her the tiniest of smiles. "I am your elder, after all."

Amusement flickers across her expressive face. "So I hear." She glances up at the sky and screws up her face. "I should turn around and head back. I'm supposed to meet my personal shopper at noon."

I raise a brow. "You are going to be cutting it awfully close, princess."

She flashes me a grin. "She'll wait for me. Or didn't you hear? I am royalty."

With that she pulls the reins she's holding, turning the horse around. Then Nika starts galloping away from me, riding fast for the stables.

I stop my horse and watch her go, acid beginning to wash around in the pit of my stomach.

16

ANNIKA

I STOP JUST OUTSIDE THE CRAVE NIGHTCLUB, BRUSHING BACK a strand of my immaculately. blown out, gleaming hair. Kalindi comes to a stop just behind me, eyeing my itty bitty shiny black dress.

"One wrong move and you're going to show every single club patron your whole butt," she says. She wrinkles her nose. "I'm not judging you, but I am very concerned about a wardrobe malfunction happening."

I roll me eyes, looking critically at her outfit. "I would say something about that white romper, but honestly? You're rocking it."

She beams at me. "Thanks!"

Behind us, Erik approaches in his same dark suit that he wore all day today. I glance back at him, a frown tugging at my lips.

Things between us have been decidedly frosty for the last two days. He says that I should find someone else to focus my attentions on.

So that's what I'm going to do tonight. Find someone else… anyone else will do.

"Come on," I urge Kal, heading toward the door. "Let's go."

When we approach the door, the bouncer looks at me. I see him dismiss me and then look again. His eyes widen and he hurries to open the door.

"Welcome, princess," he says.

We strut right into the big space. Loud dance music thrums through my blood. It takes my eyes a minute to adjust to the near darkness, punctuated by spotlights flashing high above the club. In those moments of light, I can make out the dance floor. It's packed with nameless and faceless bodies that grind and gyrate to the low, insistent beat.

"Oh," Kal says, her mouth open.

I wiggle my eyebrows at her. "Come on. Let's start with a drink."

Pulling her along by the hand, I head straight for the bar. I know Erik is right behind us, his usual scowl in full effect tonight. But I refuse to glance back at him.

Tonight is about me and what I want. And just now? I can't wait to slam down a couple shots of tequila and hit the dance floor.

Kal leans across the bar and orders us drinks, flirting a little with the hot bartender. I turn and watch the dance floor again, shivering with anticipation.

I can't wait to lose myself in between the rhythmic beats.

Erik ruins my view, stepping into my eye line. The scowl that I imagined is in place on his perfect lips. He narrows his green-brown eyes at me.

"Nika, what are we doing here?"

His voice is rough and gravelly. He looks around the night-club, as if he's searching for answers.

I shrug. "I'm trying to meet some eligible young men. I have no idea what you are here for."

He narrows his eyes on my face. "Be careful, Annika. You're coming very close to pushing my buttons."

Kal turns around from the bar, two shots in each hand. She arches a brow at Erik and hands me my shots. "Here you go. Bottoms up."

I tap the shot glasses against hers and then throw my head back, swallowing one shot and then the next. It snakes its way down my esophagus, burning as it goes.

"Blech!" Kal says, making a face. "Tequila is terrible." She looks at Erik apologetically. "Sorry, I didn't get you a shot."

Erik just crosses his arms and looks like he would rather be anywhere but here right now. His seeming detachment makes me want to punch him. But instead, I turn to Kal.

"The dance floor is calling to me!" I say, pulling at her arm. "Come dance."

I don't have to ask her twice. She grins and grabs my arm as I head out to the dance floor, sliding between people to get to the center.

Erik doesn't follow us, which is unbelievably fine with me. I throw my hands over my head and shake my ass, gyrating hypnotically to the booming bass. Kal is right beside me, giggling at the men that suddenly appear out of nowhere.

Two classically handsome Scandinavian-looking men start dancing with us. I grin up at the one I'm closest to, but I don't bother to introduce myself. If they somehow don't recognize me, I'm not about to ruin the night by telling them who I am.

I grin and keep dancing, working up a sweat. Kal seems to be hitting it off with her dance partner; he holds her by the waist as she shimmies and shakes. I grin.

This is great. Why don't we do this more often?

I glance up and realize with a note of surprise that there is an upper balcony tucked discreetly above the dance floor of this club. It's so dark that I probably wouldn't ever be able to see it…

Except that Erik is standing there, glaring at me, his expression a sullen pout. When our gazes meet, it stops me dead in my tracks.

I arch a brow, stepping closer to the guy who is dancing right beside me. The stranger puts his hands around my waist and pulls me against his body, which I could have honestly done without. But hey, I'm not a giant control freak, unlike Erik.

I put my hand around the stranger's neck, realizing that he lack's Erik's unusual height. Why that puts me off, I don't know.

Erik shakes his head and turns around, putting his back to the dance floor. I dance for another minute in my partner's grip. But when Erik isn't watching, it just seems less fun.

I turn to see Kalindi laughing as her partner whispers something in her ear. I make a 'I'm going to the bar to get a drink' gesture at her. She's so wrapped up in whatever that guy is saying that she just nods at me.

I head off the dance floor abruptly, leaving the man that I was dancing with behind. My mood is mercurial just now. I'm on the cusp of being pissed off.

Erik's black mood is contagious, it seems. Maybe if I just splash some water on my face, it'll help reset my frame of mind. Heading toward the back of the club, I find the bathrooms in a long black hallway. I push into the first bathroom, wincing at the low light. It's a single person bathroom; I start closing the door.

But someone stops me. My eyes widen.

Erik pushes the door open, glaring at me. He fills the entire doorway, his expression dark as I've ever seen it. "And just where do you think that you're going? Hm?"

I gulp, raising my chin. "What's it to you, Erik? You're just supposed to be my babysitter."

He steps inside the little room, eating up the small space. He takes a moment to close the door behind himself. The quiet snick of the lock engaging sounds loud to me.

Then again, I am used to listening to the thunderous sound my own beating heart makes. Erik rubs a hand over his mouth, looking at me like I'm his to judge. He takes a step, then another, so that he's only a few inches away from me. "What must you think of me?"

I back up until I hit the wall. He just steps forward again, his gaze dropping to my mouth.

I lick my suddenly dry lips. "What do you mean?"

He smirks, flashing me a dimple. "Do you think that I want to be here? Hmm? Do you think that I like standing guard while some other man puts his hands all over you?"

I bite my lower lip, glancing away from him with a shrug. "How should I know?"

He braces his hand against the wall next to my head, moving so close to me that we are a hair's breadth apart. Not touching… but almost.

My heart hammers in my chest. His serious eyes pierce right through me as he licks his perfect lips.

"I fucking hate it, Nika," he grates. "I hate that I'm just supposed to sit back and watch while you dance with another guy." He brings his other hand up, closing me in. And then he leans against me, tormenting me with the press of his body.

I tilt my head at him. "No one is making you do anything, Erik."

He looks down at my skimpy black dress, biting his lip. He traces a fingertip up my arm, touching a few strands of my hair.

"I think we both know that isn't true," he murmurs. He runs those same fingertips across my clavicle and down the line of my cleavage.

I squirm. "Erik—"

He interrupts me. "Are you even wearing anything under this dress?"

I swallow heavily and blush, looking up at him. It takes all the sass I can muster to say, "Wouldn't you like to know."

His lips twitch. He stares down at me for a few seconds, his expression unreadable. He leans down to my lips, placing the lightest kiss to the very corner of my mouth. He's playing with me, tormenting me.

And my response? My whole body aches. My breasts lift and tighten. My clit throbs. My pussy is damp and getting wetter by the second.

My mouth actually waters and I turn my head, trying to catch his lips with my own. But he's not interested in that.

Erik drops to his knees, making my eyes go wide with surprise. He makes eye contact with me as he touches my outer thighs, skimming his hands up the bare skin exposed by my dress. Erik presses a hand against my belly, pushing me back against the wall.

"Stay still," he warns me. "Be a good girl."

His words, spoken in such a deep and gravelly voice, make me suck in a breath. The anticipation builds as he slides his hands up my thighs.

He rucks the dress up around my hips, sucking his lower lip in briefly as he looks me dead in the eyes. I am naked before him, my whole entire pussy aching for his touch.

I've never seen anything so erotic in my damned life as seeing this man on his knees before me, bending his head toward my lower body. He raises one of my knees and exposes my most intimate parts to his view. I keep my pussy shaved completely, so I'm bare before his eyes.

I feel like if he doesn't touch me soon, I'm going to die. He licks his lips, sending a shiver up my spine.

God, he's about to eat my pussy. How long have I dreamed of this moment? I'm torn between closing my eyes and watching his every movement.

I rake my fingernails through his sandy hair, my heartbeat pounding in my ears. Erik places a single, scalding hot kiss to my inner thigh. When he nips the same soft skin, I startle, shifting my body a little.

His hands tighten on my hips. "I thought I already told you to be still." He looks up at me, his eyes promising to do dirty things to me. "I won't tell you again, Nika."

I swallow, nodding. "I'll be good," I manage.

He smirks, then hikes my knee over his shoulder. I squirm when he returns his lips to my inner thigh, kissing and gently biting his way toward my shaved pussy.

Erik splays a big hand out against my mons, gently pulling my pussy lips up and using his fingers to spread me fully. Moisture leaks from my slit. My clit throbs. Every part of me is so sensitive right now. I can feel myself beginning to tremble with need, the delicate muscles of my inner thigh shaking.

He leans in close and feathers a hot, wet kiss against the hood of my clit. I make a strangled noise, trying to tamp down my response.

He murmurs against my flesh. "I like hearing you moan for me, princess. Make all the noise you want."

He places another kiss just outside my pussy lips. I groan, shifting my weight. He just chuckles and puts another kiss below that, but still not close enough to my clit. I need more; more stimulation, more of his tongue on my clit. My hands run through his short flaxen hair, pressing him closer.

He continues trailing kisses around my pussy lips, always just outside where I want his mouth to be. I groan, whining a little.

"Erik," I whisper. "Please?"

His fingers trace the edges of my pussy, intensifying the teasing. "Please what?" he says.

He toys with the entrance to my slit, spreading around the moisture he finds there. Then he feathers a kiss over my clit once more, making my inner muscles clench with need. At the same time, he presses a single thick finger inside my pussy, pulling a hissing sound from my lips.

It feels so goddamned good.

I rock my hips against his finger, moaning when he withdraws. But before I can get too upset, he pushes a second finger inside my slit. I throw my head back and moan as he stretches me out.

Then he takes things up a notch by sealing his lips over my hot, aching clit. He sucks on it and then presses his wet tongue over it, making me cry out when he begins to lick it.

"Oh god," I whisper. "Fuck, Erik… that feels so good…"

He starts moving his fingers in and out of my slit, fingering me as he sucks on my clit. I struggle for breath as I tilt my pelvis against his mouth, moving it back and forth, experimenting with the sensations he's pulling from me body. A coil tightens somewhere deep inside me; I'm aware of my

innermost muscles shaking as I climb some invisible mountain, desperate to reach the peak.

Erik flexes his fingers inside of me, moving his hand more
forcefully. He hits a spot inside of me repeatedly that makes
me weak in the knees.

I make an inarticulate noise, my eyes closing. Clutching at
his hair, my nails rake his scalp. I'm no longer fully aware of
what is going on.

My vision tunnels down to what feels good right this second.
The press of his mouth against my clit. The movement of his
fingers in my slit, stretching me and touching that same spot
that makes me gasp out loud every time.

Erik pulls back. "Come for me, princess. Show me how good
I make you feel."

His words drive me over the edge of the precipice. My entire
body tenses, ready.

"Erik…" I cry out. "I—"

I come suddenly, shattering into a million pieces. My pussy
clenches around his fingers. My head hits the wall. I spasm
wildly, riding an unbelievable wave of sensation. Erik moans,
still working his long fingers and his clever tongue until I
pull away, too sensitive to be touched.

I feel wonderful. But I also feel like crying. I keep my eyes
closed as my heartbeat thunders in my ears, slowly drifting
down.

Erik kisses my inner thighs, drops my knee from his shoulder, and pulls my dress back down. Then he stands up.

I open my eyes and put my hands around his neck, pulling
him down for a kiss. His mouth tastes like me; my eyes fill

with tears though I am not sure why. He presses himself against my body, his hardened cock poking me in the belly.

For a minute he just kisses me, exploring my mouth with his own. I exalt in his touch and his taste, feeling… cherished.

For just this space in time, we are just Annika and Erik. Not princess and minder. Not rich and poor. There are no divisions between us, no age differences, no expectations.

But then he pulls away, stepping back. His eyes are full of sorrow and anger. "I shouldn't have done that."

I bite my lower lip, stepping close to him again. I reach out and grab at him, pouting. "Why?"

His expression darkens. He pulls away again, shaking his head. "You know why."

I draw a breath, cocking my head. "I know, yes. But I don't care. I want you to take my virginity, Erik."

He shakes his head, avoiding my eyes. "No. You don't know what you want."

I step closer. "I think I do. I like you. Erik."

"Damn it!" he curses loudly, looking at me. "No. You have no idea what you want or what you like. If you did, you would know that you and I have no future. None."

He turns away, fiddling with the lock on the door. I open my mouth to argue with him, but he just throws open the door.

"Can we just leave?" he asks, sounding angry. "Or do you have to find some more strange men to rub up against?"

I narrow my eyes. "It worked, didn't it? You couldn't stand seeing me touching another man."

His jaw clenches. "Annika— "

I shake my head, pushing past him. "Don't. If you're just going to keep telling me all the reasons why we can't fuck, I don't want to hear it."

He reaches out and catches me in the doorway, his eyes hard on mine. "I wish things were different. You have to know that."

I look up at him, at his tortured expression. "Wishing something could be different doesn't make it so."

Then I stalk out of the bathroom, intent on finding Kal and getting out of this club.

17

ERIK

I can't sleep when I get home. I'm too aggravated. By Nika, yes. But even more than that I'm just mad as hell at my circumstances.

And yeah, later when I stroke my cock, I can feel the heat of her pussy pressed against my eager mouth.

I know I can't have her. Not really.

But the fantasy of being her first, of taking her virginity, is too real... and it feels too good to stop.

That translates into a sleepless night for me, accompanied by being extremely tense and cranky the following day. I walk around with the shortest of fuses, dreading what is to come...

Family dinner.

That's right. Me, Annika, Stellan, and all the other Løve kids together with the former King and Queen. I make sure that I'm presentable - my tie straightened, my cufflinks buttoned - before I step through the door to the grand dining room.

I'm the last to arrive, by no coincidence. The room is majestic; high ceilings, plenty of natural light from the windows, a table that can seat forty people comfortably. Tonight, the table is set for eight. Goran, the former King, and Stellan, the current King, are sitting at the far end of the table. Looking as alike as a set of matching bookends, they are deep in conversation. All the men at the table look like photocopies of each other; tall, dark hair, blue eyes, exceedingly rich.

Everyone except me, of course.

To my surprise Margot sits beside Stellan, appearing as uncomfortable as possible. Her hair seems less pink than it usually is, her roots growing out.

I wonder if that's a sign of her changing style or if she caved to the Queen Mother's persistent reminders that pink hair is not ladylike.

I flash her a smile as I approach the table. She pulls a face. Good, I'm not the only one who doesn't want to be here.

Thora, the former Queen, is sitting on her husband's other side and talking to Annika. Nika is a perfect, elegant reflection of Thora's stately beauty. But for a second, as she notices my entry into the dining room, she shoots me a glare.

Then she turns up her nose at me and engages Margot in conversation. The only empty seat is next to Nika, so I slide into the seat left vacant for me. I see Nika's hand clench the glittery gold skirt of her full-length dress. It's hard not to stare at her, especially right now when she's wearing such a provocative dress. Two golden triangles of cloth cover her breasts, connected by a slinky gold chain.

I can almost see her stiff, puffy nipples through the barely-there garment. Nika wears her risqué dress as though it's not a big deal. As though there is no one that wants simultaneously to rip that dress off of her and also to cover her up with one of my jackets.

Maybe I'm the only one that feels that way, but I don't think so.

I clear my throat and jerk my gaze away, looking at Lars sitting beside me. Finn is across from me, frowning. Both of the younger brothers look like they want to leave.

I lean over to Lars. "Am I crazy or is everyone here except Anders?"

Lars' lips lift. "No, you're not crazy. No one really knows where our brother even is. Asking where he is seems to be useless. Even *Mor* doesn't remember the last time Anders touched base."

I nod, looking around the table. A servant appears over my shoulder. "Would you care for wine, sir?"

I glance up at him. "No, thank you. Water will be fine."

Finn leans across the table. "Are you living a booze-less existence, Erik?"

I narrow my gaze. "No, Finn. I just have a long day tomorrow. Annika is expected to show at a red carpet event for some fashion charity that she sponsors." I squint.

"Erik!" Thora declares. "I didn't see you sneak in. Are you excited about tomorrow's red carpet? Annika told me that it's going to be broadcast on basically every network. You're going to have to be a good escort."

I lift my head, swallowing. The former Queen never paid me much attention at all. Having her spotlight on me now is more than a little uncomfortable.

"I am," I bluff. "Although as I was just telling Finn, it's going to be a very long day."

Goran clears his throat, joining our conversation from his seat at the end of the table. "You're walking Annika down the red carpet tomorrow, I assume?"

I feel heat creep up my neck. "Actually, no. I wasn't invited to be in front of the cameras. The reporters aren't interested in anyone who doesn't have a title or isn't already independently famous."

Goran lifts a brow. "Is that so? I had no idea that the organizers even cared who walks down the red carpet."

Of course he doesn't. The former king lives in a bubble, surrounded by only the best and the finest things in life. Until he got sick and gave up the crown to Stellan, he was almost always on an expensive, amenity-filled trip to some far-flung locale under the excuse that he was spreading peace.

Stellan jumps in. "You know, Erik is going to be titled this year."

Thora's eyebrows lift. She looks over to me. "Have we not managed to find you a title already? How thoughtless of us."

I look down with a shrug. What am I supposed to say to that, exactly?

Goran coughs a few times, bringing a meaty fist up to his face. Then he starts wheezing and turning red, sputtering and coughing much more forcefully. In a flash, the focus is on the former King.

Thora gets up and presses a glass of water into Goran's hand. Annika stands, her brow drawn down as she watches her father like a hawk.

"Is there anything that I can get you?" Stellan asks his father, a concerned expression on his face.

Goran just shakes his head, his coughing beginning to subside. "No."

He takes a sip of water. Thora rubs his shoulder, looking worried.

"It would help if your father's doctors would settle on a diagnosis. We've been told that he might have multiple sclerosis or ALS... but other doctors are sure it's early onset Alzheimer's disease..."

I sneak a glance at Nika. She sinks back into her seat, her fists balled up like she's ready to fight someone. Her expression is unreadable, but I have the sense that just beneath the surface lies an endless well of sadness and rage.

Before I even realize what I'm doing, I reach out a steadying hand to cover one of her fists. Her eyes go wide as she turns her innocent gaze on me. She jerks away from my touch, her gaze sliding across the table to Stellan and Margot.

"Don't," she whispers, so quietly that I almost don't hear it.

I quickly withdraw my touch, my neck heating with embarrassment. My hand burns and I clench my fist.

What was I thinking, touching her here? It's almost like I want to get caught.

I clear my throat and look across the table. Luckily Stellan is still talking to his father. Margot meets my gaze head on though, arching a brow. She doesn't say anything, but her gaze slips back and forth between me and Annika.

I can only guess at the conclusions she's drawing.

Lars looks around. "If *dar* is going to be all right, can we eat? I'm starving."

Finn pushes his wineglass away and glances toward the doorway. "I smell meat."

As soon as he says it, servants come into the room with still-sizzling lamb shanks hot from the grill, brabant potatoes, and a cool selection of shaved brussels sprouts with slivered almonds and pecorino romano cheese. Plates are placed in front of each of us, the food artfully arranged.

I didn't even realize that I was hungry until I smelled that lamb shank. Thora reclaims her seat, and everyone digs in. The brabant potatoes and the lamb melt on my tongue. I forget sometimes that Goran and Thora have one of the world's best chefs at their disposal. The rest of the palace is served amazing food, but this… this reminds me that even within the palace walls, there are different classes.

Thora glances at Annika in between bites of food. "Annika, how are things in your world? When did you get back from boarding school? I'm afraid I'm sort of out of the loop when it comes to knowing the day to day. It's been impossible to keep up with the world while my husband has felt ill."

Around the table, all of Thora's children raise their brows. No one dares to tell Thora that her lack of parental guidance didn't start when Goran feel ill. For most of my life, I've watched Stellan and his siblings struggle with having two parents that were rarely at home with their children.

It's understandable to some degree… but also sort of laughable for Thora to even say something so out of touch with reality.

Annika clears her throat and raises her fork, gesturing with it. "I've been back for the better part of a year, mor. And…" A muscle flexes in her jaw. "I'm feeling very smothered by being a royal at this moment in time."

Thora's brows arch up. "Oh? Well, that's no good. At least you have Erik, though. That's certainly better than having some bodyguards on your tail every moment of the day."

She just glossed over the fact that she didn't know how long Annika had been back here at the palace. Typical of Thora and Goran, though. The crown just allowed them to parent from a distance, it seems.

Nika looks down at her plate with a murderous expression. "I think that Momse would agree with you on that count, mor."

I clear my throat. "Everything is running smoothly. Isn't that right, Annika?"

She shoots me a glare and takes a big bite of her food, chewing it. I send her my stoniest look. But Thora's attention has already wandered over to her other children. "And Lars, what about you? How is… what's her name? That lovely redhead that you are always running around with?"

I glance over at Lars, who frowns down at his plate. "I assume you mean Pippa. And she's fine. She's actually just taken a new job with a fashion magazine."

Margot finally pipes up. "Yes, Pippa is going to be a junior editor with a fashion magazine. It's a huge step forward in her career."

Thora smiles. "Well isn't that nice. You know, Lars, it's really too bad that your Pippa is commonly born. She would make an ideal partner for you otherwise."

My eyebrows lift. Margot's face goes a deep shade of crimson. Thora seems unaware of the fact that two of her dinner guests were not born into her same world of wealth and privilege.

Goran clears his throat. "Thora, darling. You're making Margot uncomfortable. Let's change the subject."

I don't even factor into the conversation. I keep my expression carefully blank, but inside I'm wondering why I'm even here. Finn shoots me an uneasy glance and lifts a shoulder in a shrug. Nika looks at me, her mouth tugging down into a frown.

That's the worst feeling, in my opinion. Pity for being born poor, coming my way from a fucking princess.

No, not just a princess.

A princess whose hot little body I've felt under my hands, whose perfect pouty lips I've crushed with my kiss. I can't stand the fact that she feels pity for me now.

It makes me so angry that I can't even look at her right now.

"Well… this has been nice…" Lars rolls his eyes, clearly still upset over how his mother talked about Pippa. "But I do have to get up early tomorrow."

He rises, saying goodbye to everyone before he heads out. For a minute, there is an awkward vacuum of silence. I'm focused on keeping my emotions internal and silent.

Perhaps Nika does have a point with her teasing about my strait-laced, buttoned up personality. I look around the table uncertainly.

Stellan pushes himself up from the table. "I think we should call it a night."

He and Margot say their goodbyes. I eye Annika, trying to work out my own excuse.

Thora pouts a little bit. "All my children leave me. Stay for a bit, those of you that are still here." Silence reigns for several seconds, then Thora turns to her daughter. "Tell me Annika, who are you seeing right now? Is there anyone worth mentioning to me?"

Annika eyes widen. She goes still, looking extremely nervous. Her eyes dart to me for the briefest of moments. Then she controls herself, looking at her mother.

"No, mor. There is no one." Her mouth twists to the side. "I mean, there was someone, but he ruined it."

She doesn't even so much as glance at me, but I feel my neck heat anyway. I'm a thousand percent certain that she is talking about me.

"Oh, that's too bad." Thora pulls a face. "What did he do?"

Nika tilts her head. "He was obsessed with wealth and class and status... and because of our differences in how much money we were born with, he messed things up with me too many times." She licks her lips, darting her gaze my way. "You could say that I'm taking some personal space from dating now."

"That sounds like a good idea," Goran says, nodding.

I stand up abruptly. "I think I'm going to call it a night. Thank you for inviting me, your highnesses."

Annika shoots to her feet. "Me too! I mean... I should be getting to bed early tonight."

I glare at her, but Thora just smiles. "Okay. That's all right... I wanted to speak with Finn alone anyway."

Finn's face twitches almost comically. I feel more than a little bad for him, but I've already excused myself.

"Goodnight, everyone." I bow and then stalk out of the room, feeling immense relief when I am out of the formal dining room.

18

ANNIKA

I follow Erik out of the dining room, waiting until we are in the hush of the hallway to eye him critically. He stops for a moment, throwing his head back and sighing.

"Fuck," he mutters, bringing his hands up to cover his face.

"What?" I ask, irritated with him.

He lowers his hands and looks at me for a long moment. I can feel his eyes drop to my mouth, to my barely clad breasts, to the thigh high slits in my floor length gown. Then Erik starts down the hallway, shaking his head a little. I have to hurry to keep pace with his long strides.

"You are unbelievable," he says, looking straight ahead down the long hallway.

A derisive snort leaves my mouth without me really thinking about it. "Me? How about you? Why were you even at dinner?"

He slides me a look as we reach the other end of the hallway and take a sharp right into a small, mostly disused staircase.

"I was invited by the king. It's not something that I could turn down, no matter how annoyed I am with you."

He steps out of the hallway and stops. We should part ways here, me going upstairs to my rooms, Erik going… wherever he sleeps.

The fact that I don't actually know where that is sticks in my head.

He nods. "Let's go. I'll walk you back to your rooms."

Shaking my head and rolling my eyes, I head into the service elevator. Erik ducks in after me, pulling closed the steel grating and pressing the button for the top floor. The elevator lurches upward, yanking us along with it.

I bite my lower lip and tilt my head at him. "You know, I thought we were in a good place. Then before I know it, you're telling my entire family about what it's like to… to desire me."

I blush a little as he pins me with his green-brown gaze, but I don't look away. He steps a little closer, lowering his voice.

"Do you think it was any easier for me to hear you tell your mother about me?" His lips twist. "It wasn't. It made me feel like a villain."

He moves a little closer so that we are separated by only a few inches of air. I arch a brow, looking up into his gorgeous face.

A little voice in the back of my head tells me to sass him. I feel the tension simmering, bubbling just below his surface. Something deep inside me is excited by the idea of seeing him lose him cool.

I smirk. "Aren't you the villain of this story, Erik?"

A muscle flexes in his jaw. His gaze drops to my lips, making my stomach flutter. He very carefully splays one big hand out against my waist, dropping his voice to a whisper. "Is that what you want, Nika? Do you need a villain to complete your fairytale?"

His green-brown eyes bore into mine.

I bite my lip suggestively. "How will I know unless we try?"

Erik presses me back against the elevator wall, a soft growl deep in his throat. "Don't do that. It isn't fair."

I reach my hands up to curl around his neck. His leans against me, his cock pressing into my lower belly. My pulse pounds. My eyes close.

I don't know if he kissed me first or if my lips found his, but somehow his hot mouth presses down onto mine. I moan as he slips his tongue inside my mouth, curling it against my own. The elevator jerks to a stop.

In the back of my mind, I know that I have to pull the trigger now. The moment is right. If I don't make a move now to declare my intentions, we might never get this close to having sex again.

I slide my fingers through the straps of my dress, tugging at them suggestively. Then I break off our kiss, throw my head back, and draw one of the straps down my arm. I can feel his breathing constrict as I expose my right breast. My nipple pebbles in the cool air.

Erik drags in a heavy breath, his eyes glued to my nipple. Trailing my fingers across my chest, I swirl my fingertips around the pouty, rose colored peak.

I expected him to make a noise or maybe to kiss my neck. But he shocks me by picking me up and holding me in place against the wall. I wrap my legs around him. He puts his incredibly hot, wet mouth against the pink tip of my breast, sucking and groaning loudly. The noise is hungry and needy, resonating with me on a soul-deep level.

Erik sucks and bites my nipple, causing heat to ripple outward, gathering and concentrating low in my body. My pussy throbs. He brackets my breast with a hand and takes another pull, forcing strange sounds to come from my throat.

I writhe against him, flexing my hips. He answers by rocking his own hips against me, his rigid cock making its presence known.

His free hand comes up to my bare thigh, skimming upward from my knee to my hip. When his fingers reach around to shape my ass, he grunts.

"No panties?" he husks.

I bite my lip, shaking my head.

He smirks. "You are such a bad girl, Nika."

I tilt my head. "Are you just going to tell me about it? Or are you actually going to fucking do something this time?"

His gaze narrows on my face, almost heated enough to be called a glare. He skims his hand up my arm, catching the strap of my dress and pulling it up. My breath catches.

Erik puts both of his hands on my kneecaps and lowers me to the ground. I stand on shaky legs, not really under-standing what he is doing. Then he spins, sliding the elevator grate wide and pressing the button to open the door.

For a moment, I'm crushed. Is this his way of shutting the door on the growing heat between us?

But when the door slides open, he grasps my arm and starts hauling me out of the elevator. I look at him with a bewildered expression.

He grits out. "If you don't want to lose your virginity standing upright in a shabby elevator, start walking. You have exactly one minute to get in your bedroom and get this fucking dress off. Then I call the shots, wherever we are."

My eyes widen. I hurry along the hallway toward my rooms, trying to keep up with his decisive pace. As soon as I hit the doorway to my living room, I start thinking of just how I'm going to get out of this dress. Truth be told, putting it on was kind of an elaborate production.

I glance up at Erik, swallowing. He doesn't look at me; his gaze is fixed on my bedroom door. The second we walk through it, he slams the door closed behind me and pushes me toward my elegant four poster bed. I stumble toward the crisp white linens, kicking off my shoes as I go. He grabs me from behind, nuzzling my ear.

"Time's up," he whispers. He draws my hair back from the side of my neck and bites me hard.

It feels so good, having him dominate me like this. The breath leaves my lungs. My eyes roll up in my head.

I hear a loud moan, but it's several seconds before I put it together that the sound comes from somewhere deep inside me. He walks me over to the side of the bed, taking a step back and ripping my dress down the back. I shudder at the feel of my sudden nakedness, especially when he roughly strips the dress from my body. He shoves his knee between my legs and bends me over the bed. The sheets feel coarse against my face and my sensitive breasts.

When he grips my hips and grinds into me, I moan. "Erik…"

He flips my golden mane off of my neck, running his hand from my nape down my upper back. "Mm. Do you know how long I've wanted this, princess?"

I tremble, shaking my head. Turning my head to the side, I can just make him out. "No."

His lips lift at the corners. "Longer than I would like to admit." He skims his touch down my spine ever so slowly, drinking the sight of me in. "And now, here you are." Both of his hands shape the curve of my ass. "All naked and spread for me."

He thrusts his hips against me roughly, letting me feel his hardened cock. Then he steps back. He starts unbuttoning his shirt.

"Get on your knees, princess. Face down, ass up. Let me see your pretty pussy."

My face instantly starts to glow as red as a hot coal. While he undresses behind me, I crawl onto the bed and present myself to him.

He climbs on the bed, only wearing his boxer briefs. He slaps my ass, which surprises me and makes me squeal. I can feel the stinging outline of his palm on my ass.

Then he bends down, kissing and nibbling the back of my right thigh. I make a strangled squeaking sound. He doesn't pause for a second, though.

Pushing my backbone down to bow my back, he brushes his clever fingers over my slit. I gasp, feeling a fresh wave of moisture leak from my slit.

He looks at my ass and my pussy, waiting and ready for him to touch them. "Your pussy is getting ready for me, princess." His fingers brush my slit again. "I'm going to fucking stretch you out and make you call my name. That is, if you'll be a good girl."

I shudder. *Yes*, I think. *I'll do anything you ask.*

He dips a finger the barest inch inside my entrance, making my whole body tighten with need. He moves down, trailing his kisses down my left ass cheek to the back of my thigh. I clench subconsciously as he showers kisses over my thighs, my ass, and the very outside of my pussy lips. It feels incredible, but… I know that there is more.

Hell, after he shocked me by going down on me at CURVE, I have been waiting for this exact moment. It's just… he's killing me with his slow kisses on every single place except my dripping wet slit.

Finally, I moan out of frustration. "Erik… please?"

He pauses, his lips on my inner thigh. When he speaks, I can feel his lips move against my flesh. "What do you want, Annika? I want you to tell me."

I tremble, feeling very exposed. "I—" My face burns. I close my eyes. "Eat my pussy, Erik."

He chuckles and I feel the reverberations against my skin. He grabs my hips and presses his face in, licking my slit up and down. It feels so damn good, but I want more.

I can just tell him that… right?

"Erik? Please do that more," I whisper. My face burns anew at the begging tone of my voice. But he did say that I should be vocal…

He immediately starts licking and sucking my clit, making me give a pleasured hiss.

I grab onto my comforter, needing something to hold onto.

I FREEZE UP A LITTLE BUT BEFORE I CAN PROTEST, HE SLIDES HIS hands over my thighs. Holding me down, he licks my clit in slow, lazy circles.

I am desperate for him, moaning and clenching my hands into fists in the sheets. He takes full advantage, easing his fingertips against my lower lips. I am so wet and excited that I don't need any lube. As he presses his fingertips against my pussy, entering me with a shallow thrust, I make a sound, a kind of whimper, and he takes his mouth away again.

I can feel my body weeping for him, feel the sheets beneath my body growing damp, clinging to my knees.

"Are you going to be a good girl and be quiet so that I can finish eating your pussy?" he murmurs against my bare flesh. "I really hope you are, because I can't wait to hear you call out my name."

I nod, feeling my face grow hot pink. I shut my mouth and go still, willing him to continue.

He presses against my pussy lips again with his fingertips. Then he kisses my pussy again, withdrawing himself from the bed. To my surprise, he grabs a robe and puts it on, leaving the room. He's gone for a while, a couple of minutes at the very least.

I frown and sit up, not quite knowing where he's gone. Then he returns, holding a small black silk drawstring bag and looking immensely pleased with himself.

He sheds the robe again and comes to kneel on the bed, a knowing smirk on his features. He reaches inside the bag and brandishes a six-inch-long piece of smooth, polished glass. It is the size and shape of a cock.

My eyes widen. "What… is that a dildo?"

Erik gives me a heated smile. "Lay back. Let me pleasure you, Nika."

I'm so hot for him that I bite my lip, relaxing to lie down on my back. He teases me by touching the outside of my thighs with the cold glass. I gasp, shivering. But the dildo soon warms up in his hands. He eases my legs to open again, widening them until he has a perfect view of my pussy.

He looks at me, his excitement evident as he bites his lip. "God, you are so beautiful, Annika."

Erik drops a kiss to my inner thigh as he presses the tip of the dildo to my pussy lips. I am so wet; it slides in partially with no resistance. God, the pressure of the dildo feels good, almost like his cock.

He withdraws it, kissing my clit once more. I couldn't be quiet, so I groaned softly. He doesn't pause, he just moves the dildo in again, licking my clit.

"Oh god," I gasp. "Fuck!"

I grab the sheets, knowing that I am going to come soon. I feel my thighs shake as he French kisses my clit. As he moves his tongue, he gently pulls the dildo out of my pussy, and moves it to my ass instead.

I am shocked enough by the contact to make a noise, but luckily this time he doesn't stop licking. He turns up the intensity of his French kiss as he gently presses the dildo against my ass.

Erik pauses, and I groan. When he returns, he moves the little dildo against my rear entrance once more, and I feel the slipperiness of the lube he has added. I bite my lower lip and close my eyes.

It feels so naughty but so fucking good. He slips the dildo into my ass while he kisses my clit. The sensation of being very full and very fucking ready to come washes over me.

"Oh god… please…" I beg him.

He chuckles. That is enough for me. My eyes roll back in my head, and I clench and shake. I feel enraptured, but even as I am drifting down, he is already preparing for more. He sheds his boxers, his expression intense. I shiver with anticipation as I look at his nudity, biting my lip.

He gets up, putting the dildo aside. Flipping me over on my hands and knees, he smacks my ass once. A chill runs down my spine, unbidden,

Erik actually growls his excitement, which only increases my sense of anticipation. He pushes my thighs apart and presses his thick cock against the entrance to my pussy. He feels so huge from this angle, impossibly big.

He uses a little of my lubrication to push himself halfway in. We both groan. He wraps my long platinum hair in his fist, withdraws slightly, and then hammers himself home.

I cry out, the pleasure bordering on pain. He is so big, filling every single inch of me, touching every secret spot inside.

He grasps one of my hips and starts thrusting slowly. I shudder as he withdraws and then fills me completely, again and again. Erik increases his speed, gripping my hair and fucking me harder.

I moan, feeling him filling every inch of my pussy. He shifts a little, and suddenly he is hitting my g-spot. I tighten and clench instinctively around his cock.

"Ah!" I call. "God, right there!"

"You like that?" he growls. "I want you to come so hard. I want to feel you cream all over my cock."

I groan as he hits my g-spot over and over, his thrusts as rapid as gunfire. Everything inside my body tightens.

"Oh god… oh god, Erik, I'm— I'm—" I cry, clenching around his cock. I feel like I am exploding, my eyes rolling back in my head.

He groans as he comes, finishing with a final thrust. I can actually feel his cock twitching, hot spurts of come releasing as he buries himself deep in my pussy.

"Fuck," he mumbles, struggling for breath.

He loosens his hold on my hair, leaning forward to kiss my lower back.

When we are both lying on our backs, struggling for breath, his expression contorts. He puts his hand over his eyes, making a quiet sound of distress. I look over at him, pulling in a breath.

"What?" I ask.

Erik rolls onto his side, sliding his legs off of the bed, and then sits up. "Nothing."

I arch a brow as he stands. "Where are you going?"

A pained expression crosses his face. "To my bed. This was…" He squints, stretching. "We can't do this again, Nika. This was a one-time thing."

I sit up, tilting my head. "We both wanted it. There's no issue of consent or anything, if that's what you're worried about."

He grabs his dress pants, hauling them up his legs. He doesn't meet my gaze. "It's not."

I'm a little taken aback by how dismissive his tone is. "Did I do something wrong? Did I… not…"

His expression darkens. He looks at me, his eyes filled with so much guilt and regret and shame that the breath freezes in my lungs.

Erik sits on the bed, looking me in the eye. He takes my hand. "You were perfect, Annika. Really. You blew my mind. I feel lucky to have shared your bed."

I bite my lip, my brow furrowing. "So, what is the problem, then?"

A muscle ticks in his jaw. He glances away, taking a deep breath. "When I'm with you, nothing ever seems forced or contrived. It all just seems so natural. But as soon as I take a step back, I see all the cracks in our foundation."

My lips twist. "Are you talking about Stellan?"

His hazel eyes swing around to pin me in place. "Annika. That might be the biggest reason that we shouldn't be together. But that's not the only one. I'm too old for you. I'm too poor. I was born in a different world. My father— "

Furious, I shake my head. "If you repeat that you weren't born a royal one more time, I swear I will scream."

He lifts a single shoulder in a shrug. "Okay. But just because I don't say it doesn't mean that it isn't true."

I can feel angry tears beginning to prick my eyes. I'm frustrated by his rejection and angry at his reason for it.

There is nothing I want less than to cry in front of Erik, but it seems like it's about to happen. I stand up, grabbing my robe from the back of a chair that I keep by my bedside table. I can feel Erik's probing glance as he just stares at me.

I head for my bathroom, hoping like hell he will get the message and make himself scarce.

"Where are you going?" he demands to know.

I inhale a shaky breath, but I don't look at him. "I'm going to take a bath and sulk."

He looks mildly offended. "What? Are we just done then?"

I stop, my body tensing, my hands clenching into fists. My jaw tightens as I whirl around on him. "Erik, get out of my room. You don't want me, and you don't want to be here… so just leave!"

My voice gives out on the last word and I turn, shaking my head. I feel so ashamed and unwanted. Tears prick my eyes. I just need to be alone. I run the last few steps toward the bathroom, ignoring the way that Erik calls my name.

Entering the cool white marble bathroom, I slam the door behind me. A sob escapes my lips as tears start to pour down my face. Covering my eyes with my hands, I lean against the door and sink to the floor in despair.

I'm officially in full meltdown mode, crying on the floor like a lovesick little girl. What has this guy brought me to?

I hear Erik as he taps against the bathroom door. "Nika…"

His voice is muffled but I can sense the frustration there too. I don't answer. Or maybe I can't, I don't know. I hiccup and continue to ugly cry. Crying feels almost relieving at the same time as it feels like a knife twisting in my guts.

I hear him just on the other side of the door, his discomfort complete and obvious. He stands there for several beats. Then I hear him step back.

"I'm sorry," he says. "I'm the one that allowed things to go this far. It won't happen again, Nika. I swear."

It feels like he is physically shredding my heart. But the worst thing is the leaden feeling in my chest when I hear his footsteps receding, his presence vanishing in the blink of an eye.

My heart sinks. Closing my eyes, I let the tears stream down my face.

This.

This is what anguish feels like.

I need to remember this the next time that I am feeling flirtatious.

19

ERIK

I SIGH AND RUN MY HAND DOWN THE FRONT OF MY TUX, glancing around the press junket. It is a madhouse right now. There is a large white backdrop set up across from where I stand, complete with designer logos of the companies that are providing support for this charity event. Before the backdrop is a red carpet, laid out like an offering from the gods.

Women in barely-there, skimpy black dresses teeter on sky high heels down the red carpet. Men in tuxes just like this one I'm wearing walk beside the women, doing their best to keep the women upright and steady.

It's always a little surreal to be invited to one of these events. On television, it's so seamless and glamorous. But in person, you can see how frantic everyone is behind the scenes. There is a chaotic energy as assistants and reporters hustle back and forth, preparing for the red carpet event to take place.

Usually the royal press office politely declines. But this event is for one of Annika's favorite fashion-related charities. So here we are, me watching with anxious eyes as a camera crew begins setting up to my right.

Nika took a separate car to get here, presumably because she doesn't want to be around me at all. And I don't blame her for that, not in the least.

After I left her chamber last night, I laid awake in my bed, restless. I tossed and turned the whole entire night, unable to get the sound of Annika's muffled tears out of my fucking head.

Even sobbing and messy, she was so damn beautiful. I swear, I started to crack.

Today, in the cold light of day, I feel like an empty vessel, poured out and left to lie on its side. All that is left over is a little bit of anguish on the very bottom, amplifying whatever emotions I've been feeling the last few days.

It's an empty hollowness more than anything, a numbness which I am fairly sure that I didn't intend to feel.

Hell, I didn't plan to feel any of this.

I fuss with my bow tie and look at my cell phone. For someone that got exactly what he said he wanted last night, I'm acting like I am dying. I don't know what to do about that but it's still a fact.

I hear her arrive before she even gets out of the car.

I know that Nika has just arrived because a hush falls over the entire red carpet and the press pit. There are people whispering about it from this distance. The red carpet runs all the way down the steps to where the celebrities are supposed to get out of their cars. And the second that Annika gets out and looks around, a hush falls over the people around me.

I turned my head, looking at her. My eyes widen the little bit. If her grandmother sees just what she is wearing, that beautiful hot mess is a dead woman walking. She wears a short length of gold chain which has somehow been converted into a dress. It shows off her collarbone, her breasts, everything from her thighs down. And when she turns around for just a second, I get a glance at the back of the dress, if it can even be called that. The dress is fastened at the back with gold chain and a barely there bit of fabric covers her ass. That's it.

My breath leaves me in a huff. The guy to my right adjusts his bow tie and gives me a look. "I know, right? Who would've known that the princess was so…" He bites his lip. "Well, you can see for yourself."

I shoot him a glare and hurry out of the line of press that I've been hiding behind. I should stop Nika before she even steps on the carpet. That's the only way to make sure that her grandmother doesn't lose her mind afterwards.

Elbowing my way through the crowd, I keep my eyes fixated on Annika's long flaxen hair. She seems to notice me only at the last moment that I push towards her. Her guileless eyes take me in and coolly dismiss me. I grab her elbow, pulling her closer.

She turns towards me, opening her mouth as if to argue. That's when I smell the whiskey on her breath. Leaning closer to her, I narrow my gaze on her face. "Are you insane? Just what do you think you're doing?"

She pulls her elbow from my grip, her expression unreadable. "I'm walking the red carpet."

I growl under my breath. "Annika, I swear to god…"

Her head swivels as she searches the crowd. She lands on a tall, dark-haired man in a tux. He turns and brightens; he begins to nudge his way through the crowd to get to her.

She points her long arm at him. She teeters, her balance thrown off. Clearly, she is even more drunk than I gave her credit for. When she speaks, she slurs her words. "There he is now. He's my date. If you will excuse me?"

I grab her arm before she can walk away. "You think that I'm going to just let you drunkenly wander around here? You may be a princess, but I am your minder. And if you think that I am going to just let you embarrass the royal family by appearing on television right now in your current state, you've got another thing coming."

Gritting my teeth, I start to pull her back toward the limousine that she just left. The chauffeured car has long since pulled away from the curb, but I can still make it out, stuck in traffic.

Nika pulls herself from my grip once again, this time hissing at me. "What are you doing? Let me go!"

I don't even look at her. I just use my overwhelming size to push her through the crowd, trying to ignore that people are definitely turning their heads to see what the fuss is about. Honestly, it wouldn't even be that big of a deal, except that Nika is so well known.

I'm man handling the country's princess, after all.

So, while I'm doing my best to shield her from prying eyes, everyone is probably whispering about the fact that the Princess is being forcefully removed from this event. That isn't what I want per se. But if it comes down to deciding between making Annika angrier with me or protecting the royal family from embarrassment, I know what I will choose.

I make it down to the street, all but carrying Nika. She doesn't even try to resist, really. She just looks mad and flushed as she glares up at me. Her mouth is screwed up like she's just bitten down on a lemon.

A hand lands on my shoulder, pulling at me. I glower, turning my head to see that Nika's dark-haired date has followed me. He is looking between me and Annika, a little bewildered.

This close, I realize that he's actually taller than me. I raise a brow.

"Could you fuck off?" I bite off.

He flushes, looking at Nika beseechingly.

"Princess Annika. Do you need help?" he asks, his voice unusually high and grating for someone so big.

I shrug out of his grip and step backward, pulling Nika into my body protectively. The last thing I want is to cause a scene here where everybody can see us. But I don't have time or the inclination to explain myself to this random dark-haired stranger.

Annika looks at me, arching a brow. "I don't know. Do I need assistance, Erik? Or do you want to just let me go right now? Because I will cause a scene. That much I assure you of."

A man wearing a tuxedo, a headset, and a clipboard cuts into our argument. "Excuse me, Princess Annika? We need you to walk the red carpet now so that we can prevent the back up of celebrities as we begin our event. We want to go ahead and get you seated in the front of the room, at the table of honor."

Annika looks at me with a little smirk and wrests her elbow from my grasp. Then she straightens her dress and looks at the dark-haired man she's chosen as her date. She holds her arm out and smiles, showing off her teeth. "But of course. Let's go, David."

Her date takes her arm, leaning close to whisper in her ear. "It's Ben."

She pats his arm and starts walking back towards the red carpet, climbing the stairs once more. She doesn't spare a second look for me. I am left to follow in her wake, having the depressing realization that this is what babysitting royalty is all about.

If it weren't for Annika being so interested in flirting with me, this is exactly what it would have been like the entire time that I had been tasked with this duty.

I suck in a breath and hold it as I trail after Annika and Ben down the red carpet. No one is interested in me, which is not surprising at all. Everyone is interested in Annika, taking their microphones out for a comment and peppering her with questions. She smiles in a way that does not seem genuine and somehow manages to walk down the red carpet, despite the fact that she is drunk and those gold heels that she is wearing look like torture devices.

Sexy, yes. But they definitely look like she could die at any moment.

She pauses on the carpet, posing with Ben at her side. Her saccharine smile never leaves her face. And if there were no questions from reporters, I think that maybe Annika would've gotten away with the next incident. But unfortunately for her, they are still pressing in on her with a thousand questions.

One pretty female reporter steps forward out of the line and pushes her microphone close to Annika's face. "Princess Annika, who are you wearing? And who is your date?"

Annika leans against Ben and licks her lips apprehensively. "I'm wearing Greta von Grissel and my date is my lovely friend…" She pauses. It's clear to me that she has forgotten her date's name. She blushes a bit. "You can just call him my friend. That's okay."

The dark-haired reporter raises her brows slightly. She steps a little closer to the Princess. She must get a whiff of the booze on Annika's breath. I can see a split-second decision being made on the woman's face. She smiles at Annika, her expression turning a little cruel.

"Princess Annika, are you drunk right now?"

The crowd falls under a hush, heads turning. Everyone strains to see Annika's response. Annika's eyebrows go up, and her mouth tightening a fraction.

I see her shake her head, frowning just a little bit. "No. Why would you ask me that?"

The reporter presses closer, pushing her microphone into Annika's face. Annika reacts, stepping backward. But those gold heels betrayed her. She tips over and trips over the carpet. It's only a moment of quick thinking on my part that saves her from total disaster.

I move forward, neatly catching Annika by the elbows and hauling her up against my chest. She shoots me a glare and tries to shake off my touch. But I lean in close to her ear, pressing my lips close. "Are you really going to make this worse than it already is? This clearly isn't going to go your way. So, let me just take you home."

Annika bares her teeth at me. Her eyes lose focus for just a second, reinforcing the fact that she is drunk as hell. "Yeah, like I'm going to let you take me anywhere. That's just not going to happen," she hisses.

In the next second I step back from her. Letting her go so suddenly removes some kind of stability that she relied on, apparently. Because when I take my hands off of her arms, she goes down like a lead filled balloon.

And there is no stopping her from falling.

I belatedly realize what is already happening when Annika is looking at me with a bewildered expression, slumping help-lessly to the ground. My eyes widen as she collapses.

Ben is right behind her, picking her up off the ground. But the damage is already done. Reporters crowd around her in a circle, shouting questions and fighting to be the closest one to the disaster.

That's it.

I go into auto mode, grabbing Annika and hauling her back toward the limousines. I grit my teeth and let my expression do most of the talking.

It's simple math. I'm much bigger than most of these reporters... and way more determined, too. I just haul Annika along, wishing like anything that it wouldn't be unto-ward to scoop her up and carry her.

But honestly, I'm not even sure that she's wearing anything underneath that tiny gold dress. Besides, I don't want to risk showing the world her privates any more than I want there to be pictures of me and Annika together.

Rumors have been started over the last couple and all I need right now is for this event to start them up again.

Reporters press in from all sides, seeming to circle like sharks. Right now, it's Annika's blood that they're tasting in the water and they move forward as I do, eager to get their stories.

"Annika! Annika! Who is your handsome savior?"

"Princess Annika! Are you going to a rehab program? Are you relapsing? Princess…"

"Annika, why do you keep embarrassing the royal family?"

Gritting my teeth, I keep moving, ignoring the camera flashes and shouts. By the time I get down to the cars, I open the back of the first limo that I see and shove Annika in. I don't even say anything to the reporters trying to push in and ask their questions. I just wrestle the door shut, closing it on them. Then I order the limo driver to pull away from the curb. I don't even care that it's not our car, either.

As soon as we begin to move away, I glance at Annika, my expression stern. She looks at me for a second, then her expression crumples and her eyes begin to shine with tears.

"I hate you," she whispers tearfully. She balls up her fists and hides her face behind them. She can't seem to decide between hatred, fury, and sadness when she delivers the killing blow. "I fucking hate you, Erik."

Her words are like a knife twisting in my guts. My heart sinks.

Do I deserve that? Yes. I deserve everything she could ever give me, every slur and barb she could ever throw.

Absolutely, without reservation. I never should have touched her. And now I'm just stuck between a rock and a hard place. Damn if it doesn't feel like my stomach is filled with lead.

Nika's body goes rigid for a second. Her eyes widen. She tenses.

Then she suddenly grabs the ice bucket from its resting place, hanging her head over it. She gags for half a minute.

I'm frozen for a second. I don't know what to do. My hand hovers on her back and she retches, throwing up into the ice bucket.

Then some instinct kicks in, some foreign knowledge of what to do in this exact situation though I've never even come close in practice. I lean forward and tuck her hair back out of her face, smoothing my hand over the bare skin of her back.

God, this is all wrong. Once, Stellan was the only one of the Løve siblings I had to worry about. But now Nika has had too much whiskey to drink and she's vomiting it all up. And though I have resisted taking care of her for so long, I rise to the occasion presented to me.

"It's going to be okay," I murmur to her. Raising my chin, I call out to the driver. "Do you feel like taking a ride? Because I think it would be best if we got out of the city for a bit…"

20

ANNIKA

FOR A WHOLE DAY AND A WHOLE NIGHT, I JUST SLEEP.

I'm exhausted from just being myself.

From having so many damn feelings.

From trying to put on my smiling public mask and not let anybody see the cracks that have formed in it.

From being one thing to my adoring fans and another to my mess of a family and still another thing entirely to Erik.

Erik, who rejected me. He did it as soundly as a person can be told that they are not good enough or pretty enough or... well, enough.

I wake up with the realization that I have apparently been quite busy while I was passed out. There is a trashcan beside the couch that I'm sleeping on. It smells like the stench of alcohol and gastric juices. It's a very unique smell, one that makes me gag a little.

Pushing myself up on my arms, I try to breathe in deeply and not throw up the contents of my stomach, which by now are surely just acid and bile.

My head throbs as I look around. I haven't seen this room before. Where am I exactly?

I move to the other end of the couch and stand up shakily, wishing like all hell that I had not done quite so many shots of whiskey the night before. Or the day before…

I squint around the room, but there are no windows. Nothing to tell me if it is night or day. I feel like I've been asleep for a while, but I have no idea where or even when I am.

One thing that the room I'm in does boast aside from the couch is a small bathroom. I drag myself into it, peeing and brushing my teeth with a brand new toothbrush and a tube of toothpaste. I look down to find myself wearing a rolled up old button up and nothing else. I frown at that.

What happened to my dress that I wore earlier? What happened to the heels that I strapped on?

Then I clean myself up, running a damp washcloth over my armpits and privates. It's not the classiest thing I have ever done, but it's not the least classy either.

God, my head aches. How did I come to be here?

It's only then that I think of Erik. I get a flashback of the last time I saw him. In the back of a limo, patiently holding my hair back as I vomited.

Oh, god.

Erik is the last person I want to be vulnerable in front of. And yet, I have a vague memory of him lifting me from the backseat and carrying me into a house.

The sharp scent of saltwater overlays my hazy memory. The tang of saltwater, the cool breeze on my back, light wood a dark room.

A puzzle piece clicks into place. I go to the windows and throw the heavy curtains open, revealing the beach splayed out below me. Crisp, clean, all but virgin sands. In the distance, the blue-black sea spreads out as far as I can see. The waves crash on the beach, hissing as they retreat.

It's not quite the same view as the last time I was here but there is the neatly kept patio, leading out to the beach.

Erik brought me here.

He could've taken me anywhere in the world and yet…

Here I am. I can't think of why he would bring me here. I can't actually think of anything at all, not without my head aching.

Desperate for water, I venture to the doorway.

I heave open the door and stick my head out, nearly blinded by the golden daylight that pours in on me. If I had to guess, I would say that it was seven or eight in the evening. Not super late, but not nearly the time that I last remembered it being.

I squint around, looking back and forth down the hallway. It's lined with wood, ceiling to floor. I can see the huge plate glass window at the end of the hall, the sand and light green grass blending in with the décor of the house.

I press the heels my hands against my eyes, wishing like anything that this would all go away. But after leaning against the doorframe for half a minute, I realized that nothing is going to be resolved by me just hiding up here. So, I take the next step and wander down the hall, going downstairs. I find the downstairs living area airy and full of white furniture and the same light wood as I found upstairs. Everything is still and silent.

Water is still calling my name, so I venture into the kitchen, where I find Erik at last.

His back is turned to me. He has a radio on that plays some classic rock very quietly. And he is frying something, I can hear the sizzle and smell the butter as he hums to himself gently and agitates the frying pan. It's only when I step into the open area between the kitchen island and the countertop that he even looks up.

He bites his lip and looks me up and down, a little frown appearing on his face.

His gaze on my legs makes me realize that he probably undressed me and put me in his button up. There's something so intimate and personal about that, while at the same time it makes me a little sad. It also makes me think of the fact that I am naked beneath this oversized shirt and he knows it.

I don't know quite what to think about that. My head aches and I press my palm to my temple. He continues to look at me, finally making a comment.

"I see that you made it. I was starting to wonder."

He turns back to the stove and flips the sandwich he's making in the pan. I take a deep whiff of the smell of cheese and bread toasting. My stomach lurches and I take a step backwards. Not knowing quite what to say, I go around Erik, giving him plenty of space. I retrieve a bottle of mineral water from the refrigerator.

Then I sit down at the kitchen island, watching him. His light-colored hair is slightly askew, as if he has styled it by shoving his hands through it. He wears a T-shirt and dark jeans, slung low at the hips and looking quite like an advertisement for designer jeans. His mood seems lighter too, although you can never tell quite what is going on behind Erik's eyes.

I guess that being here, away from the city and closer to the beach, makes him more relaxed.

If I'm honest, it is a look that really suits him. He essentially ignores me and hums along with the song playing on the radio.

I sit in silence and drink my water. He transfers the grilled cheese sandwich from the pan to a plate, turning to look at me. "Do you want one?"

Just looking at that sandwich makes me feel queasy all over again. I swallow and shake my head. "No thanks. I have a rule about eating after I have vomited. It's usually not a good idea."

Erik looks at me for a long second and then sets the sandwich down on the counter. He leaves the room for half a minute, returning with a can of coconut water and a couple of aspirin. He leans over the counter and puts them in front of me, then goes back to his sandwich.

I take the aspirin and the chilled coconut water, washing one down with the other. He doesn't look at me, just takes a big bite out of his sandwich.

We sit like that for several minutes until I finish the coconut water and the bottle of mineral water. And then I scrunch my face up and look at him. "Where's my phone?"

He doesn't look at me. He doesn't make a face exactly, but I have an idea of what exactly he is thinking. He squints off into the distance, looking out the large windows toward the beach. "You don't need to check your phone. I called the press office and canceled your upcoming engagements. I think you should just relax and take it easy."

I blanch a little. He wouldn't say that unless the press was really swarming. "It's that bad, is it?"

He raises a single shoulder in a Gallic shrug, his expression unreadable. He looks down at his plate for a moment and I have to wonder what in the world he is thinking.

"I think we should stay here for a while. Maybe a month. Maybe more. I think…" He looks up, his tawny eyes pinning me in place. "I don't think that the spotlight is really a good place for you, Nika. I know you grew up with the press outside your window. I know you've always felt like you were on display. But I don't think that has served you very well, so far."

My mouth puckers. "What? What are you saying?"

He shrugs again and looks me dead in the eye. "I think it would be a good idea if you took a break from being in the public eye, that's all."

My cheeks flush. I toy with the rim of my water bottle, trying to guess at what he is really saying. I definitely blacked out earlier when I was at that red carpet event… How bad was my behavior that Erik is now advising me to retreat from public life?

The fact that I don't know what happened really puts things in perspective for me. I should never feel this way, not because of something that I did. That much is clear.

The real question is whether or not I am actually stuck here with Erik babysitting me or if he's just watching me temporarily. Biting my lip, I look up at him.

"How bad was it? Like are we talking about something that I should make the daily rounds on TV and do an apology tour? Or…"

He shakes his head, looking somber. "I don't think we should talk about how the press perceives you, Nika. We both know that when you live your life under a microscope, things can get distorted and blown out of proportion so easily."

My head pounds. I lean my face on my hands, shutting my eyes for a second. "So… what are you suggesting? We just take a break from the outside world for a while? We just… hole up in this house and don't listen to any outside news?"

He cocks his head, studying me. "Doesn't that sound… I don't know… like a kind of relief?"

I pull a face. "You are ignoring the fact that I would rather be trapped with a pack of wild dogs than spend time with you. I pretty much hate you."

In the next moment, Erik grabs me and shocks me by pulling me close and giving me a shake. "Don't say that," he growls. "Don't you dare start in on that again. You know you don't hate me. Apologize to me, right now."

I blink up at him, startled. A flush begins creeping up my cheeks. "Again? When did I say I hated you?"

His gaze narrows on my face. "What, you don't remember?"

The flush that has been creeping up my neck slowly turned into a full on blush. My cheeks heat and I bite my lip, looking away as I try to remember. Maybe it was something that I said when I was blacked out. "I…"

He gives me another sharp shake. "Of course you don't remember. That's your whole life, isn't it? You're so used to being a princess and getting everything you desire. You don't even realize that the things you say and do have effects in the real world to real people." He pushes me away from him, shaking his head with a disgusted look on his face. "You know what the worst part of it is? I'm not even that surprised. I just… It's always two steps forward one step back with you. And I am getting tired of this little dance."

He storms out of the kitchen, turning right and heading outside. I watch him go, my mouth opening a little with surprise.

What just happened? Somehow, it seems like I've managed to hurt the feelings that I didn't even think he had.

So what am I supposed to do about that?

Sinking back into my chair, I stare at the doorway that he disappeared through, my eyes welling with tears. I'm frustrated. With myself, first of all. But also with this situation in general.

First Erik and I sleep together. Then he tells me that it was all a mistake, that his feelings for me don't run that deeply.

And now this?

This… whatever this is.

It feels almost self-indulgent to cry right now, but that's exactly what I do. Laying my head down on my arms, I have a good long cry.

Unfortunately, I end up feeling like I am dehydrated by the end of my little crying jag. When my tears slow, I help myself to another can of coconut water before heading upstairs.

I try to think of how I should console myself, how a healthy person would do it. I have a choice of sorts. I could either dig myself deeper into this hole and spend hours looking at the internet, reading all of the comments about my appearance and my behavior.

Or… I can try to use one of the… what are they called again?

That book about radical self-love called them coping strategies, I think. One of the main coping strategies is self-care. Taking a bath, taking time to do my nails, or maybe doing some yoga.

Baby steps. I decide that before I do anything else, I need to take a bath and consider all my options.

That's the only way that I can see forward and out of this mess at this particular moment. Sucking in a deep breath, I raise my chin and head towards my favorite bathroom in the house.

21

ERIK

I STALK OUT OF THE HOUSE AT SUNSET, MY WHOLE BODY vibrating from tension. I swear, one of these days, Nika will finally do or say the wrong thing… And I will just completely fucking lose it.

I'm so mad right now that I'm shaking as I storm out across the sandy beach. The sun is low in the sky but still present enough to make me shade my eyes as I trudge toward the horizon. I have to get away from Nika and away from that house. I don't know exactly where I'm going but anywhere is better than there.

I break into a run, just now realizing that I am barefoot. The grains of sand are a little coarse underneath my feet. When I go farther out, toward the water line, it seems like a good place to stop.

I turn and look back at the house, only now realizing that I have actually left the house quite a way behind. It looks very small in my peripheral vision, just a black, squat blip on my radar.

I suck in a breath and close my eyes, turning back toward the setting sun and the coolness of the sea. I wade out just a bit. I stand and let the waves lap against my feet. For some reason, it helps sooth the angry, injured being that lives deep inside me.

I take another breath and let it out very slowly.

It doesn't help that thoughts are pounding at my head, relentless as the waves themselves.

I hate you.

Nika said that yesterday, over and over again. I feel like that was just her way of saying what she couldn't when I left her bed that night… She might've been huddled and crying on the floor of her bathroom, but in my heart, I knew that she harbored black thoughts about me.

Hearing them said to me out loud is something I hope never to hear again. When she said that she pretty much hates me just a few minutes ago, it was the straw that broke the camel's back.

I just snapped. And rather than unload all of my anger and resentment and the confusing amalgamation of sadness and sorrow onto her… I just left. Which is how I came to be standing here just now.

But God, even hung over as she was, she looks so damn good that I nearly lost control of myself. Especially wearing nothing but my wrinkled white button up.

She was angelic for a moment there.

But in the next second, her smart mouth reminded me of exactly why I wanted to avoid all of this in the first place.

Because she's essentially a spoiled little brat. Yeah, maybe she has her own reasons. But nothing really overwhelms the fact that she has had everything in her life handed to her and has lived without repercussions.

In fact, I think I'm part of the problem...

Instead of making her stay in Copenhagen and face her colossal mistakes... She could have owned up to the fact that she made a complete fool of herself in front of the press. But instead I'm helping her hide out here.

Hell, I even thought of it myself. There is no one that made me do any of this. I just did it on my own, for her benefit.

And I would probably do it again if given the same situation. Because I have definitely developed some sort of crush on Nika...

Maybe crush isn't even the word. I guess a crush is something unrequited. What happens when a crush is returned, and you get exactly what you have longed for?

Man, I am starting to have this sinking feeling in the pit of my stomach. Do I have feelings for Nika?

Surely that can't be the case... Right?

But the fact that I'm standing out here, all angsty and brooding, indicates that I do have something to be worried about.

I grind my teeth and take another step into the shallow water that swirls then washes around my feet. I raise my head to the sky and bring my arms out, yelling wordlessly. It's the only way that I can express all the things that I am feeling.

My phone begins to buzz in my pocket. I'm irritated as I pull it out because I have almost everyone on silent. The only person that my phone would even notify me for is Stellan...

I swallow as I realize that that is exactly who is calling. Gritting my teeth, I answer the video call.

"Hello?"

Stellan's face appears, his dark eyebrows drawn down quite severely. It looks like he's at the palace, though with the low lighting behind him it's hard to be sure. He tilts his head to the side and looks at me quite seriously.

"Hey. I was just calling to check in on you and Nika. I'm wondering if we need to start talking about some kind of alcohol treatment program. Maybe somewhere far away on the beach?"

I sigh. "She's just young. That's all it is. I don't think that we have anything to worry about in the alcoholism department."

He pins me with his deep blue gaze. "Did something set her off? Because we can't have a reckless princess out there, running around and representing the royal family so poorly. It's just not something that is going to work."

My neck feels hot all the sudden. I squint off into the distance and try to think of how to explain it without telling Stellan that I definitely banged his sister. I feel a little queasy having to lie to him.

Maybe I should just tell him the truth and get off this babysitting duty. Of course, it would most likely have way more ramifications than that.

How do you tell your best friend that you have developed feelings for his little sister? How do you say that she is acting out because of something that you did?

"Erik. Pay attention."

I look at him, his white button up rumpled, his shirt sleeves rolled up. "Sorry. I just think that Annika needs some time out of the spotlight. From what she's been telling me, it sounds like every time she has to interact with the press, something goes wrong. So, my solution would be just, don't interact with the press."

Stellan looks tired, rubbing his face and sighing. "That isn't a permanent solution. That's temporary at best."

I nod absolutely. "Yeah, I know. It just isn't fair. If she were anyone else on earth, I would tell her to just walk away from the royal family. She would be happier if she did. But I know that that's not an option in real life."

"Nope. It's not." He pauses, screwing up his face. "You really don't think that she needs to be in rehab?"

My lips lift a little at the corners. "No, I don't think so. I just think we're going to have to find a way to distract her. Maybe there's some kind of retirement from public life or something…" I pause, though occurring to me. "You know who would know?"

He perks a brow. "Momse?"

"That's the one. She has knowledge of what the royal family has done in the past. I mean, there has to have been someone somewhere that opted out of the spotlight."

A thoughtful look appears on Stellan's handsome face. He runs a hand through his short, dark hair and exhales. "I'm sure that Momse does have some opinions about Annika. But honestly, I don't even want to give my grandmother that kind of power. I just finished setting some boundaries with her over the whole Margot debacle. I hate to take steps backward at this point."

I scrunched up my face. "Very true. Right now, it is a bit of a strange time for Momse. She is going through something, not being allowed to pull all the strings anymore. It's got to be an adjustment for her."

The corners of Stellan's lips quirk a little. "I'm sure. But I think that my parents let her run the kingdom of Denmark, essentially. And the fact that I'm taking control back is a rather prickly subject for her. I might be her favorite grandchild but I'm still her competition, in a sense. She's held the strings too tightly for too long."

I bite my lip. Somehow, we've drifted onto Stellan's favorite topic again. He loves to think about how the power dynamics are shifting in Denmark with his succession to the throne. But that's not why he called.

Did he just forget about Nika entirely? I press my lips together and sigh. He gives me a sharp look. "Am I boring you, Erik?"

I roll my eyes and give him a light smile. "Not at all. I was just wondering how we ventured on to this topic. I remember you calling about your little sister. That's all."

I hear a woman in the background, asking Stellan a question. He looks away from the phone. When he looks back, his expression seems distracted. "I have to go. Margot needs my attention. Are you guys going to be okay out there for now?"

I nod. The sun is all but set and I start walking back toward the house. "Yeah. We're fine. As long as I keep Annika away from the press, I think she will be content."

I hear Margot's voice again, clearly calling for Stellan. He rolls his eyes and says goodbye. "I have to go. If you need to get a hold of me, you can always call my new secretary. I'll talk to you later."

I think about how I should answer that. But Stellan has already hung up the phone. A blinking red icon on my screen indicates that the line has been disconnected.

I glare at the screen and shake my head, shoving my phone in my pocket. I'm not even mad or that surprised at his behavior. That's what you get when your best friend is the King of Denmark, apparently.

As I walked back to the house, that little quip about how I should get in touch with him through his new secretary rings in my head. I think he was joking… But in all seriousness, if I'm going to leave the service entirely, this could be my future. I could be facing a lifetime of missed calls whenever I try to actually talk to Stellan.

That fact has not escaped my worried thoughts. All the way back to the house, I walk over the sandy beach and feel the weight of that knowledge in the pit of my stomach. It is heavy and bitter, and it leaves me feeling more uncertain than usual.

I walk up to the house, heading through the French doors that I left open. To my surprise, I find Nika right where I left her. Although she has a bowl of cereal in front of her now. I glance at her and she takes a bite of her cereal, shrugging a shoulder. Through a mouthful of cereal, she apologizes, which takes me back.

"You were right," she says. She chews the bite of cereal and then swallows. "I shouldn't have said that I hate you. That was unfair. I'm sorry."

Exhaling loudly, I meander into the kitchen, stopping when I am opposite where she sits on the counter. Leaning back against the counter behind me, I fold my arms across my chest and look at her somberly. "Thanks for that."

She wrinkles her nose and pushes her bowl away, stretching her arms over her head. I can't help the fact that her movement draws my eye down to her breasts. They look particularly amazing under that loose white button-up shirt she is wearing. If I stare hard enough, I'm pretty sure that I can even make out her nipples. I lick my lips and yank my gaze back up to her face.

I find her giving me a flat stare. "Do I need to go put on real clothes? Because that kind of staring is not allowed. If we are just friends or I am just a babysitting assignment for you, that's fine. But don't stare at me like I am the juiciest steak and you haven't eaten in a year. It's not fair."

I feel my neck get hot. Tucking my head, I shrug a shoulder. "I'm trying. But we both know that the other is attractive. There's no denying that. It's just a matter of doing what is right as opposed to what I might want at this moment."

She pushes her cheek out with her tongue and looks annoyed. Nika stands up, grabbing her cereal bowl and stalking to the sink that is right behind me. I slide over a little to make room, looking down as she puts her bowl in the sink. When she's done, she looks up at me, her pale eyes narrowing.

"I don't understand how you think that the two of us can just coexist like this." She pulls her arms over her chest, framing and emphasizing her breasts. That isn't helping anything at all as far as I'm concerned.

I shouldn't lean closer. I shouldn't use my intimidating height as a weapon. I shouldn't play with fire by using the electric current that runs between us like this.

And yet, I do exactly that. I step closer to her until we are toe to toe, gazing down at her with a stormy expression.

"We only have to stay in the same place and stare at each other for three more weeks. Then it will be Stellan's wedding. And then you and I can quit this little babysitting routine. As far as I'm concerned, I'm only accountable for you until then. After that, you can do whatever you like."

Nika's head falls back and she looks up at me defiantly. "Oh yes. I haven't forgotten that you accepted the bribe that my grandmother offered."

I smile at her evenly, showing all my teeth. "If you weren't such a problem child, she wouldn't have offered anything at all. So, I guess I can thank you for my title-to-be. Without you, I would be a commoner for the rest of my life. Luckily, you're such a pain in the ass that no one wants to deal with it..."

She laughs coolly. "Gold digger."

She just tosses that accusation out like it's nothing. Like her words don't mean anything at all. It makes me angry. But the curl of her lip also turns me the fuck on.

I lean in very close to her, so that there are only a few inches between our lips. "Troublemaker."

"Opportunist."

One corner of my mouth hitches up in a smile. "Spoiled little rich girl."

Her nostrils flare and her eyes widen. I can smell her excitement perfuming the air. "How dare you."

I can't seem to stop myself from kissing those gorgeous, pouty, mouthy lips. I pull her against my body and stop her talking with my mouth, making a soft noise at the taste of her as it bursts across my tongue.

God, I can never get enough of her.

Her hands clutch my shirt, balling into fists and then relaxing just for a second. Then she suddenly shoves me away, taking a shaky step back and drawing in a breath.

Her eyes shine with lust, but she looks so distraught and angry. "Erik, we know where this leads. And I for one have had enough rejection in the last few days. So, if you don't mind, fuck off and leave me alone."

With that she spins on her heel and heads toward the staircase, trotting up towards her bedroom. And I just stand here, feeling the heat from her body and her mouth, knowing that she is right but wishing that she was dead wrong.

22

ERIK

It's been a week since I took Annika from Copenhagen to hide out from the press. A very long week full of heated glances and angsty looks. The only bright side is that I completely forgot about the trip to Santorini until literally hours before we were supposed to leave.

It's Lars's birthday and I dropped a ton of money almost a year ago to get just the right spot to celebrate.

And the private plane ride to the Greek Isles is as awkward as can be. Silent. Angry. Full of her annoyed sighs.

But now… we're here. And we're not alone. Lars, Finn, Kalindi, and Pippa now stand between me and Nika, thankfully letting some of the tension out of the situation.

"Oh…" Lars says as he climbs the ramp and steps onto the gleaming white deck of the palatial estate I've rented in the Greek isles for the weekend.

Our mansion is made of perfectly sun-bleached white stone and topped with a brilliant copper dome. Heat snakes up from the perfect sapphire and cerulean water as it glistens all around us. A servant appears, taking our small party's bags into the house.

"Man, this is seriously swanky," Lars says, looking out at the small village of sun-bleached white buildings and rounded copper roofs.

He looks back at me, his grin bright. "You organized this for my birthday?"

I can't scowl, which is the only thing I feel like doing. So I keep my expression neutral. "I did."

I planned this almost a year ago, back when I was still Stellan's private secretary. Back before I realized that dragging a very uncomfortable Annika on this overnight trip would be so… tense.

To put it mildly.

I slide my gaze over to Annika now. She catches my gaze and whirls away, her cheeks turning a dusky rose color.

The color looks good on her. But it's also been her only reaction to me for days and I'm really starting to wonder just how far over the line I took things the other day.

I could've easily taken it so much further… just thinking about it makes my body harden.

Pippa tosses her red hair, looking stately. "Annika, Kalindi, do you want to go sun ourselves on the front deck?" She points to where she means, but Annika already has an answer.

"Yes!" Annika says. She glances at me, flushing prettily, and then hurries away.

Kalindi casts a dour look at me and follows her friend. Pippa looks around at Lars, Finn, and I. She shrugs and then moves off after them.

Oblivious to the tension simmering between Annika and me, Lars claps me on the back and points to the house. "I think I see a bar set up just inside the window there. Let's go check it out."

He takes off. Finn follows, always the darkest, quietest one of the Løve siblings. I don't think of Finn very often or really ask him to things. I'm not even sure who invited to this trip, but I'm glad he's here. One more person between me and Annika can't hurt anything.

Then again, you could put a whole country between us, and somehow things would still be stifling. With a sigh on my lips, I start heading after them.

The second we step into what appears to be a rather extravagant library, a servant hurries to pour us each a glass of bourbon.

"Thank you," I murmur. The servant bows his head. I turn to Lars, toasting. "To Lars, the reason for this little getaway."

Finn merely cocks his dark head and raises his glass. "Hear, hear."

We all sip what I am sure is remarkably fine bourbon, wandering back out onto the broad terrace. I look down at the private dock, which is only probably a hundred feet down from where I'm standing.

It's beautiful outside today with azure waves and little white peaks as far as the eye can see. There isn't a cloud in the sky either.

If I wanted to be here, it would be perfect weather for sailing. I look at the all-white power boats bobbing at their docks, calling to me.

Lars looks at the boats too, turning toward me. "We're going to race those, right?"

I wiggle my eyebrows. "I was only waiting for you to suggest it."

Finn chuckles and Lars grins, sipping his whiskey.

I love boat racing. Actually, I love any kind of adrenaline-pumping, action-packed sport. The idea of taking one of those boats out and pushing it full throttle excites me beyond reason.

Finn finishes his tumbler of bourbon first. "I'm ready. I should get the girls, *ja?*"

Lars laughs. "Definitely at least offer to take one of them in the boat with me. I don't know if any of you have seen Pippa or Kalindi in a bikini, but the idea of having one of them clinging to my arm while I win the race— "

I snort. "Dream on, Lars. You'll still have to race against me… and I don't usually lose."

Lars rolls his eyes. "Get ready to eat your words, Erik."

A smile tugs at my lips. "We'll see about that. I do like a challenge."

We head down to the docks, Finn lagging behind to get the girls on board. Each of the boats already has the keys in the ignition. I'm standing behind the steering wheel and gunning the engine when I realize that Annika is standing on the dock, glaring at me. She looks particularly fierce just now, with her long wavy hair falling to her waist and her very skimpy black bikini. She wears a white sarong around her waist, but almost every other inch of sun-kissed skin is on full display.

A shudder runs down my spine just looking at her. I raise my brows, turning to check on the other guys. Both of them are helping a girl onto their boat... leaving me with their little sister.

"Shit," I mutter. Looking back to Annika, I step to the side and offer her a hand up. "Come on."

Her mouth twists a little, but she accepts my help, her warm palms slipping beneath mine. She weighs virtually nothing as I help her aboard; when she makes the jump onto the deck, I steady her with a hand on her waist.

There is a split second where I hold her, staring down into those guileless eyes.

For just a second, I see something in her eyes... some kind of carnal interest that makes my hands tighten on her waist.

But then in the next second she brushes off my touch and tosses her hair. "Can I drive?"

My eyes narrow on her as she turns and walks over to the steering wheel. She walks right up to the wheel and turns around, a pout already on her lips.

"I don't think so," I say, rolling my eyes.

"Hey!" Lars calls. "Are you guys ready? The last boat to reach... twenty miles? The loser makes drinks tonight, ja?"

I jog a few paces until I stand right behind Annika. "*Ja!*"

Annika turns around, pinning me with her fiery gaze. Her full lips smirk. "Don't just say no. I need you to teach me how, Erik."

My heart stutters. My mind goes blank, short-circuiting. I can tell that she's teasing me. She definitely intended to get exactly this reaction from me.

As soon as I regain some amount of control over myself, I scowl. The other boats pull out, so there really isn't time to argue.

Stepping up to the helm, I just shake my head. "Fine. You steer, okay?"

Annika shoots me the most mischievous look ever over her shoulder. Putting the boat into gear, I move my hand under her arm to the throttle, which is to the left side of the steering wheel.

As the boat shoots forward out of its slip, Annika's lithe body pushes back against mine. I'm already hard for her and I grind against her ass. She freezes up for a second and her muscles lock up… but after a second she relaxes, leaning her head back against my chest. She grins as we take off and gives an excited whoop.

God, she feels so good right now. Her scent is everywhere for a second as we speed up, her hair blowing in every direction too.

Using one hand to steady the wheel, I keep the other on the throttle, pinning her in place.

I try to keep my eyes on the horizon, or at least the other two boats which are the best part of a mile ahead. But with Annika pressed against my torso like this, all I can think of is her incredibly soft skin.

It's as smooth and soft as silk, as warm and gently scented as fresh honey. I'm so close to burying my whole face into her shoulder, to biting and teasing her flesh until she pleads for me to touch her…

She turns her head, shouting for her words to be heard over the rush of air all around us. "Are we still in a fight, Erik?"

It takes all my self-restraint not to nuzzle her neck and nip at her ear. I frown, having to actively work at not letting my eyes stray down to her tits. I mean, they are right there.

Just waiting for me to fondle them, to cup them and pinch her nipples.

"No, Nika," I grate out.

She grins. "Okay. That's good, I guess."

She shifts her weight against my torso, pressing against my cock. My eyes close briefly. My face screws up. I let out a soft sound of interest that she probably can't even hear.

When I open my eyes though, I see her biting her lower lip and looking at me like…

Well, her expression is one of pure want. She's giving me these fuck me eyes and I literally can't think about anything else.

"Annika… we can't," I say, slowing our boat.

She narrows her eyes. "Why, because you're the king's best friend and I'm just his emptyheaded little sister?"

Shaking my head, I separate our bodies. "That's one reason. There are about a million more. Now if you don't mind?"

Annika's expression screws up. I can tell that the next thing out of her mouth is going to be a protest. Pulling her by the arm, I push her behind me. "Sit down and be quiet."

Her expression turns stormy. But before she can say anything, I stop her with a begging look and two simple words. "Please, Annika."

Her eyebrows lift. Then she gives in, stops pushing against me.

I turn around so that I can't see her anymore as I start to re-engage the throttle. But she doesn't utter another word of protest. She just sits down behind me and glares at my back so hard that I swear a hole starts to form between my shoulder blades.

All I can think is that when we get off of this boat, I'm probably going to get a fucking earful from her. Pushing the boat's throttle all the way, I shake my head and try to focus on the task at hand.

2 3

ANNIKA

LOOKING OUT OVER THE MOONLIT SHORE, I TILT MY HEAD. THE sea is so beautiful and calm just now, a great black mass that seems utterly still. The rocky white coast cuts into it at the edge and bleeds as far as the eye can see. The whole village of Santorini is asleep, the white buildings seeming like nothing so much as jumbled teeth jutting out, reaching toward the night sky.

I stand on my private balcony and shiver just a bit though it isn't cold. I'm wearing nothing but a filmy white négligée and feeling as though I nearly blend in with the white sandstone mansion behind me.

"What are you still doing up?"

Erik's deep voice nearly gives me a heart attack. I whirl, backing up against the little balcony railing. He appears out of the shadows in my room, stepping into the moonlit-drenched doorway.

God, he's handsome. His flaxen hair is messed up just a little bit. His hazel eyes and aristocratic nose war with his too-expressive lips. All that on top of a mountain of a man… a mountain elegantly carved from the richest stone, his muscles making him a true work of art.

And he's shirtless at the moment, clad only in a pair of low-slung jeans that show off his chest hair and his entrancing happy trail.

"What are you doing in here?" I ask, frowning. "And why aren't you wearing a shirt?"

He shrugs a muscular shoulder, the very picture of grace and power. "I'm not sure."

I bite my lower lip. "I can't sleep," I say. My head falls to the side as I look him up and down. "I mean, I usually struggle to fall asleep at the palace. But here, far away from all the noise, I find it too quiet."

He steps out onto the balcony and looks out toward the sea. "Me too," he admits. "I thought the sound of the sea so close by would lull me, but instead it just makes me…"

I exhale, knowing just how he feels. "Restless?"

That serious gaze finds me, narrowing on my face. He nods slowly. "Yes."

I toss my head, scrunching my nose. "Same here."

He is quiet for a moment, scanning the beach below. "I thought you would still be fuming about what happened between us on the boat."

I arch a brow. "Would that help either of us?"

A smile tugs at Erik's lips. "Definitely not."

Shrugging, I perch on the edge of the railing, carefully tucking the ends of my silky négligée beneath me. "I have to say, I'm sort of baffled."

He looks at me, surprised. "About what?"

I pluck at the hem of my nighty. "Well… you said there are a million reasons why you can't… *be* with me again. I was wondering what those are, exactly."

His brows rise. "You still need me to list them?"

I stare at the hem of my négligée. "Well… yes. I think I do."

He chuckles. "Okay…"

Wrapping his arms across his chest, he leans against the railing, just an arm's length away. "God, where do I even begin? Aside from you being the little sister to my best friend in the world, of course."

I tilt my head, considering him. "Naturally."

Erik sighs. "You're also so young."

"I'm almost twenty." I straighten my spine, trying to seem… old enough, I guess.

A rumble bursts from somewhere low in his chest. "You make me feel old, Annika."

I roll my eyes. "We're not even a decade apart in age."

He slides me a disgruntled look. "There is the fact that you are the only Danish princess. And I'm a commoner."

I push out my cheek with my tongue. "At least you are Danish. Stellan fell for an American journalist."

He squints. "Yes, but he is the king."

"And I am, as you pointed out, the only princess. Besides, you're practically one of us."

Erik cocks his head, looking at me. "I'm very far away from that and we both know it. And anyway, shouldn't we both be disgusted by the fact that we essentially grew up together?"

I press my lips together into a thin line. "Hah! Very funny. You didn't even acknowledge my existence until I returned from boarding school. I hardly think that qualifies."

Erik's gaze focuses on my face. "What do I have to say to make myself perfectly clear? Nothing will happen between us. I mean, nothing *more*. Even if none of those things were the truth, there would still be a fundamental difference between us."

I tilt my head. "Are you talking about our personalities?"

His lips twist. "Yes. You're off playing fashionista and preening while I'm just— "

"Being boring?" I suggest, cocking a brow.

He rolls his eyes and shakes his head. "You're attracted to me. Either you have bad taste or I'm not as stiff as you claim."

I bite my lip, trying to hide my smile. A blush creeps up my cheeks, warming me. "Oh? You're not stiff? Is that really what you want to claim?"

Wiggling my eyebrows at Erik makes color rise in his cheeks, setting off the jade in his eyes.

He glares at me. "That's not what I meant, and you know it. But yes, there are some fatal flaws in our… attraction to one another."

"I see. You want to just break everything down into simple thoughts. Black and white. Cats and dogs. Either it is raining or it's not. X or Y. It must be frustrating to live in that kind of a codified world."

He raises his eyebrows at me. "Do you think that I'm wrong?"

I suck in a deep breath and let it out, taking a second with my answer. "I'm saying that there are lots of things in between black and white. There is a whole world of colors and you have limited it down to just the two. So yes, I do you think you're wrong."

I turn toward the French doors that are open behind me. He reaches out and grabs my arm as I start moving in that direction. I give him a hard look. "Easy. I'm just getting a drink. Do you want some champagne?"

His fingers tighten on my arm and I bite my lip, looking up into his face. His eyes sparkle like twin tiger's eye gemstones, making me feel more seen then I ever have in my life.

He's angry, I can tell.

For second, I think he is going to break, to sweep me off my feet and kiss me.

But he doesn't. Erik releases me and I give him a smirk, shaking my head as I head inside. Once I go in the living room area, I look around and find the bar.

It's the work of a minute to find a suitable bottle of champagne and two glasses. As I pop the bottle, Erik saunters in the house behind me, making a striking silhouette against the bright moonlit night sky behind him. I smile and pour the champagne, handing him a glass.

He accepts the flute with two fingers, watching me carefully as he prowls around the living room. I take a sip of my champagne and crinkle my nose in surprise at the bubbly, acidic flavor. Erik swirls the champagne around in his glass, looking at me while he takes a sip.

I brush past him, smiling and shaking my head. He follows me out to the patio again, looking at me while I take a seat on the white wicker patio furniture. I glance up at him and pat the seat beside me. "Join me on the couch. Come on, the view is very nice."

After a second, he moves around to sit on the couch beside me. He looks out at the beach, the rolling sea relentless as ever in its pursuit of reaching the beach.

Erik doesn't say a word. He just sips his champagne and looks off into the horizon. I bite my lip and put my feet into his lap, stretching out. He looks down at my feet and then looks at me, his expression one of surprise.

I shrug shoulder. "What? I'm just being comfortable. I'm comfortable around you. Is that okay?"

He stares at my feet again and only and then smooths the top palm of his hand over the top of my foot. Even this slight touch warms me from inside out. He glances up at me, our gazes connecting. And then he just keeps stroking my foot, my ankle, my lower leg. All the while, he seems like a caged tiger ready to pounce.

I've driven him to this, I know it. There's no question that tension has been right in the air between the two of us for some time. If I am honest about it, the tension started to build the second he walked out on me after we fucked.

This is overdue.

I smirk at him and finish my wine, setting my glass aside. His gaze drops to my legs, where the silky fabric of my négligée meets my bare thighs. It's a powerful thing to be looked at in that way by a man like Erik.

He glances up at me, licking his lips, his expression tortured.

"Nika..." he whispers. "I meant what I said before. All the reasons that I listed for why we shouldn't even be touching right now... They are still real. If we slip up and fuck each other's brains out, the reasons will still be between us when we wake up in the morning."

I bite my lip. I know that he is just waiting for a sign, something urging him on. So, I open my knees a little wider, using two fingers to draw up the silky white négligée up my leg. Inch by creamy bare inch, my thighs are exposed to his view. Soon I reach the apex of my thighs, but I don't stop. I draw all the négligée up until my pussy lips are bare before him and widen my knees a little more.

Erik looks at me, swallowing. His gaze is so brooding and intense that meeting his eyes is more difficult than it should be. But I don't look away.

When I speak, my voice shakes more than it ought to. It's only then that I realize how badly I want him, how badly I want to feel his touch and all the things that come along with it. I want to feel the pleasure that I know that only he can give me.

A whisper leaves my lips. "If you want me, I am here for you. All you have to do to get me is just reach out your hand and take what is on offer."

He reaches out his hand and glides it up the inside of my thigh. He licks his lips, his gaze focused on my pussy. Then he reaches out a single finger and runs it up my wet slit, biting his lip as he gathers my moisture.

Shudders of electricity run up and down my spine. My breasts feel like they are achy and throbbing, just like my clit. I let my head fall backward and release the breathiest little moan, my lips parting.

He glances up at me and brings his finger up to his lips, popping it in his mouth and moaning at the taste of me. I swear, I've never seen anything sexier than a man who is that turned on by the way I taste.

When Erik sits back, pushes my feet out of his lap, and stands up, I don't know exactly what's going on. He offers me his hand and I take it, my heart going crazy in my chest.

I lick my lips and allow him to pull me to my feet. He gives me a little tug and I come into his arms so easily, like a choreographed dance move executed perfectly. I press up against the shelter of his hard body and I look up at him with wide eyes. He looks back at me with nothing but desire. It's all over his face, written so clearly that I could scream.

"I do want you, princess. I always want you, even when I shouldn't. That's my secret." He tucks a strand of my hair back behind my ear and tips my head up, leaning down and brushing his lips over mine. His kiss is burning, his touch so rough that I'm sure it will leave marks. But it lights a fire deep inside me, a burning inferno that I can't deny even if I wanted to.

"Yes," I say against his lips. "Please, Erik. Please…"

And just like that, he scoops me up in his arms and heads inside, leaving me shivering in his arms while he finds the bed.

24

ERIK

I STRIP WITHOUT THOUGHT. WITH ONE HAND, I CUP HER CHIN upward towards my mouth. The other pulls her close against me. My hardness slips with ease between the heat of her soft thighs.

That little négligée teases me, looking so perfect against Nika's tanned skin.

I need more, want more, and by the way Nika responds, I know she does, too. I start to walk her backward, through the open bedroom door. When the back of her knees hit the bed frame, she sits down, her cherry red lips inches from my cock.

Before she can react, I lift her négligée over her head. I take a long moment to admire her, all that naked skin bare before my hungry eyes. I bend her back and bite my lip. Her pink nipples are already hard, her pussy damp, and my length hardens more, desperate for her.

But I am not about to give in yet. Instead, I twist the silky white négligée around her wrists like makeshift handcuffs.

Slowly, I lower her bound hands and gently push her onto her back. Nika lifts her head to watch while I lower my lips to the full breasts I'd fantasized about non-stop since the last time I got her naked.

As I begin to nibble on one nipple, I pinch and squeeze the other. Nika lets out faint gasps and wriggles against her cuffs, which hold her captive. My cock presses against one of her thighs, covering her skin in a thin coat of wetness.

"Please," she whimpers. She begins to whip her head from side to side while I move down her stomach with soft kisses. When I get down to her glistening pussy lips, I place a single light kiss on her clit. She lets out a loud groan, spreads her legs wide, and presses herself to my mouth. I smile up at her, though her eyes are screwed shut.

God, I love the way she makes me feel. This? This moment?

This is everything.

I kiss her again, deeper, using just a little flick of my tongue. Her clit is swollen and plump. With my every touch, she responds. I trace my tongue up the inside of her thighs and across the crest of her mound. Nika pants my name when I come close to her glistening clit, but I tease her mercilessly. Instead of the kisses and licks she clearly craves, I blow across her clit and order her to open her legs wider.

She calls out my name. It has never sounded sweeter than when it trips off her tongue.

She is so ready, her juices already starting to drip from her opening. I test her with a finger, which she pushes against greedily. As my finger enters her, ever so slowly, I taste her clit and feel her muscles tighten around my knuckle. I pull my finger out, though she does her best to press against my hand and keep me inside.

My index finger is covered in her clinging wetness. I hold my hand up to her and press my thumb and forefinger together so she could see just how wet she is. Nika leans up to suck my hand, but I pull away and trace her areola with her sweetness.

"More," she murmurs.

"More what?" I ask. I tighten my grip on the négligée as she starts to struggle again. At the same time, I tease her opening with two fingers and kiss her clit.

"Erik… Please, give me more," she demands breathlessly.

I slide two fingers into her. Nika cries out as I begin to work her clit, licking and sucking. When she begins to fuck my hand, writhing her hips against me, I let her. I match her rhythm with my mouth. Her inner muscles begin the tremble. When I can tell she is close, I make her slow down. I raise my head, switch my mouth for my thumb, and let my eyes feast on the glorious sight of Nika about to come.

With her head tossed back, eyes shut, and mouth open, she is an absolute vision. "Are you going to come for me?" I ask as I start to fuck her faster with my hand.

"Yes," she says. Nika opens her eyes and looks at me. I release her wrists just enough so she can prop herself onto her elbows and watch. "I'm close," she says.

"I want you to come in my mouth," I command. "I want to taste you."

"I can't—"

"Come in my mouth, Nika," I repeat. My tongue returns to her clit. I explore every crevice of her. When I can tell she was close to coming, I slow down again. I remove my finger from her even as she cries out in frustration—only to begin to moan when my tongue dives into her center.

"Please," she says when I trail my tongue from her opening to her wet clit.

"Come for me, Nika," I whisper. "Come right now."

Immediately, she weaves her fingers into my hair and pulls my lips against her center. I grip her hips on either side of my face and meet her furious pace. She fucks my face, my mouth, like it is all she'd ever wanted. Every time she cries out my name it makes me harder, makes me want her more. "I'm coming," she says. "Oh, fuck, right now."

I ready myself for the flood of her sweetness, but what she gave me I'd never have expected. Along with the gush of her coming, the juices that pour onto my tongue, I feel the stream of her squirting across my lower face. It drizzles along my throat and to my chest.

Holy *fuck*. That was surprising in the best way.

She is wetter than anyone I have seen before. Carefully, I lick up every last drop of her moisture. When I kiss her clit one last time, she shivers.

As I raise my head, I saw that she is flushed. Nika clutches the balled-up négligée to her face. "I'm sorry," she says. "That's never happened before... It just feels so damn amazing and—"

"Sorry?" I interrupt. "For what? That was the hottest fucking thing I've ever seen."

"Really?" she asks. Nika chews at her lower lip and gives me a half smile. I get up from my knees and she looks down my body. "You're still hard," she says, almost surprised.

"After making you come with my mouth and feeling you squirt? I'm harder than I've ever been in my whole life," I say with a laugh.

She brings a hand to my package, caressing it, but I catch her wrist. She looks up at me, piercing me with her gaze.

"Please?" she asks.

I smile at her. "I need you to tell me what you want," I say. "Please, what?"

"Please… let me have your cock," she says. She reaches for me with her other hand, but I catch it, too.

"I don't know," I say. "What do you want to do with it?"

"You'll see," she purrs. "Please."

Nika leans forward and takes my tip between her lips. I can't resist anymore. I drop her wrists and comb her hair back with my fingers so I can watch her swallowing my cock. Those lips I've dreamt of for the past two weeks are finally on me and feel better than I could imagine.

Nika licks the full length of my shaft and sucks gently on my tip. With her hand at my base, she takes me slowly all the way to the back of her throat. "Jesus," I mutter, unable to resist the urge to hold her head and guide her.

She makes satisfied little sounds in the back of her throat as she licks and sucks. "You're going to make me come," I warn her, my fingers twisting in her long hair.

Nika releases me. "Come in me," she says as she strokes me with a hand slick with saliva.

I pause. "What?"

"Come in me," she repeats. "Please. I need you to fuck me." She pushes herself back along the bed and opens her thighs to me. One of her hands pulls at her nipple while the other circles her clit.

"Say it again," I demand as I crawl toward her.

"Please fuck me," she whispers into my ear.

Positioning myself between her legs, I slide into her with ease and exhale at how fucking good she feels. Tight, wet, and warm.

Nika digs her nails into my lower back to keep me deep inside her. "Slow," she says. "I want to feel you."

I start to fuck her, slow and controlled, while I kiss and suck at her neck.

"Stay," she says suddenly as she pulls me as tight as she could against her. "Fuck… damn, I'm already coming again."

I feel the waves of her orgasm squeezing against me, stroking my cock rhythmically. It feels so intense that I can feel the edge approaching.

"Nika," I say. "Jesus, you're going to make me come right now."

"Come in me," she pants through her waves of pleasure. "Please, I need it."

I release myself into her with a cry, pumping my orgasm into her willing body. Nika calls my name as another wave of orgasm hits her.

"Oh my God," she repeats over and over. "Oh, Erik…"

I feel the aftershock of orgasms roll through her, each one squeezing out another drop of my cum.

As the sweat cools on my body, I just stretch out beside Nika and look at her. Her blonde hair is messy, her cheeks are flushed the loveliest pink I've ever seen. She pulls the soft-looking white sheet up from where we managed to kick it off and tucks it around her body. She seems a little embarrassed to have me look at her naked now that we are not actually having sex.

Turning on my side, I reach out a lazy hand and trail it down her hip, tugging the sheet down as I go. She looks at me, her pale eyes suspicious.

"What are you doing, Erik?"

My lips twitch. "I just like to look at you. Is that so wrong?"

Her cheeks turn bright red for a second. "I think you just like to wind me up."

I think that she expects me to crack a joke or maybe say something dirty. But instead I move little closer and brush a few strands of hair back behind her ear, cupping her jaw tenderly. I brush a kiss over her lips, thinking how much I like her.

"I like looking at you. I like the way that you have little freckles all over your body. I like your breasts and ass. I like your face. And when you aren't busy being mad at me, I really like your sense of humor and lack of pretentiousness. I think it's a shame that you try to hide things that are so magnificent. That's all."

She looks me deep in the eyes and swallows a little nervously. "I think you are handsome too."

I smiled a little and kissed her good. "I wasn't fishing for compliments. It just seems like there are so many parts of you that are beautiful and yet, you don't even seem to notice. That seems wrong."

Her eyebrows lift an inch. Her cheeks flame. If she could squirm out of the bed and hide herself, I'm pretty sure she would take that option. "Well… thanks, I guess."

I brush one more kiss over her luscious lips and then settle back on my side, studying her. She looks away for a moment and then pulls the sheet back up, tucking it in around her body.

I exhale deeply and prop my head up on my hand. She doesn't look at me, can't meet my gaze. I reach out to touch her sheet-covered hip again, moving my hand along the neat line created by the piece of fabric.

I'm not sure why she is so shy. She's gorgeous and I think you would have to be crazy to not realize it. Maybe it's just because she's so young. In the back of my mind, I rebuke myself again for being attracted to her, for sleeping with her. But I can't help what I feel.

And I definitely don't regret having made the decision to bring her into my bed. At least, not now. Not while I am still in her thrall.

I run my hand up her arm, just enjoying the feeling of touching her soft skin. It feels luxurious, lying in bed with her in this mansion in the Greek Isles. My whole life is pretty decadent… But this takes the cake.

I glance up and catch her staring at me as if she is trying to puzzle something out. "What?"

She bites her lip, hesitating for a second before she speaks. Her voice is husky, reminding me of the fact that we just had sex. She shrugs a shoulder. "Nothing. I just... I think I just realize how much I like you. And I'm trying to figure out if saying that aloud will make me look like a little girl or not."

I flash her a smirk. "I like you too, Nika."

She blushes bright pink. "Yeah?"

I pull her closer with the hand to her lower back. Just touching her like this, pulling her close to my body once more, I can already feel myself getting hard for her again.

"Yes, I think it's fair to say that we are on the same page. I can't go five minutes without thinking about you. If that's not some kind of infatuation, I don't know what is."

Nika rubs her hips against mine and presses her lips up against my mouth. "Will I ruin it if I tell you I've never felt this way about anyone else before?"

God, she's looking at me with those pretty, innocent eyes and touching me with those dainty little hands. It's enough to make a lesser man tremble.

"No," I whisper. I kiss her again. "God. If I never stopped kissing you, it wouldn't be enough for me. I just can't get enough of you."

Wrapping her arms around my neck, she smiles into my kiss. "It feels like this is..."

She trails off, an echo of uncertainty crossing her face. I reach out and brush some of her hair back, looking at her amazing features.

"Don't censor yourself for me."

She pins me with her gaze. "I was just going to say... This feels like more than a one night stand. I mean, I could be wrong. I've never been with anybody else. But..."

I look her dead in the eye, completely serious. "It can be more than that, if you want it to be. I'm having trouble imagining how I'm supposed to just let you walk away after what we just did."

Her smile is slow, but it definitely grows on her face. "Really?"

I nod, flashing her a dimpled smile. "I'm serious as a heart attack. We can't be together in a long-term sense, but that doesn't mean that we can't... explore each other, I guess."

She kisses me then, so eager and so hot that I nearly forget what I just said.

We can't be together in a long-term sense.

That bit is vital to keeping my life plan on track. Though just now, with Annika in my arms, it's unbelievably hard to focus on that fact.

I deepen the kiss and we are quickly swept away in a storm of our own passion.

ANNIKA

AT THE END OF THE WEEKEND, EVERYONE IS PACKING TO SAY goodbye. I stand next to Pippa, folding a barely-there bikini and giving her side eye. She tucks a strand of her red hair behind her ear and straightens her giant flouncy skirt, shooting me a questioning look.

"What?" she asks.

I turn my head, checking that the door to the sunny bedroom that we are in is mostly closed. Then I shrug. "I was wondering when you and Lars were going to come out and admit that you're a couple."

Her eyes widen and she looks up, a bit surprised. "What? We're not a couple. We're just friends. I thought that you of all people would not fall into the trap that everyone else does. You have guy friends, don't you?"

I scrunch up my face. "Not really."

Pippa up rolls her eyes and straightens her spine. In the strappy black tank top and the long black skirt she is wearing, she looks like a model. She even has a couple of inches on me and I fancy myself unusually tall for a girl.

"Sure you do. What about Erik?"

A laugh bubbles up from inside my chest. "I don't think of him as being a friend. He is..." I pause, trying to figure out exactly how to phrase it. What is Erik, anyway?

My lover? My babysitter? My mouth twists. "He's just working with me and keeping watch over me until Stellan gets married. That's the deal. My grandmother has worked out a plan with Erik in which he will get a title for doing her bidding." I roll my eyes. "It's all very upper crust royalty stuff."

Pippa looks down at her skirt, picking a piece of lint off and biting her lip. Her British accent is particularly strong just now. "I have eyes too, you know. I saw you and Erik kissing yesterday when you thought no one was looking. It's all very cloak and dagger but you can't think that it will go unnoticed by anyone for too long. That's just not the way that things work."

Kalindi comes to the door, knocking before nudging it open. "Are you guys ready? Because the cars are waiting outside to take us to the airport."

I shoot Pippa a smile and pick up my linen-covered suitcase, setting it down on its dark wheels. "I think we're ready. Right, Pippa?"

Pippa smiles and then nods. She picks up her suitcase and rolls it out of the room. When I go to follow her, Kalindi stops me with an arm across the doorway. I look at her, raising an eyebrow. "Yes? Is there something that you want to talk about?"

Kalindi's eyes narrow. "I saw you and Erik together this morning. How could you keep this from me?"

I look at her, my cheeks flushing. This is the second time I've been called out on this exact thing in this exact room. God, Erik and I are really doing a terrible job of hooking up in secret. I blow out a breath.

"It just happened. I just... I didn't tell you because it's all still very new. We don't even know what this is yet."

Kalindi opens her mouth to say something, but then Lars comes clattering down the hall, looking like he means business. "Are you guys kidding right now? We're all waiting on you. Let's go."

He points down the hall, ushering both of us toward the front of the house. Kal gives me a look that says that we are definitely going to talk about this later. But I just give her a soft smile and don't feel any need to continue the conversation.

As I pull my suitcase along behind me, I find Erik in the kitchen, his phone pressed to his ear. His expression looks intense and he is pacing back and forth. He spots me and puts his hand over the phone's speaker.

"Do you mind waiting for just another few minutes? Let the others go. They are on a different flight anyway." He doesn't even wait for me to nod or say anything, he just goes back to arguing with someone on the other end of the phone. "Yes, I'm still here. I'm trying to talk to someone about my father..."

His father? My eyes widen a little. I've met his father once, which was enough for me. I was 12 and his father dressed me down for what he called inappropriate riding gear, whatever *that* means.

How Erik managed to escape that man without ending up with a nasty temper of his own, I have no idea.

Leaving my suitcase by the door, I shoot Erik a single backward glance and then head out to say goodbye to my brothers and my friends. It's a relatively quick affair; as soon as I say my goodbyes, they are hustled into the back of a big white limousine and then the vehicle trundles out, heading down the steep driveway.

I stay put for a second, squinting out towards the ocean. It's looking especially blue today, just an azure hue that makes all the white buildings and tan sand of the beach stand out.

I hear Erik shouting into the phone. "Why not?" He pauses. "Then get him back on the phone!"

I turn, surprised. He is quiet for a second. I'm aware of the hot Grecian sun on my shoulders as I float back toward the front door.

"Are you kidding me? He's an old man. Make him do it! He—"

Erik falls silent. I can't stay away now, not without knowing more of what is going on.

When I follow his angry voice back inside, I find Erik furiously tossing his phone down on the counter. He walks away, pressing his fingertips to his golden hair just beyond his temples.

I bite my lip, hesitating to say anything. Erik gets upset like anyone else. But I have rarely ever heard him yell at someone… and never on the phone. He is just radiating this angry, frustrated energy right now and it's freaking me out.

I frown as I approach him.

He looks up at me with an irritated expression. Clearing his throat, he shakes his head. "I'm sorry. That… that was someone from the hospital closest to the palace. My father was taken in yesterday. It took them a full day to get in contact with me."

My eyes widen. I step closer to him, reaching out and touching his inner arm. He looks at me, still scowling.

"Is your father okay? What happened?"

He pulls a face. "Apparently my father had a heart attack."

It takes me a second to fully absorb that fact. "Heart attack… how bad?"

He frowns. "I don't know. The doctors can't really tell me much. Apparently, my dad is awake, and he is clamoring to leave the hospital already. I thought… I thought that I was going to have to rush to get on the plane and fly back to Copenhagen. You know, to be with him. But as it turns out, he doesn't want to see me. In fact, he forbade the doctors from contacting me. I just got lucky that there was a rebellious nurse on my dad's case. I guess she felt like someone should know where to find him."

I'm at a loss for words. I know that we don't have a language worked out between us for how we comfort each other. But now seems like a good time to start figuring that out.

I hug him, using my lightest touch and looping my arms around his waist. I rest my head against his chest, feeling a little overwhelmed by his news.

"I'm sorry," I murmur.

I feel his arms come around my back, holding me a little closer. His lips find the back of my head and he takes a deep breath. When he lets it out, I look up at him. His expression is nothing short of tortured.

"We should go to the airport. If we leave now, we can be back in Copenhagen this afternoon."

He flinches. "My father doesn't want me to come to the hospital. He told the doctors and nurses that he is fine. Which is just not true, obviously, but…"

I rock back and forth ever so slightly as I hold him, because that feels like a comforting gesture. "Do you want to be there?"

His expression turns bitter. "I don't know. I would like to be able to make that choice. I mean, I would like for once to just be a normal kid with a normal parent. But I guess I should've given up on that a long time ago."

I bite my lip, frowning. "If you want to go, or you want to at least be in Copenhagen right now, we should go. No matter what your father's mental status might be… we should go. If your father isn't giving you what you need, you have to take it. Sometimes, you just have to take what you deserve."

He pulls back an inch, looking down at me with the most intense expression. He scans my face. "How did you become so wise?"

I suddenly feel awkward. Shrugging a shoulder, I give my head a tiny shake. "I don't know. It doesn't really matter, does it? We can be at the airport in twenty minutes and be in the air in forty. That's enough for me."

He frowns, looking pensive. "You know what I just figured out? I just realized that there is a lot more to you than meets the eye. You're way, way deeper than you want people to think."

I give him a sad little smile. "Maybe."

He takes a deep breath and closes his eyes ever so briefly. Then he drops a kiss on my lips and steps back, turning toward where he left his phone.

Before I know it, we are bundled into the back of the limo, heading for the private airport. I keep looking at Erik, needing to reassure myself or maybe comfort him. But he just looks worried, not paying any attention to me. We pull up to the tarmac and he slides me a look, giving me a brief smile. Then he squeezes my hand and opens the door.

He slides out before I can even think of what to say. And I follow him after a second, reminding myself that his needs come first right now.

26

ERIK

I LOOK OUT OVER THE CITY LIGHTS OF COPENHAGEN, STANDING on the penthouse balcony of this building that is near the hospital where my father is staying. I have always known that this place was owned by the royal family, but it's Annika's first time here. She's somewhere behind me, through the open patio doors and in the lavish luxury loft. If you can call this place a loft…

After all, it may be only one room, but it's also the entire floor. At some point, you reach a place where it's just ridiculous to call any place like this something so silly as a loft.

I suck in a breath and shake my head. I picked this place because of its proximity to Copenhagen's best hospital. But my father is still refusing to see me. I flew back to Copenhagen and put Nika at risk of the paparazzi finding out that she is in town. I did all that for no reason, as it turns out.

Why is my father such a bastard?

"Erik?"

I turn to find Nika just steps behind me, looking concerned. She beckons me inside. "Come on. You haven't eaten all day. Let me make you a sandwich or something, at least."

My eyebrows raise. Lured by her offer and no little amount of curiosity, I step inside and close the doors behind me. The walls of the loft are all glass. Everything inside is sleek and light colored and modern. The overlarge living room area that is to my left, the dining room table set up to my right, and straight ahead is a truly luxurious kitchen that any chef would die to have.

I follow Annika toward it, noting the stainless steel appliances and the huge marble island. She walks to the refrigerator and opens it, biting her lip as she frowns at the contents.

"Oh, I thought… I assumed that there would be… like sandwich things or something." She flushes, looking up at me. "It looks like we are out of luck unless we want some expensive wine and cheese."

I exaggerate my eye roll for her benefit. "Move over, Princess. I'll make something very simple for us. You need to eat as much as I do."

I catch a tiny frown on her face, but it's gone as quickly as it appeared. She relinquishes her space at the fridge. I quickly assemble a platter of the expensive cheeses, bread, sliced fruits, and cucumbers. I add a couple glasses of sparkling wine, sliding it all onto the marble countertop.

Nika cants her head at me. "We should eat in the living room. Come on."

She picks up the platter of food and her champagne flute and makes her way to the living room. I snag the bowl of bread and my own drink, following her. I would never think to eat on the expensive looking white fabric couches that line the corner of the penthouse. But Princess Annika does it without thinking about it. She and I are just fundamentally different, I suppose.

She throws herself down on the couch, putting the wooden platter of food down beside herself. I take my own seat on the other side of her with more caution, settling the bread down between us. She glances at me, tucking her fair hair back behind her shoulder. She raises her glass, biting her lip.

"Is it tacky to toast right now?" That same little frown appears on her face.

I shake my head. "I don't think so, no. Cheers."

We clink our classes together and then I lift my flute to my lips, taking a long pull of the wine. It's extremely sweet but there is a certain satisfaction that I feel, a poor man toasting with the most expensive champagne in all of Denmark. That's nothing to sneeze at.

I sip my wine and look out at the dark landscape of Copenhagen. There are a million thoughts playing over and over again.

How my father is a bastard.

How I feel like I've done something to let him down, even though a part of me knows that that's not the truth.

How I'm sitting in this penthouse, surrounded by all of this obscene wealth and yet I know that none of it is mine.

So, I brood. I drink my champagne and nibble on a piece of cheese. And I think over all the things that have been bothering me ever since I got the fateful call this morning.

Nika sets her glass down and looks at me carefully. "I can see that you have a lot of things on your mind. Do you want to talk about it?"

I squint at her, finishing the last of my wine before setting my glass aside. "You don't really want to hear it. It's all just noise."

She bites her lip, a wrinkle appearing in her brow. "Yes, I do. I want to hear whatever you are thinking."

I arch my eyebrows at her and tilt my head. "Really?"

She rolls her eyes at me. "Yes, really. I'm here for you. I'm listening."

She adjusts her position on the couch, pulling her short white skirt down an inch and looking at me quite seriously. I shrug my shoulders, looking away over her shoulder at the darkened city skyline.

"I don't know. I was just thinking that…" I pause, trying to think of how to word what I am feeling. "I know that this emergency isn't about me. But I'm just so mad at my father. He is such a bastard. *Of course* he doesn't want the nurses fussing over him. He just wants… He just wants to go back to his little cottage and drink himself to death."

Nika frowns. "That has to be frustrating. It's hard to care for people that don't care about themselves."

I inhale a deep breath and nod. "My father makes it next to impossible. One minute he curses me for how invested I am in the royal family. He says that I am too uppity, and I need to learn my place. He seems to think that I belong back with him, working in the stables. And the next moment, he pushes me away, saying I'm a lost cause. It's definitely hard to be around him."

Her brows rise and she scoots forward, frowning at the platter of food between us. She gets up and moves to the other side of me, settling herself on the couch, one knee overlapping my own. She presses herself close, leaning her head against the couch.

I find myself grabbing her hand, twining our fingers. She gives me a squeeze, shooting me a comforting look. "I'm sorry that you have to deal with this. It isn't fair."

I squint off into the distance, uncomfortable just now with meeting her gaze. "I mean, it is what it is. Everybody has their things. If the royal family has taught me nothing else, it's that everyone's life is hard, no matter how glamorous it might seem from the outside."

The ghost of a smile crosses her lips. "That's very true. It doesn't lessen the burden for you, though."

I glance at her, scanning her face. "Ah, shit. I wish I hadn't told you any of it. I don't want to seem… I don't know. Weak, I guess."

Her eyebrows fly up. She leans close to me, her hand clutching my own. "Erik, look at me."

I still, my gaze latching onto hers. She looks so perfect and so untouchable in that moment. She grips my hand.

"When you are vulnerable with me, it makes me trust you more. It makes me feel like you're letting me in. It makes me feel so special. It's important to me that you understand that."

My eyes widen the little. I cocked my head, not quite knowing how to respond to that. I end up chuckling. "Okay… That sounds a little crazy but…"

"But nothing. It's how I feel. And that is the only true thing that I know." She leans in and offers her mouth up to me for a kiss.

I press my lips to hers, my thoughts in a mess. Her mouth feels so damn good beneath my lips, like honey and cinnamon and something utterly unique. She draws back after a second, her eyes shining with tears.

I didn't expect her to cry. That's the last thing in the world that I want right now.

I cup her face, using my thumbs to brush away the tears glittering in the corners of her eyes.

"Hey, hey. I thought we were getting along. What's the deal with the tears?"

She gives me a slow smile. "We are. I just... I guess I'm overwhelmed."

I take a moment to kiss her lips again and then whisper gently against them. "Is that a bad thing?"

She's shakes her head, putting her hands on my shoulders. "No. I think it's just a part of us growing closer. I think it's pretty natural to experience some wild emotions when you're... I mean... you know, whatever we are."

I trace my hands down her neck to her shoulders and then continue down until my hands grip her waist. I look at her, her beautiful, powder blue eyes seeming like they know my innermost thoughts. "And what are we, exactly?"

A hint of surprise shows on her features. "What do you mean?"

I bite my lip and smirk at her just a little. "Is this a relationship? Or are you going to leave me the second you get your freedom back?"

She closes her eyes for a brief second. I was only kidding, but now her hesitation has me sucking in a breath. When she opens her eyes again, there are wet with a fresh batch of tears.

When she speaks, it sounds like a threadbare whisper. "Are you asking me to be your girlfriend?"

My gaze tightens on her face. Am I asking that? I take a few seconds and exhale.

"I don't know. I mean... I know we aren't going to last forever. But it would be nice to pretend for a little while, wouldn't it?"

She launches herself into my arms, hugging me with such force that I can't breathe for a moment. She giggles and pushes me backwards on the couch, kissing me soundly. It's strange to feel her taking control for a moment. So, I wrested the control from her hands and flipped the script on her.

I reach up and grab her face, fisting both my hands in her hair and kissing her so hard that I swear I can almost taste blood. She doesn't lose an ounce of her eagerness, either.

She moans under my touch, writhing against my body like a heathen.

I pick her up and carry her into the first bedroom I find, stripping myself bare and then doing the same to her. And then I proceed to fuck her until we are both unable to move, hours and hours of skin to skin and clutched sheets and sultry moans.

In the dark, many hours later, we lie in bed together, me on my back and her on her side, pressed against me. Whatever anguish I was feeling before over my father's hospitalization, I feel empty now. I fucked it all out of my system, apparently. I lie on my back, sweat cooling, and think of absolutely nothing.

She's pulled the sheets up, very insistent on that fact. And I let it go because there isn't a damn thing I care about outside of this bedroom.

She surprises me by bringing up the same topic that we were talking about hours before.

"Can I tell you something?" she asks, her voice a frail thing.

My voice has gone to gravel. I clear my throat. "You can tell me anything, princess."

In the dark, I can just make out her shy smile. "I was just thinking about you and your father. And I realize that we have something in common."

I turned my head to look at her. "Oh yeah?"

She nods. "I think we both longed for approval as kids. Right?"

I shrug. "I guess so."

She makes a face. "We looked around for the people that were supposed to love us, namely our parents. And they weren't there. I know we had very different childhoods, but I think we have more in common than we think."

I give her a surprised look. "That's some pretty heavy thinking that you been doing."

She ducks her head. "After I read through that book on body positivity and self-love, I picked up a dozen more self-help books. It's slow going, but I'm finding out new things on every single page."

I stare at her for a beat. "I didn't realize that you were interested in all that. I mean, more than the radical self-love stuff."

She looks away for a moment. I imagine that her cheeks are glowing red by now. "Well, I am."

I reach out, turning her face back towards me. I place a gentle kiss on her lips and then look at her meaningfully. "I think it's great. I have almost no interest in that, but I support you being curious."

She bites her lip. "Do you think I'm right though? About how we had similar childhoods?"

I think about that for a second. "I don't know. I mean, I guess so. My father was never around because he was busy working the stables or passed out drunk. My mom left when I was very young. She never came back. And when your father offered to take me off my father's hands, my father jumped at the opportunity."

She rubs circles on my chest, nodding. "Yes."

"And your family obviously had their own set of issues. I mean… Not to speak badly of them, but they didn't give a fuck about anyone other than themselves."

Nika scrunches her nose. "I know. They really were just not around almost all of my childhood. I had mom. And I had all my brothers… But I never really had a family. I mean, not in the traditional sense of the word. It's funny to think of the King of Denmark having such a mess of a family."

I reached my arm around her, squeezing her waist. "I'm sorry that your parents missed out on you, Nika. You're pretty wonderful for having essentially raised yourself."

That same shy smile comes over her face again. "You too, Erik."

I kiss her one more time, then close my eyes and let my breathing even out. It's nice, laying here with my... well, my girlfriend. It's the first time for that, at least.

I settle in, opening my eyes a crack. Just to check on her before I fall asleep. But to my surprise, I find her wide eyed and frowning, as she lies on my chest.

"Hey. Whatever you're worried about, it can wait until tomorrow."

She raises her eyes to me, her frown deepening. "I guess so."

I sigh and open my eyes a little bit more, continuing our talk even though I'm basically exhausted. "What's on your mind?"

I can feel the hesitancy rolling off of her in waves. She sighs, bringing both her hands up to cover her face. "I don't mean to be a bummer."

I groan and raise myself up on my arm, frowning down on her. "Well now you have to tell me. What are you thinking about that has you all worked up?"

She lowers her hands and looks at me. "Our relationship."

"I'm going to need a little bit more to go on than that."

She scrunches up her face. "People won't understand. The world will judge us. And... I don't even want to think about what my brother will think?"

Stellan.

Thinking about him is like a punch to the gut. I can just imagine his face when he finds out that I am dating his little sister. Some combination of fury and outrage will run across his features, I'm sure.

Still, that doesn't change the fact that I have feelings for Nika. If anything, it makes my feelings more pronounced.

I glance at her. "Does that make a difference to you?"

She bites her lip, hesitating again. My heart starts to pound. And then she shakes her head, tucking her platinum hair behind her ear. "It doesn't. It should, but it doesn't."

I gather her up in my arms, shifting onto my side and kissing the top of her head. "Good."

She places her small hand on my upper arm and buries her head against my bare chest. If she continues to have doubts, she doesn't say anything about them. Soon her breathing slows and evens out, letting me know that she is near sleep.

But she has unintentionally infected me with her worries. Because now I can't get Stellan's enraged face out of my head. And even as I close my eyes, he follows me into sleep…

27

ANNIKA

JUST A COUPLE DAYS LATER, I AM SITTING AT THE KITCHEN island, sneaking a look at my iPad. I haven't had any contact with the outside world other than a phone call with Kal. And so far, I've been pretty much happy. But some part of me, some self-destructive little voice in the back of my head, is screaming at me to check my social media accounts.

I bite my lip and open twitter, my heartbeat already pounding in my ears before the page even loads.

Is Annika drying out somewhere?

Maybe she is on a permanent vacation where she can just eat and booze all day and all night...

Good riddance. Denmark is better without her.

What will we do without our very own Princess Piggie?

Each snide comment is captioned on a different unflattering picture from the red carpet event. I look like a hot mess in those photos, drunk and a little too thin and completely out of the loop. My artfully done make up is marred by my tears.

And of course, there is a picture of me in full breakdown mode, being scooped off my feet and into Erik's arms.

Ugh, I hate myself so much. Why did I even look at Twitter?

I turn off my iPad and leave my head down on my arms. The cool marble countertop receives my tears, the stone unflinching. I don't even remember my eyes welling up. I just feel like everything in the world is piling on top of me, forcing me down, caging me in.

I struggle to draw in a breath. Shit, it's happening again.

One glance at social media and I'm in a tailspin, having a panic attack.

What should I do?

I feel my chest tightening and I'm aware of my hands turned numb.

Shit. Shit. If Erik sees this, he will probably freak out.

I push myself to my feet, looking around the house. My vision is wonky, going black at the edges. I try to stagger to the couch, but I don't make it all the way. Instead I tumble to the ground in the middle of the room, crying and sobbing and gasping for breath. I curl up in a ball, praying like hell that this will pass.

It feels like I'm dying, though.

And this exact moment is when Erik decides to come back in from taking a shower. He is clad in only a towel and his wet hair is slicked back. He takes one look at me and breaks into a run, scurrying over to my side and dropping to his knees.

"Nika? Nika, what's going on? You have to tell me. Are you okay?"

He sounds frantic. I can barely nod. I can't speak. I can't move. I am struggling for breath and there's nothing that Erik can do to help.

Erik scoops me up in his arms, groaning as he climbs to his feet. He carries me into the bedroom that we've claimed as our own and carefully places me on the bed. He sits right beside me, worry etched on his face. "Is this a panic attack? Are you having another one? Because if you're not, I have to call someone. Just nod if you are having a panic attack."

I nod frantically. He blows out a breath and looks down at me, his hand coming up to my back. He rubs small circles into my flesh, seeming to think about what to do. "I read that panic attacks only last five or ten minutes at most. And I'm going to stay right here. I'm not going anywhere, Nika. You're going to be okay. You're going to be fine."

A sense of doom claws its way up from my chest and I close my eyes, sucking in breath after breath. In the back of my mind, I am embarrassed that Erik has to see me this way again. But that feeling is shoved to the side by more immediate concerns.

Erik doesn't even hesitate. He just keeps up his calming touches and reassuring words. "Everything is fine. Everyone is fine. This will pass. Everything is fine. Everyone is fine. This will pass..."

I tremble and sweat drips off my body. Squeezing my eyes closed seems to help, in some small way. So, I do that, eventually reaching up and grabbing Erik's free hand, twining his fingers with my own.

I'm okay. I know that I'm okay. I feel like I'm going to fucking die but I'm okay...

I repeat those words to myself like a mantra, waiting for the panic attack to subside. After a few minutes, it seems a little easier to breathe. I don't feel the sense of approaching doom anymore. I take a deep breath and blow out a breath, opening my eyes.

Erik is looming over me, his green-brown eyes deeply concerned. "Nika? How are you feeling?"

Not trusting myself to speak just yet, I nod. I'm thirsty, maybe thirstier that I've ever been before. I manage to squeak out the word. "Water?"

Erik looks beyond relieved. He lets my hand go and stand up. "I'll be right back with a glass of water."

I close my eyes and only reopen them when he sits down beside me again on the bed, pressing a cool glass into my palm. I sip from a glass very gratefully, my heart still pounding. It takes another minute for me to regain full use of my voice.

"Thank you, Erik. I'm starting to feel a little bit more normal now."

He looks down at me, his expression somber. He starts stroking my back again, looking worried as ever. "You scared the shit out of me, Nika. I know you didn't mean to. But what set this whole thing off?"

I look at my glass, avoiding his eyes. I shrug a shoulder. "I might have… gone online and checked Twitter."

His expression turns sour immediately. "What would make you do that? Why would you do this to yourself?"

I push out my cheek with my tongue. "I don't know. I guess… I was just feeling like things were good. You know, things between us, things with the royal palace..." I make a helpless gesture. "I'm not used to things feeling fine. Maybe I just... needed to dip my toe back in reality for a moment. And the quickest way that I knew how to do that was to check Twitter and see what people were saying about me."

His brows rise. "I thought you were dying. I felt helpless. I don't like feeling that way. You have to find some other way of dealing with this, Nika. If that's what really set you off..."

He looks a little angry and pretty disappointed. My cheeks flush.

I exhale loudly. "I know. I think... I mean, I didn't know that it would cause a panic attack. But I am not used to being so... happy."

He takes my hand, placing it against his heart and pressing it close. "I'm glad that you're happy. But this self-destructive little habit of yours? It won't work. I can't deal with it. I won't."

Pushing myself to a seat, I reach up and touch Erik's face. "I'm sorry. Really, I am. I'll try to figure out another way to deal with it, I guess."

He frowns. "For the record, I'm happy too. And my father is resting at the cottage, although apparently, he has turned several nurses away at the door. And so, I am just taking it as it comes, trying to keep my mind off of it. And because I need the distraction, I am extra happy that I'm here with you."

I turned my face up to him, seeking a kiss. He brushes his lips against mine very briefly. Then he pulls back, brushing back a few strands of my hair. "I don't want to see you hurt like that, Nika. I think you should see someone professionally. For the panic attacks, I mean."

I screw my face up. "I did talk to a psychotherapist. For a little while, anyway. When I was a preteen, I started to realize how distorted the mirror that the press holds up to the royal family really is. And the press almost always had something to say about me. How much I did or didn't eat. How I looked in jeans. One time, they wrote that a dress I wore made me look 'extremely plump'."

His eyebrows shoot up. "They called you fat?"

I nod. "Yeah. Can you imagine calling a twelve-year-old 'extremely plump'? I still remember how miserable I was. I used to eat chocolate and…" I pause, not sure how much to tell him. Glancing up, I take a deep breath. "I binged on foods and then threw them up. At times, I grew tired of that, so I restricted my food intake very severely."

Erik's eyes narrow on my face. "Are you saying you had bulimia?"

I look down, embarrassed. "Not had. Have. I don't believe that kind of disordered thinking about food ever goes away completely. If you think that I don't know exactly how many calories I've had today and how many we've burned off fucking, you're *nuts*." I frown. "My point is, I talked to a therapist trusted by the royal family then."

He's silent for a second. I glance up at him, feeling a nervous shiver slide down my spine. He looks somber. "I'm glad you told me."

Feeling awkward, I shrug. "Whatever."

"Nika," he says, shaking his head. "I hope you realize that there is more to you than just a pretty face."

I roll my eyes. "Yeah, yeah."

He gives me a little shake. "You're intelligent. You're deep. You're compassionate. If anyone ever so much as breathes a word to the contrary, I'll fucking kill them."

He looks dead serious when he says it. My eyes widen a little bit.

Erik nudges me. "I mean it. And I meant what I said about you seeing a professional." His face crinkles. "Maybe you could see someone that has nothing to do with the palace."

I arch a brow. "You are so quick to turn your back on the royal press office."

He smirks. "They'll be glad to see the back of me."

"What, are you leaving?"

His smile vanishes. "Eventually."

My brow hunches. "Do you want to tell me your plans?"

He stretches, looking down. "Maybe later. What I really want is to get dressed and then make us some breakfast."

He presses a final kiss to my lips then gets up, heading to dress. I collapse on the bed, thinking to myself that telling him about my eating disorder wasn't at all terrible. He just makes the past seem…

I don't know, far away and out of focus.

And that's a good thing, so far as I can tell…

Making a mental note to look up therapists, I close my eyes for a few minutes and wait until Erik calls me to breakfast.

28

ANNIKA

TODAY IS A SPECIAL DAY. NOT ONLY DOES THE DAY MARK THE one month anniversary of Erik and I officially dating. But it also happens to be my birthday.

I know, I know. It's definitely passé and gauche to make a big deal out of what is essentially just another day on the calendar. Especially my twentieth birthday... I don't even get any special privileges for turning twenty. But even before I open my eyes, a shiver of excitement runs through me.

I can't help it. I just love celebrating holidays and my birthday definitely counts as one of those.

I open my eyes to find the space beside me in bed empty. I reach out my hand, touching Erik's side of the bed. He has obviously been gone a while because his side isn't even warm anymore.

I sit up, looking around sleepily. From the sun slanting in the windows of the loft, I would guess that it's still early, probably only eight or nine in the morning.

I hear some vague banging in the main area of the loft. Pushing off the heavy satin coverlet, I get up and pull one of Erik's black T-shirts on over my head. Then I pad barefoot over the cool stone floors, my eyes widening when I realize that Erik is already in the kitchen.

He looks up at me from spreading preserves on toast, his face lighting up a little. God, the way that he looks at me just now, his warm green-brown eyes and his cool yellow hair against the backdrop of his big muscular body... I feel lucky suddenly.

I have warm shivers all over my body and I beam at him.

"Hey," I say, shoving a hand through my thick sinuous hair. I look at him, trying to decide whether or not to tell him that it is my birthday. It feels a little ridiculous to make a big deal out of it but there's a part of me that definitely wants to.

"Hey. I thought I would surprise you with a little breakfast in bed. After all, it is your birthday."

My eyes widen. "How did you even know that?"

He finishes coating the toast with some kind of glossy fruit preserves and smiles up at me, bringing a plate full of eggs and toast over to me. Then he presents me with a little white vase with a single white rose inside of it, placing it beside my breakfast with a flourish. "I'm a mind reader, that's how."

I roll my eyes a little, but I can't keep the stupid grin off my face. "Well... Thanks. Not to be ungrateful, but is there coffee?"

He nods. "There is. Sit down and I'll pour you a cup."

I noticed that there are mylar balloons and several gift boxes on the far counter. I nod at them as he delivers a fresh cup of coffee. "What are those?"

He smiles lately. "I think they are all gifts and notes from your family. Kal made a special gift too, and I had it all delivered here."

I arch my brow. "Nothing from you?"

He rolls his eyes. "I didn't get you anything so tame. You can't unwrap my present. Hope it wasn't crazy, not getting you designer jewelry for your birthday."

Shaking my head, I shoot him a shy smile. "You're not wrong."

I pick up a piece of toast, biting into it. It's crispy and buttery and sweet. I close my eyes, enraptured for a moment.

I don't know how I'm going to tally that in my calories for the day but damn if I'm not glad that I tasted it.

When I open my eyes, Erik is staring at me. His expression is intent.

"What?" I ask.

He shrugs. "You're just beautiful when you enjoy yourself, that's all." He pushes off the counter and starts heading toward the bedroom. "You should open Kalindi's present first. Then hurry up with your breakfast because we have a lot to do."

I shoot him a questioning look, but he is already gone, vanished into the hall where the bedrooms are. I stuff another half piece of toast in my mouth, crunching happily, and I stand up to head to the presents.

True to form, Kal's present is perfectly decorated. It's the one with the mylar balloons attached, balloons that probably are supposed to be for a younger girl's birthday. But they are the right shade of hot pink with big white bubble letters that say happy birthday. I pick up the hot pink and pale green polka-dotted box that the balloons are attached to. Untying the perfectly knotted green ribbon, I find an assortment of toffees and other sugar free sweets. Under that, there is a picture of me and Kal at age 11, attached to a very heartfelt poem.

It makes me smile. My best friend has my best interests at heart, no matter whether we see each other on our birthdays or not. Something about that makes me very happy.

All the other gifts are from Momse and my parents and other palace officials.

A matching diamond tennis bracelet and diamond necklace. That would be from Momse. I sigh and shove it to the side, rifling through the remainder of the presents. Everything else is neatly wrapped and obviously a luxury item, but there is little evidence that any thought was put into it aside from 'would a twenty year old girl like this?'.

It's not surprising. And I am grateful. But I soon move on, finishing up my toast and eating a couple bites of the eggs. I slurp down half the coffee and then put my dishes in the sink, heading back towards the bedroom.

I'm surprised to find Erik fully dressed and in dark jeans and a dark T-shirt, laying out clothes for me. He chooses something casual, a pink flouncy baby doll dress and a pair of white flats. I cock my head, narrowing my eyes at him.

"What is this?"

He winks at me. "Get dressed. I'm not saying that you need to wear this outfit exactly, but you don't need to go overboard on getting dressed up. We are not going to see anyone else today. We're just going to your birthday surprise."

"Well." I wiggle my eyebrows. "Whatever I can do to make that happen, I guess..."

In a matter of minutes, I'm dressed. Other than swapping out his practical white flats for just a strappy black heel, I take his suggestions to heart.

He holds out a length of white silk, just big enough for me to make a blindfold. He nods at the silk. "I'm going to need you to wear a blindfold. Then we can go. We are not going very far."

Crinkling my brow, I allow him to tie the blindfold on me. I can't see anything, but I can make out my surroundings and tons of sunlight pours in through the blindfold.

Then he guides me out of the apartment, down the elevator, and out onto the street. I assume that we will get in a car of some sort, but Erik surprises me by just walking a very short distance, maybe three blocks or less.

I grin as he directs me, holding me by the waist every step of the way.

"Watch the door, there's a step there..."

He leads me into a building and up another elevator. Then we step off the elevator and he comes around behind me, steering me to the exact place that I need to be. I can't see much but the place Erik guides me to is filled with sunlight, at least.

"Okay," he says. His hands are still on my shoulders, his big body behind mine. "You can look now."

I reach up and push the blindfold up, pulling it off entirely. My eyes widen as I take in the scene before me.

I'm in a bedroom, standing right in front of a huge four-poster bed. The bed is draped with colorful hanging curtains and covered in soft white comforter. All around tiny twinkling lights are strung around the ceiling. They are mirrored by the candles that are lit on every surface: the dresser, the side tables, the low white satin chaise in the corner.

The room screams cozy and then whispers *expensive*.

The walls are covered with fairy lights and pieces of stiff linen paper, each one with a photograph attached. I'm drawn to the closest one, a photograph of me looking happy on the beach. Frowning, I turn to see another picture. This one is from the arcade, it's me and Erik, clinging to each other and looking breathlessly happy. I step back and look at more pictures... Pictures from our recent trip to the Greek Isles, pictures from our everyday lives at the palace, pictures from the Greta von Grissel fashion show. There are even a few pictures from the last few days. I turn my head and look at the next wall, which has the same pieces of linen paper but instead of the photographs, they have words.

Kindness. Compassion. Humor. Fun. Style. Intelligence. Snark.

Each one has a different word, but they all contain something positive.

Frowning, I look at Erik. "What are these? What is this place?"

He takes a deep breath, meeting my eye. "It's my house. Newly acquired, I guess you could say. And someday, I hope that you could live here too. I think for now it could be a good place to hide out from the press. I... I want you to love it."

He draws my attention to a jar of my favorite toffees and a door that obviously leads into a closet that is empty.

My heart starts pounding. "Is this all for me?"

He gives me a funny look. "Of course. Who else would it be for? It's the very beginning of your personal hideaway, I hope." He scrunches up his face. "I paid cash for it so if you don't like it, please say something now."

My eyebrows fly up. "What, you're kidding? This place must have cost you a fortune! How... How can you afford this?"

He rolls his eyes little. "Let's just say that I have been known to play the stock market and win big."

I absorb all of that for a second. Nodding my head, I look around in awe. I didn't even notice that there are the same linen pieces of paper up on the third wall, listing facts about me.

Loves coffee.

Hates waiting in line.

Graduated at the top of her class.

Would choose the ocean over mountains anytime.

I raise my hand, walking over to touch one of the cards. For some reason, this is the most touching thing that I've seen yet. My eyes mist over as I read the facts printed on each card.

"So?"

I blot at my eyes, turning with a question on my face. "What?"

He looks down for a moment. And when he looks back up, his gaze is smoldering, threatening to burn me alive. "I know we haven't been together for that long. But… I was just thinking about your rooms at the palace and how happy you've been for the last month, since I took you away from there. I want you to know that you will always have another place that you can live. You don't have to be a trained seal for the royal family, Nika."

My heart pounds.

My mouth is dry.

I don't know quite what to say.

"This place… it's for me?" I say again, wide eyed. It's just so hard to wrap my head around.

I am officially swept off my feet. I put a hand over my heart, my mouth crumpling.

"No one has ever done anything like this for me," I whisper. It's the hardest thing not to just break down in tears of gratitude right now.

Erik shrugs a shoulder. "Well, I see us living here, eventually. Assuming you don't get tired of me first. I… I like spending time with you."

I stare at him for a second, not sure I'm hearing him right.

No one has ever asked for me to spend more time with them before. No one has ever cared enough about me, not even my family. My mouth opens, but no words come out.

Erik makes a face, coming over and wrapping his arms around my waist. "I need you to say something, princess."

I bob my head, burying my face against the solid wall of his chest. "Yes. Yes! I would love to live with you, Erik. I mean… more permanently than I do at the moment."

He tips my chin up with a finger, kissing my lips. I kiss him back fiercely, really moved that he did all of this for me. He smiles against my lips.

"I'm glad you like it," he whispers.

I break into a grin. "I love it… I really…. I love you, Erik."

He freezes for a second. His expression is one of complete surprise. His hands tighten around my waist. "Oh, Annika…"

I bite my lip and blush. "I'm sorry. That kind of slipped out."

He shakes his head. "Don't apologize. I care about you too, Nika. More deeply than I can say."

I bite my lower lip. "Yeah?"

He shakes his head and kisses me tenderly. "I do."

I take a deep breath, feeling a little off-center. Does that mean that he loves me and just can't say it aloud? Or am I being optimistic to think so?

Erik takes my hand, guiding me back to the bed. I sit down, enjoying how squishy that mattress is.

"I'll be right back," he says.

He returns with a huge silver tray and sets it between us on the bed. It's been made up with a silver ice bucket with champagne chilling, a platter of French macarons and hand-made chocolates, and two champagne flutes. And right in the center of all of it is a single pink cupcake with a candle, just waiting to be lit.

I grin as he sits down on the other side of the tray.

Erik pops the bottle of champagne and pours us each a glass. I pick up a pink macaron, nibbling it delicately. It's sweet and light, made of almond flour and raspberry cream.

He holds up his glass to me. I pick mine up and clink it against his. He smiles.

"Happy birthday, Nika."

I wiggle my eyebrows at him as I taste the champagne. "Thank you for doing all of this, Erik."

His lips twitch. "It was nothing." He takes a sip of his drink then looks at me. "Isn't this the part where you tell me your goals, birthday girl?"

I shoot him a smirk. "My goals?"

"Yep." He reaches over to the platter and touches the edge of the cupcake, taking just a little frosting off of it. Then he pops his finger in his mouth, smacking his lips appreciatively.

My lips twist. I sigh, tilting my head and leaning back on the bed. "I'm not sure. I..." Pausing, I bite my full lower lip. "If I weren't a princess... if I could break away from the royal family, I would live a very different life."

His eyebrows rise. He sets his glass on the floor and runs a couple of his fingers along the outside of my arm. "What would you do?"

I push out my cheek with my tongue. "I would probably focus on charity work? Maybe something with fashion... or maybe raise awareness for people with eating disorders? I don't know. I would just be excited to go out without the paparazzi following me everywhere."

His lips quirk. "Like this morning?"

I nod. "Exactly."

He screws up his face for a second. "We could break away from the palace, you know."

I give him a funny look. "What?"

He shrugs, looking down at the platter. "I'm just saying. You can do anything you want to do, if you are willing to pay the price."

I give a half-hearted chuckle. "What about you? Where are you in this scenario? Because I don't see you being Stellan's secretary if you encourage his little sister to run off and become a *former* royal."

He looks up at me suddenly, spearing me with his deep, serious gaze. "I don't plan on being his secretary for much longer. Before all of this, I was trying to find the right time to tell him that I wanted to leave. Now, I have even more moti-vation to leave."

I stare at him. My heart pounds. "Are you saying you would go with me if I made the jump?"

He nods. "I would. In a heartbeat."

I frown. "And what would our future look like together? How would we live?" I scrunch up my nose. "I imagine that I would receive some sort of stipend from the royal family but— "

"We don't have to worry about money," he says, tilting his head at me. "I have enough. I mean, it's nothing like the kind of money that the royal family has. But it'll do. I can take care of you for the rest of our lives, Nika."

I narrow my gaze. "I don't want you to feel like you have to take care of me."

He shrugs. "It's just money. I would rather spend it on making a life with you than anything else."

I bite my lip and frown at him for a few seconds, taking it all in. My heart lurches in my chest. "You're serious? You would break off from my family if I agreed to go?"

He trails his touch along my arm, nodding. "Yes."

I scoot around to be close enough to kiss his gorgeous lips. For a minute, we just explore each other's mouths, languorously kissing. When I finally open my eyes and look into his face, my heart is so full that I can't help but grin.

He smirks. "How should I read that? Is that a yes?"

I nod, biting my lip. "I would be a fool to say no. I'm not promising anything, but… I will leave if you're propping me up."

"I can't think of anything better." Erik pauses, his brow wrinkling. "We should wait until after Stellan's wedding to make any announcements. Right?"

"Yes. That would be the polite thing to do." Reaching up to his sideburn, I run my fingers through the short hair that I find there. "It would be even more polite to wait until after he gets back from his honeymoon."

He pulls a face. "It would be polite, yes. But I don't want to wait that long. Do you?"

My lips twitch. I kiss his lip for a second before shaking my head. "No."

Erik moves closer, kissing me more deeply. We get lost in the moment and I sigh breathily as he starts to brush his lips against my collarbone...

29

ERIK

ANNIKA IS LOOKING AT ME LIKE A FUCKING ANGEL. I CAN'T not touch her. I put the tray of food on the floor and pull her closer. She moans with this breathy little voice that makes me wild and crazy.

Shaken to my very core, I drag my thumb across her lower lip, then follow the caress with the press of my lips against hers. She responds immediately, ravenous for my touch.

Fuck.

Echoing her sentiment with an appetite all my own, I bend her backward, trailing kisses down her neck. I grab her by the waist and bring her down to the floor, spreading her thighs and bringing us together. My mouth descends upon hers, hungry and demanding.

She opens her mouth and her thighs for me, drawing me in without a second of hesitation. Her hands slip around my neck, fingernails lightly scoring the flesh of my shoulders. I palm one of her breasts, then pinch her nipple, drawing a cry from her lips.

I trail kisses down her jaw, skipping over her neck, and bend down to nuzzle the space between her breasts. I feel her legs wrap around me, her heels digging into the backs of my legs, pulling me as close as possible.

I reach down and hike her pretty dress up, finding her bare underneath. I groan as I rip off her dress, kissing her exposed breasts. I know I'm not being delicate with her, but I'm too entranced to care.

She doesn't seem to mind, her head thrown back. She's making these little oh sounds that are killing me, every second I'm not inside her.

Fuck. I need to have her, right this second.

She kisses me, and I bite her lower lip. She grabs my head and bites me on the neck, which I swear makes my cock pulse.

"Talk dirty to me again," she whispers. Her words are another turn on.

"Fuck!" I grit out. "You are such a bad girl, princess."

I squeeze one of her breasts hard, and she gasps.

"Bad enough to get punished?" she whispers.

"Ohhh fuck," I say, pushing her down against the floor. I look at her for a second, searching her face. "You don't really want that."

She struggles under me, trying to push me off. "Maybe I do."

I bring my hand up to her neck, fitting my fingers around the slim white column of her neck. I apply just a little bit of pressure, making her gasp and writhe beneath me. When I release her, she tries to pull me closer for a kiss. I allow it for a moment, but then I pull back. There is much more I want to do to her.

I move back, kneeling on the ground. I strip off my own jeans and T-shirt.

Her eyes are immediately drawn to my cock, which jumps at the attention she pays it. She looks up at me, biting her lip.

"Can I taste you?" she asks quietly, seeming unsure.

God, could Nika be any sexier? I reach down and stroke my cock with one hand, nodding. Her eyes twinkle a bit, and she pushes herself up on the bed. "I have been dreaming about your taste..."

She reaches out, brushing her hand along my length. I grit my teeth as pre-cum leaks from the tip of my cock.

"If you insist," I say, amused. She presses her free hand against my chest, turning me onto my back. I go willingly, trying not to flutter my eyes closed as she moves down, kissing as she goes.

When Nika circles her wet tongue around the head of my cock, I can't breathe for a second.

"Like this?" she asks, looking up at me. She shifts so that she's on her knees.

"That's... perfect. Jesus, you're hot when you're on your knees like that."

Swallowing, I look down at her heart-shaped face. Her pouty lips part as I guide my cock to her mouth. The second I touch my cock to her lips, the sensitive head probing the wet heat of her mouth, I have to close my eyes for a moment.

My dick twitches, and it takes everything in me not to just bury myself in her hot mouth. I imagine how I would do it. How good it would feel just to put my hand in her hair, to let go and fuck her mouth and throat.

But no. I open my eyes again, breathing hard. She's looking up at me, her lips on the very tip of my dick, her eyes telling me that she trusts me. I have to remember that.

"Open your mouth a little, and stick out your tongue," I encourage her, pressing the blunt head against her lips.

She does, rolling out the velvety tip of her tongue. It caresses the head of my cock and sends tiny lightning bolts of electricity down to my feet. My toes curl.

"*Fuuuuuuck,*" I whisper. She nudges my hand out of the way, closing her little fist around my cock. I put my hand into her hair as she sinks her mouth down on my dick.

She starts to work her head forward and back, fucking me oh so slowly. I groan as she picks up the pace a little, closing my eyes and leaning my head back.

Usually when I'm fucking a girl's pussy, I'm in a position of complete control. I can stop or slow down as often as I want, which helps me to keep from blowing my load before I'm ready. Even with throat-fucking, I am in control more than I am now.

And control is something I desperately need to have, especially now. Especially with Nika.

I can't scare her off of going down by grabbing her and fucking her throat. And as much as I'd like to cum in her mouth, I know that I can't. It's too much.

"Fuckkkk," I hiss. Her mouth feels incredible, it's going to be hard to restrain myself. "Okay, okay. You have to stop, otherwise I'm going to finish in your mouth."

I gently grab her face and push her back. She sits back on her heels, wiping at her mouth with the back of her hand.

"You taste good," she says, her eyes scanning my face. She licks her lips. For a second, my eyes are on her mouth, watching her tongue.

Yeah, I would've finished there without a problem.

"Your mouth is incredible." I pin her onto her back. "I just didn't want to come in there, when there are so many other places that call my name."

She giggles for a second. I grab her knees and force them apart, leaning down to kiss her breasts. Then I go straight for her pussy, spreading it with two fingers, and licking her clit.

Nika cries out and buries her hands in my hair, her back bowing. I trace figure eights around her clit and dip my tongue into her pussy, loving the scent and taste of her. Just as she gets worked up, her juices flowing, I press her knees up and lick my way around the tiny pucker of her ass.

"Oooh!" she cries, startled.

I kiss and lick it for a second, penetrating her ass with the tip of my tongue. Then I break away, kissing her inner thighs, kissing and biting her breasts.

"I want you to touch yourself again," I whisper in her ear. "While I'm taking you from behind, I want you to make yourself come."

She nods eagerly, and I flip her over. She braces herself on her knees and elbows, showing her pretty pussy and ass to me. I grasp my cock, pressing the head to her entrance.

"Touch yourself," I order. She reaches under her body and starts to play with her clit.

I plunge inside her and hear her gasp. She feels so hot and so tight that I have to go slow, otherwise I'll come right away.

"Oh my god," she gasps. "Erik, your cock feels so good."

I grab her hips and use them as leverage while I fuck her, working my cock in and out of her pussy. She begins to tighten her innermost muscles even more as she plays with her clit. I focus, closing my eyes, and try to hit her g-spot every time I thrust.

Finally, she bursts, coming with a shout. I speed up as soon as I feel her begin to spasm, letting myself pound into her like a jackhammer. She cries out my name, which has never sounded better.

I feel my cock start to twitch and pulse as I drive home again and again. I feel like I'm coming like a fucking fountain, her pussy milking my cock for everything it's worth.

"Fuck!" I shout. "God damn, Nika."

We collapse in a sweaty, laughing pile. I kiss the side of her face and she beams at me. "You know what I want now?"

"I hope it's a cupcake," I say, still catching my breath.

She looks at me for a long second. "That's exactly right, Erik."

I laugh and roll over to grab the cupcake from the floor. And we enjoy it together, savoring the moment.

30

ERIK

"WE ARE ALMOST THERE. JUST A LITTLE FURTHER."

With my hands over Nika's eyes I walk behind her a few more steps. I look up at the soaring factory ceiling above me, wetting my lips. It's bright in here, everything is painted white. The stainless steel machinery in the center of the room makes surprisingly little noise. Just a gentle whirring sound, mostly.

"Are we there yet? I'm dying to know where you brought me. My birthday was a week ago…" she reminds me.

I nibble at her ear and laugh. "Okay, okay. You can look now."

I pull my hands away, dropping them to her shoulders. She looks around with wide eyes, inhaling fragrant wafts of toffee-scented air. She looks at me with a surprised little grin. "Are we at the factory where they make toffee?"

I give her a slow grin. "Yup. We're here to see how the toffee is made and to try some of their test flavors. I called ahead a few weeks ago and they said that today would be the perfect day to come and visit."

She squeals, hugging me hard. "Oh my God. I had no idea that you had this plan! Thank you, thank you, thank you…"

She hugs me one more time then pulls away, grabbing my dark green plaid button up shirt by the hem and towing me along. We are all alone on the factory floor, walking to the left of machines that make the toffee. Just in front of us is the one that stirs the melted sugary goodness. As we walk down the catwalk a little further, I can see that the candy is poured into little molds and cooled down by yet another machine. We keep heading around the outside of the factory line. We look through a clear plexiglass windows at a spot where the candy is freed from the molds and dropped straight into the shiny gold wrappers. Annika looks up at me, taking my hand and squeezing it hard.

"I can't believe you did this for me."

I smile. "It wasn't that big of a deal. I only had to name drop the royal palace once."

Nika grins. "Still. I wouldn't have even thought of this. I didn't realize that I wanted to come here but now that I've been, I don't know if I ever want to leave. Why go anywhere else?"

I slide an arm around her, pulling her closer as we continue walking. Spotting a gray-haired gentleman in a hairnet and a white laboratory jacket, I nod towards him. "I think that man is waiting for us."

Nika looks like I've just told her that she's going to get to fly to the moon or something. "Is this the part where we get to taste the weird flavors of toffee?"

I grin at her. "I think so."

She makes a little fist, pumping it in the air. "Yes…"

We head down to meet the man waiting for us, who introduces himself as Noah, the factory manager. We might be here on a lark, but Noah is all business right now. He has a face like a weathered apple and if he has ever felt joy, it isn't readily apparent.

"If you will just follow me this way, I can show you to the room where I have all the samples laid out for you to try."

He hustles us into a brightly lit room with a giant metal table. On the table are two dozen samples, laid out neatly and labeled. I follow Nika's lead and wait patiently as she tries different flavors of toffee out.

Banana, coffee, butter rum, maple, vanilla, raspberry… So on and so forth.

I drift along in her wake as she samples each flavor, excitedly offering half of whatever she has just tasted to me.

I'll admit it right now, I don't like toffee at all. I don't like caramels or anything that is sticky and sweet. But I keep trying them because I don't want to ruin Nika's excitement. So, I make pleasured sounds whenever I put them in my mouth even though I want nothing more than to spit them out.

"The coffee and butter rum flavors are my favorite. Where do you get them?" she asks Noah.

He clears his throat and looks dour. "I prepared a goodie bag for your highness to take with you. Unfortunately, it's impossible to purchase many of these toffees here in Denmark. There are flavors that are more popular internationally."

Nika's eyebrows go up but she just nods. "Wow. Well, thank you."

Noah bows. "There is one more thing, if you don't mind. We have a very special flavor that we would like your highness to try. It's brand-new."

Nika's eyes widened and she looks at me, her excitement evident on her face. "We would love to. Thank you!"

Noah bows again and produces a final sample, a brownish toffee on a white plate. She goes ahead and picks it up, biting half of it off and offering me the other half. I shake my head gently. "It's for you."

"Mm. Oh my God, I love it. What is it? Chocolate and… some kind of pecan?"

Noah nods. "You nailed it exactly, Your Royal Highness. If you like it, the candy company would like to offer you your very own flavor. You could name it as you like, but we were thinking of just calling it princess's blend."

Annika's eyes widen with excitement. She tosses her hair and looks at me, a goofy grin on her face. "This is the best birthday present anybody could've ever gotten for me. I don't know how anyone could ever top this."

She steps closer and hugs me, while responding to Noah's question. "I love it. Noah, I would be extremely proud to have my name on your product."

Noah smiles briefly, his face creasing for only a moment. "Thank you, your highness. We are happy to oblige. I know I speak for everybody in the company when I say how thrilled we all are that you are a fan of toffees. I know they are a bit stuffy and boring."

"No, no. I don't feel that way at all. Can I ask, is there any chance of you making this toffee low calorie or sugar free?"

Noah smiles again. Bowing his head, he answers her. "It already is sugar free. The fact that you can't taste it is a good sign, I think."

Nika grins at both of us. "I would say so. Thank you for helping us out today, Noah. Can I sign anything for you? I'm sure that you have some little girls in your family that would like an autograph."

He bows his head. "Thank you, Princess. My niece would love your autograph."

I shoot Noah a little glare, but Annika doesn't seem to mind signing a couple of company brochures. She carefully scrawls Noah's niece's name, signs a few more brochures, and then hands them all over to him.

I gather up the bags of samples that we are taking with us and Noah sees us out of the factory. He is very diligent but still quite grateful.

As we leave, heading down the stairs and out into the parking lot, Nika slides her arm around my waist and gives me a hug. "Thank you for doing that. It was really a once-in-a-lifetime treatment."

I smiled down at her, kissing her lips for a moment. "You're welcome. Admittedly, I didn't come up with the idea of naming a flavor after you. When I called to make the arrangements for a factory tour, the company was very gracious. I didn't do much of anything, really."

Nika chuckles. "You knew me. You knew how much this would mean to me. That's really the essence of why I am so blown away. That's it."

Tugging her to a stop, I leaned down and brush my lips over hers. "I'm glad you got what you wanted."

She pulls back, looking at me. For second, I feel her gaze as it rakes up and down my face and shoulders. "You know, I think that I got a lot more in the bargain than I asked for. And I'm not talking about the candy."

The corners of my mouth turn up a little. "No?"

She's shakes her head. "No. I'm talking about you."

I don't really know how to accept her complement straight on. So, I just grab her hand, kiss her on the lips, and pull her toward the car.

31

ERIK

It's been ten days since Nika agreed to move in with me. Ten days of delirious happiness. Ten raunchy, dirty nights.

Every time I look at her, all the good chemicals in my brain start listening, trying to convince me that I love her.

The sound of her laughter.

The way she presses her face against my chest, burying her head.

The feeling of completeness I have at the end of the day, holding her in my arms.

Is it love? I have no idea.

But I know that I'm not ready to say anything to her, lest she be let down by my inevitable flip-flopping.

Still, I think that everything is going pretty well for us. I make an early morning run to the palace, scooping up a few of Nika's things and checking in on Stellan. I don't even get the chance to talk to the king.

So, after I stop for some fresh bread and nice piece of salmon, I head back upstairs to the penthouse loft that I own. When I get inside the door, I am aggravated for about the twelfth time by a loose floorboard that's sticks up a quarter of an inch.

I grit my teeth and remind myself that I just have to call someone to fix it. Living in the new loft is a little weird because it's the first time that I've ever had to think about things like that. I've never owned anything before, certainly not pieces of property with such obvious flaws.

Carrying the groceries with me into the kitchen, I make a mental note to call someone to fix it today, before Nika notices that it's a problem. For some reason, the idea of her noticing such a tiny flaw really kills me. I had the same realization this morning when I noticed tiny, hairline cracks in the porcelain of the bathroom sink.

I set the paper sacks of groceries on the counter in the kitchen, absently wondering where Nika is. "I'm home!" I call.

She emerges from the bedroom, wearing nothing but one of my gray T-shirts. She holds her iPad, which I didn't even realize she had here. I raise an eyebrow.

She stops me before I can say anything. "I wasn't looking up myself. Kal texted me a link to some press about Stellan and Margot. Here, have a look."

She saunters over to the kitchen counter, setting her iPad in front of me.

I squint down at the tablet, taking in the headline and the matching photo. In the picture, Stellan and Margot are at a market and they look extremely unhappy. Stellan is raising his hand to point at something, shouting. Margot has her arms crossed across her chest and looks extremely pissed off. The caption reads, "Are King Stellan and his new Queen already on the rocks?"

I scan the first few lines of the article, the corners of my mouth turning down. As far as I know, there is no trouble in paradise. But then again, what do I know? I've been isolated from Stellan and the whole royal family for almost two months now. Still, it doesn't seem like something I should have to worry about.

Stellan is completely in control at all times. I doubt that that has changed much since I was last his secretary.

I push the iPad away. Glancing up at Nika, I shrug a shoulder. "I don't see a problem. It's just the press making things up. You should know about that, shouldn't you?"

She puts her blonde hair in a long, messy ponytail and winces a little. "Apparently Stellan and Margot have been the talk of the Royal Palace lately. Wedding planning is really getting to them, it seems."

I roll my eyes a little. Turning toward the refrigerator, I fish out a bottle of sparkling water. "Do you want a glass?"

She frowns at me. "No. What I want is to know whether you're going to call Stellan or not. This is a pretty big deal, if it's true. And I think that it is. I mean, Kal did send it to me for a reason."

Cracking open the bottle, I take a long pull. Then I shrug. "It sounds like the press is trying to sow the seeds of discontent between the two of them. And you, who should know better and who should have their back no matter what, are falling for the press's tricks."

Her eyebrows go up. "You're not going to talk to my brother about this? I mean, no one is saying that you have to flourish this article in front of his face. I just mean… I'm sure he needs someone to talk to."

I tried to set the bottle of sparkling water down, but I am a little too forceful and I manage to shatter the bottom of the glass. "Shit. I can't believe I did this."

Nika frowns and heads over to the nearby closet, opening it and handing me the broom and dust pan. I sweep up every last piece of glass, mindful of the fact that she has no shoes on and probably will walk in here in short order.

When I'm done cleaning, I look up to find her staring me down. "What?"

She shrugs. "So, you're just going to abandon my brother?"

I glare at her. "Your brother isn't taking my calls. Or at least I imagine so. I tried to say hello to him just a few minutes ago and he was mysteriously absent. No one seemed to know where he is. So no, I'm not abandoning my best friend. He abandoned me."

Nika folds her arms across her chest and cocks her hip. She levels her gaze at me. "What if it were us?"

Her question stops me dead. "What?"

She jerks her head toward the iPad. "It could just as easily be us that the press is picking on. I would hope that in that position, Stellan would pick up the phone and call you."

I snort. "I don't even think that he has noticed that I'm missing from the palace. And anyway, it's not like we are in the exact same position as Stellan and Margot. They are engaged. They have real problems."

She frowns and rubs her palms together. "What is that supposed to mean? I thought that you and I were moving forward."

It's everything I can do not to roll my eyes. "Forget I said anything. We are moving forward. Let's just... move on with our day."

She stalks a few steps closer to me, staring me down. "What do you mean they have real problems?"

I rub the back of my neck. "I don't know, Annika. I'm just saying that they have married people problems and we don't. We don't have any idea of what the king and the future queen will have to deal with. That's all I was saying."

"Do you not think that we will face similar challenges? I mean... This is all because Stellan is King of Denmark and Margot is a commoner. If that doesn't ring any bells for us, I don't know what would."

A commoner. That's the line that makes me lose my cool. I don't know why exactly, since I've said it a thousand times myself. But the way she says it, it sounds... dirty. And not the sexy kind of dirty, either.

I grit my teeth. "Well, maybe they are crazy to be getting married. Hell, maybe we're crazy too! Maybe we are living in a bubble and not being practical. Have you thought of that?"

Her brow hunches. "What is that supposed to mean?"

"It means that I have no illusions about our future together. You are going to marry a real royal and I am going to be cut loose, eventually. It's just what people do. People who aren't Stellan, that is."

Her eyes widen. "What? You can't possibly think that I'm going to just leave you. I'm not a different person than I was five minutes ago or five hours ago or five days ago."

I shake my head. "We shouldn't be arguing. Let's just enjoy what we have while we have it."

I turned away, taking the dustpan to the glass recycling. When I turn around, she is right there, glaring up at me.

"Are you saying that you don't think that we can make our relationship work in the long term?"

I glare at her, moving her aside. "Let's not talk about it right now."

She makes a frustrated growl. "You are so stubborn. Just… I could strangle you right now."

She turns away, she storms out of the room. I call after her. "Annika… Annika?"

I clench my fists. I didn't mean to start a fight or whatever the hell just happened. That was definitely not my intention. But it seems like I have really put my foot in it.

I head back to the kitchen counter, spotting her iPad. I turn it on and read a little more of the article, which is obviously full of hot air. It's just more royal headlines to earn the paper more clicks.

It's not worth calling Stellan about, that's for sure.

Nika comes storming out of the bedroom, tucking her gray T-shirt into a pair of sleek black jeans. She shoulders her purse, looking pretty angry. As she starts heading to the apartment's front door, I called after her.

"Where you going?"

"Out for a drink."

Before I can say another word, the front door slams, leaving me alone in the apartment.

32

ANNIKA

It's dark outside by the time I stumble out of the elevator and into Erik's loft. It's cool and quiet up here right now, the lights dimmed. Maybe Erik has gone out as well…

It's been a full day since I walked out this morning. A whole day that I have just been trying to disguise my appearance, flitting from bar to bar.

I know, it's beyond old news that I shouldn't drink and play over the scene from this morning in my head, again and again. I just can't get my head around the fact that he said that he doesn't expect us to ever be engaged. It boils down to the fact he doesn't believe in the potential for longevity of our relationship.

Which I knew, I swear I did. But hearing him say it?

It killed me.

I lean against the front door and take my shoes off, sighing with relief. I'm more than a little drunk and still revved up from the argument. I head to the fridge, opening it and helping myself to a pint of fresh berries and a bottle of sparkling water. When I close the fridge door, I'm surprised to see Erik standing not two feet away from me, a glower on his face.

"So, you're alive."

I rolled my eyes at him. "Yup."

"What were you thinking, Annika? You know you can't just go out alone."

I pop one of the berries into my mouth and make a face at him. "I can do whatever I want."

Sliding the berries across the counter and in front of a chair, I sit down and pull the top off of the sparkling water. I take a big gulp and eye him. His face is tense.

"What's your problem? I thought we were getting along."

I shrug a shoulder. "Who says we aren't getting along? For right now, anyway. Who knows what will happen tomorrow?"

He glares at me, making a disapproving sound. "What is that supposed to mean?"

I pick up a strawberry, biting into its succulent fruit. "Why did you even ask me to move in here with you?"

Apparently, my question was unexpected. He tilts his head, trying to puzzle out what I mean. "Why? I don't know. I guess I felt like we were spending all our time together anyway… So why not?"

I snort. "How utterly unromantic. Here I was, feeling like it was a sign that things are going well between us."

He holds his arms across his chest. "They are."

I arch a brow at him. "For how long? Because if we are not building something that can last... I'm not interested. I am trying to shape my future here."

He pushes his cheek out with his tongue. "Let's not get ahead of ourselves here. That's all I am trying to say."

I glare at him. "What do you see for us in the future? A year from now. Or five years from now. Do you see us getting married someday? Starting a family?"

He frowns and looks pensive. I'm forced to wait for a full minute while he thinks about my questions. I take another sip of water as he considers what to say.

"I don't know, exactly." He shrugs. "I try not to think too much about what will happen in the future. It's easier just to focus on what is right in front of me."

I toyed with the cap of the water, unable to look at him. "I'm asking if you think that we will be together. That's it."

There's a note of hesitation on his face. "What do you want me to say? I don't know. I feel like there are so many factors working against us. If I had to make a wager, I would probably bet against us in the long term."

My heart sinks. I knew that he felt that way. That's a big reason why I disappeared all day to mope on my own.

But it's a whole different thing to say it out loud.

I can't meet his eye anymore. "You're getting in your own head. That's what this is about, isn't it? This morning, when I said that you needed to talk to Stellan, it shook you. And now you're not even sure that we should be together. Do I have all that right?"

A muscle in his jaw tenses. "Why are you so worried about the future? Why can't you just be happy with what we have right now?"

I put my hands on the counter, pushing up from my seat. "Because that isn't good enough for me. What woman wants to hear that you like her right now, but you don't know about what the future holds? That's how relationships fail."

He arches a brow at me. "And you're the expert, are you? Admit it. You don't have any idea of how relationships work."

"Neither do you. Obviously."

His gaze narrows on my face. "So, what, then? Where do we go from here?"

I give a humorless laugh. "I don't see how we do anything together at this point. If you don't believe that we will be together for the foreseeable future, I think I would rather just call it what it is right now. Because if you think that something is going to die, it usually does."

He squints at me. "I'm not saying that we will not last."

I shake my head and roll my eyes. "That's not good enough, Erik. Either you believe in us or you don't. And it sounds an awful lot like you don't."

He flexes his fingers and tightens his fists.

"You know just as well as I do that when the press gets ahold of the existence of our relationship, we're done for. That's not even talking about what Stellan will feel when he finds out that I'm banging his little sister. And your grandmother? God, I can just see the expression on her face right now."

I level a gaze at him. Crossing my arms, I walk to the hallway, pausing. "It's funny. Your worries are all related to how you feel that people will perceive us. I thought that I was supposed to be the one that was so worried about appearances. I guess that was all wrong, too."

With a heavy heart, I head into the hallway, planning to grab a bag full of my stuff. Erik follows me, glowering at me the entire way.

"Where are you going?" he demands.

I huff at him. Pulling a tote bag out of the closet, I start stuffing it with necessities. "Where do you think? It's not like I have many other places to go to."

He leans in the doorway, folding his arms across his chest and frowning. "You're being crazy, Nika. Why don't you just take a while to cool off and then we can approach this more logically."

My eyes mist over. Even though part of me very much wants to stay, to spend as much time with him as he will allow me to, I know I have to go. And that breaks my God damned heart.

Blotting at my eyes, I pick up the tote bag and turn to face Erik. "The thing is. You either believe in us. You believe wholeheartedly that we can make it... Or you don't. It's just that simple. So, tell me. Do you believe? Or are you still caught up in what other people think about us that you can't see the forest for the trees?"

He pushes out his cheek with his tongue. "Nika... Don't. Please. I'm asking you to stay. Isn't that good enough?"

Sucking in a breath, I shake my head slowly. "No, Erik. I don't think it is."

I walk towards him, waiting for him to move, to get out of my way. But he doesn't. He just stands there, an immovable brick wall of smoldering anger.

"You're making a mistake." His voice is rough, gone to gravel. "If you walk away, that's it. We're through."

A tear breaks free from my eye, running down my cheek. I step up to him, a hair's breadth away. Peering up at his face, I utter the words that will echo in my head for a long, long time.

"So be it. I would rather be alone than be with someone that doesn't believe in me."

Erik shakes his head, pushing himself off the doorway and backing out of the way. I push past him into the hallway as tears begin to run down my face freely.

I raise my head and stalk out of the apartment, reminding myself that I am a princess. No matter that I can't see because I am blinded by my own tears and my own weak heart.

The last thing I see before the elevator doors close is Erik, his face tortured, his big body looming just outside the elevator door.

I open my mouth to say something to him but the doors close before I can get it out. Pushing the button to take me to the ground floor, I promise myself I won't break down until I am out of the building.

33

ERIK

"Are you sure you're ready for this?" I whisper to Stellan. He adjusts his tux, giving me a hard look. Behind him, a whole cathedral full of dressed up wedding guests sit, chatting and laughing, their voices low like ambient noise.

Stellan runs his tongue over his teeth, wiping his hands on his expensive tuxedo pants. "I'm as ready as I'll ever be. I'm very excited to have this part over and done with so that Margot and I can rule the country. That, and we have a hell of a honeymoon awaiting us."

I smile at him. "It sounds like you have your priorities in order. You have any second thoughts?"

He clears his throat, looking behind me at his brothers. He will always be the oldest son, the one in charge. There's no getting around that.

"None whatsoever. We've already done a private ceremony with just the family. This is just an elaborate show for the public."

I nod, casting an eye over the church. "Fair enough."

Behind me, the organist begins playing a hymn. I look around, as if the person that I'm the most anxious to see will be in the crowd. But I know for a fact that Nika will be marching down the aisle with the other bridesmaids. Just thinking about her, my palms begin to grow sweaty.

Lars edges over to me and leans in close. "You look like shit. When is the last time you even slept?"

I probably haven't slept for four whole hours at a time ever since Nika left me. I toss and turn every single night, trying to piece together what happened and figure out if there is a way back for the two of us.

There has to be, right? That is very much on my mind at the moment.

I wince. "I haven't slept much this week."

Lars raises an eyebrow. "That bad, huh? Our little Annika seems to have you wrapped around her little finger…"

I shoot him a glare as the first bridesmaid makes her way down the aisle. It's a random brunette woman that Margot and Pippa know from New York. Pretty enough in her own way, she swishes down the aisle looking like a cupcake. She winks at me, hinting that she is available. Although that's the last thing on my mind right now.

I turn away, clearing my throat and keeping my eyes on Stellan.

Next is Pippa, looking breathtaking as usual in a pretty pink gown. When I glance over at Lars, I see him watching her with a crackling gaze that seems almost electric.

Those two are definitely going to get together. The question is when.

I forget all about Pippa and Lars and their weird friendship that is on the verge of breaking into a full-blown lust. Because Annika steps out into the cathedral at that moment, literally stealing the breath out of my lungs. I can't look away from her: her hair is piled atop her head, her makeup subdued, her body looking unbelievable in her strappy pale pink dress.

I school my expression. No one else here needs to know that I have been turning myself inside out every day and every night since she left. No one else here knows that we were even a thing.

But when Nika looks at me, pinning me in place with her frost-tinted eyes, I forget all of that. I can only focus on how amazing she looks and how much I want her to run straight to me.

When our gazes meet, her cheeks turn pink and she looks away immediately. She walks up the aisle towards me, avoiding my gaze. At the last moment she turns right and climbs the stairs to stand beside Pippa.

I keep my expression blank, but I can't help the fact that my gaze is drawn to her over and over again throughout the ceremony. In her barely-there strappy sleek dress, she displays miles of bare, glowing skin. Skin that I know, every single inch of it.

I swear, I can feel her skin against mine, her warm body pressing against my flesh.

When Margot comes in and the music changes, I have to rip my eyes away from Nika. Margot does look beautiful, wearing a gorgeous white gown and a long, glamorous veil and train that are carried by two young men.

No one walks her up the aisle, which is a little odd. But when I look over at Stellan, he has tears in his eyes. I'm reminded of his engagement party, of the fact that Margot and Stellan look at each other like they are the only two important planets in their tiny universe.

What they have is truly special. Even I can admit that.

Margot walks up the stairs, bowing slightly so that Stellan can peel back her veil. She's all smiles today, already in tears. Her cupcake pink hair has never seemed so coiffed.

And yet, my eyes keep wandering over to Nika. I listen as the ceremony proceeds, but I keep darting my gaze over to her again and again.

I have to do something. I can't let her walk away again. Not this time.

Stellan leans back towards me, looking at me clinically. "The rings," he prompts.

I pat my pocket before reaching in and producing both of the rings. Stellan doesn't seem to mind the fact that I wasn't paying a bit of attention. Then again, he seems to be wholly caught up in his own world.

Before I even realize it, the wedding ceremony is almost over. There is a moment where Stellan and Margot kiss.

My gaze finds Nika. And to my surprise, she is looking right at me. She blushes and looks away, but I have the satisfaction of having caught her.

The priest announces the new couple and they head down the stairs, walking down the aisle like they are floating on air.

I follow them out, heading down the aisle, Lars at my side. I give him a look and he shrugs.

"Weddings give girls ideas that we actually want to marry them," he jokes.

I roll my eyes at him. "Can you not just be happy for your brother? Besides, we all know who you are going to end up walking down the aisle with. There is no suspense or mystery to be had there."

He glares at me. "I'm going to tell you this for the one billionth time. Pippa and I are just friends. That's all we will ever be. Should just take your lamentations about dating someone in this family and shove them up your ass."

I shoot him a look. It's better to avoid the entire subject of dating someone in his family, I think. "I'll race you to the reception."

He smirks and elbows his way past a group of older women who have just gotten up from the pews. "You're on."

Rolling my eyes, I hurry after him. For the next two hours, the wedding takes precedence over anything I want to do. There's the receiving line, walking to the reception at a very posh hotel, and then there are speeches and the first dance between Margot and Stellan. I see Annika several times throughout the preceding events, but she always looks away and pretends to be busy with someone else.

Honestly, it makes me grit my teeth. It's not until after I deliver my rousing best man's speech that I can slip away unnoticed.

I corner Annika in a quiet hallway, just off the main room. As I approached, she looks up at me, her eyes going wide. Her gaze slides around the hallway. She bites her lip.

"Erik…" Her voice sounds like a shaky warning. "Today isn't about us. You would do well to remember that."

I pace over to where she stands, looking at her amazing body in that perfect little pale pink dress. I breathe in, catching a whiff of her natural scent.

It's maddening.

"Your brother is happily involved with his new bride. Now I have all the time in the world." I reach out, brushing my fingers along her upper arm. She shivers and swallows, her wide, innocent eyes seeming to spear me.

"Have you changed your mind, then?"

I smirk at her. "You still think I'm the one that was in the wrong?"

Her gaze hardens. "Yes. I thought I was pretty clear."

Sliding my big hand around her tiny waist, I pull her flush against my body. I hear her sudden exhalation of breath. She feels so good in my arms. I'm sure that there is not a single woman on earth that I would rather be with right now then Nika.

I lean my head down, brushing my lips over hers. I whisper against her mouth. "You want me. I can tell. It's written all over your face."

Her hands come up to push at my chest, but I kiss her again and they relax a little, her nails digging into my skin through my tux. I bend her back and kiss her properly, not even thinking about the fact that we are in a public space.

No, I'm only thinking about the girl in my arms, about how much I have missed her. When Stellan himself comes rushing over, I take too long to pull back from her lips.

And that second of hesitation allows him to land the first punch, nearly a knockout blow. I stumble backwards, still holding Nika in my arms. She pushes me away and stumbles backward, her wide eyes on her big brother.

Stellan is furious with me. "You fucking asshole. You're… what, you're sleeping with her? You stole something from my family. What the hell?"

I raise my hands, only now aware of the crowd forming behind Stellan. I definitely don't want to get into a fist fight with him, not today of all days.

"Just go back to your wedding, man. Look, Margot's waiting for you." I nod to her, feeling my jaw where he punched it. It's achy.

Stellan doesn't look satisfied with that. He rounds on Nika, pointing his finger at her. "You should've known better. You should have stayed out of his bed. I don't want to see you anymore today. Just go." He looks at me, his fury evident. "As for you, consider yourself fired from the royal family service. Good riddance to bad garbage." He spits on the floor, his face going red.

My hands bunch into fists. He called me garbage. Nobody does that to me as an adult and gets away with it.

Nika scowls at her brother. "Don't call him that. He may have ruined my life but he's not garbage."

Stellan raises his head and sniffs. "I said what I said."

"You're wrong," Nika says, facing him down. "You've never seen him for the prize that he really is. That's been clear to me from the jump."

He sneers at me. "Are you just going to let my little sister fight all your battles?"

I take a step towards him, baring my teeth. But Nika raises her hand to block me, looking at Stellan. "We will go. We don't want to make trouble, honestly."

He squints at both of us. Then he relents a little bit, or so I think. "Nika, you can stay. But Erik, I want you gone. I won't have someone that would stab me in the back so eagerly hanging around. That's what you've done your whole life. You hung around. Now it's over. So I want you gone. From this event. From the palace. From my life. Just go."

Stellan cuts me to the core, skewering me with his words. And because he is the king, I'm pretty sure that he can follow up on his threats.

Just like that, I have lost the life I've built over so many years. I look to Annika, wordless and beseeching.

She presses her lips into a thin line and looks like she is about to die of embarrassment. Then Stellan turns around, storming off toward where he left Margot on the dance floor. Nika looks at me, swallowing tensely. She shakes her head at me, like she doesn't even know me. When I try to reach out to her, she just shrugs out of my touch.

"Don't. Don't touch me. I think you should leave now."

As she says it, two blue jacketed guards approach me. They both have serious looks on their faces, like they are ready to throw down. I try to protest but one of the guards grabs me by the elbow and shoves me toward the exit door, taking me to the stairs at the back instead of through the crowd of people gathered and watching.

Just before the door swings closed on me, I look back and catch a glimpse of Annika, her expression nothing short of tortured.

And then I am being pulled down the stairs, telling the guards to take it easy.

I turn forward and stumble along, feeling so overwhelmed that I can't process any of it at all.

34

ANNIKA

I STAND AT THE VERY CORNER OF THE BALLROOM, LOOKING OUT the huge plate glass windows. The wedding reception is still going on behind me although it is winding down by now. I look out the window to the sun setting on the Copenhagen skyline and try not to cry.

There are so many thoughts and feelings going on in my head right now.

But this is not the time or place to air them out... Especially not when my big brother is brooding and twirling his new bride on the dance floor. I turn and eye the ballroom, trying to guess when I can slip away and not be noticed.

My misery is complete, the source of it has been escorted from the premises. And yet, I am more alone than ever.

I spot Kal coming towards me, looking chic as always in her lavender gown. She arches a brow at me as she approaches, handing me a flute of champagne. I accept it, giving her a sad smile.

She lifts her glass, clinking it against the rim of mine. "To Stellan's wedding, I suppose."

My mouth lifts a little, but I repress an eye roll and take a sip of the wine. "I'm sure that Stellan probably hates me right now. I interrupted his wedding with my personal drama. How perfect."

Kal wrinkles her nose and looks around. "What do you say we get out of here? Just for a little while. I think I saw a sign that said you could get to the roof from here."

I sigh. In the normal course of events, I would say no. But today, I have royally screwed up. No pun intended.

So, I just nod. "I think that sounds great."

Kal leads me to the same stairwell that Erik was escorted out of just a little while ago. She opens the door, waving me inside.

"Wait!" A woman's voice calls. Kal and I both turn and find Pippa making her way towards us. She flashes us a gentle smile and follows us through the door into the stairwell.

"Wherever you guys are going, I want to go to. I am tired of having Margot and Stellan's love rubbed in my face. It's enough for one day at least."

Kal's lips twitch. "We were just going up to the rooftop. Come on."

She leads the way up the staircase, opening the door that leads onto the roof. It's surprisingly peaceful up here, the rooftop bar and patio area set up but empty. It's balmy outside, the late Copenhagen summer evening still nice. Pippa leads the way to an empty table, pulling up a chair to it.

When we both sit down, Pippa looks around at both of us. "So? Spill the beans. Dish the dirt. What happened with you and Erik?"

I take my seat and lean my elbows against the table, pressing my hands against my face. "I don't even know where to begin, honestly."

"I didn't even realize that you guys had broken up!" Kal protests. I sigh heavily and drop my hands, putting my arms on the table. "

I screw up my face. "Yeah. I mean... It got a lot bigger than just sleeping together and it happened fast. I..." I stopped speaking, my eyes misting over. I swallow. "Sorry..."

Kal gets up and leans down to hug me, which is exactly what I needed just now. I turn towards her, my hand resting on her shoulder as I fall apart against her collarbone.

She shushes me, murmuring that everything will be all right. She has no way of knowing that, of course, but it's still comforting to hear.

Pippa frowns. "I'm sorry to see you so sad over this. Do you want to tell us about it?"

I suck in a breath and shake my head. "Not really."

Kal gives me a squeeze and pulls her chair next to mine, sitting down. She looks at me, her mahogany eyes piercing. "Let me just ask one thing, then. How far did things progress? I mean, did you guys say those three little words, or are we talking about something less?"

Pulling away from her chest, I waved at my eyes. "I told him I loved him. He didn't say it back, though."

Kalindi and Pippa both look surprised at that. My cheeks heat and I look down at the table, embarrassed. Pippa reaches out and takes my hand, squeezing it.

"I'm so sorry. That isn't very fair."

Blotting my eyes, I sniff. "Thanks. You are nice to say it."

Kal frowns and leans back in her seat. She seems unsatisfied with that answer. "What did he think he was going to gain by kissing you today?"

I slowly shake my head. "I don't know. He seems to want me to take him back. But he doesn't believe that there is a long-term relationship in the cards for us. Why would I do that?"

Tilting her head, Pippa pulls a face. "I can tell you one thing. Men suck. Maybe you're better off without him."

A door opens up behind me. I turn and look to see who it is and am surprised to see Margot and her beautiful white wedding gown. She blushes a little as she comes outside, looking between all of us. "Is there room for one more?"

Pippa is the first to grin and wave her over. "Today, you get whatever you want. Come sit down by me."

Margot walks over, showing off a champagne bottle that she brought up from the wedding. "I come in peace and I bring gifts."

Kal smiles at her, getting up and grabbing for champagne flutes from behind the empty bar. Margot sits down and Kal puts the flutes down in front of her. Margot pours a little champagne into each glass, looking at me with a small smile.

"I gather that things aren't good between you and Erik."

Taking the glass that she offers me, I exhale loudly and take a sip of the champagne. Rolling it around in my mouth, I savor the sweetness of the wine. "You could say that. Of all the things that I intended for today, telling Stellan was the least among them. I'm very sorry that Erik and I made a scene."

Margot scrunches her nose up and tucks a strand of her pink hair behind her ear. "He'll be just fine, believe me. I'm sorry that he reacted so poorly. He feels bad about punching Erik in the face. Or at least I think he does."

Kal tilts her head questioningly. "Has anyone heard from Erik?"

Pippa shakes her head and Margot just sighs. "Not that I know of. It's better if he and Stellan have a cooling off period from each other, anyway."

I look at her for several long seconds, finishing off the glass of champagne in one long pull. "Go ahead. Say it."

Margot's brows delicately rise. "Say what?"

I look down at the table, dropping her gaze. "Whatever my brother sent you out here to say to me... What is it? Is it about how Erik betrayed him? Is it about how Erik is way too old for me? Or maybe it's the fact that I am seen as just a baby, and he thinks that Erik somehow took advantage of me? What is it?"

Margot waits for me to finish, sipping her champagne. She takes a full breath. "Stellan has a few issues with you and Erik hooking up, not the least of which is the fact that he worries that you are being naïve. He said that he's worried about the appearances of it, that people will think that Erik is using you for a title or some kind of money somehow. But I don't run errands for my husband. I just came out because I know that you are very important to Stellan and would like for us to be close too. I wanted to make sure that you were okay. That's all."

I glance up at her a little sheepishly. "Oh. Well... Sorry. I think I am just still a little confused and defensive."

Pippa interjects. "Margot, Annika was just telling us that Erik doesn't seem to know what he wants. Apparently, she told him that she loved him and that sent him into a tailspin somehow."

"Really? You love him?"

Margot appears thoroughly surprised. I nod, unhappy. "I do. Or I did. Whichever way makes me sound less pathetic."

She gives me the soft smile. "I think I know one way to make you feel a little bit less miserable." She reaches underneath the table and then shows me her palm, a heavy skeleton key sitting in the middle of it. She picks it up and offers it to me.

I take it, frowning. It's made of ancient wrought iron and inscribed with old, worn letters. "What is this for?"

She wiggles her eyebrows. "A Tuscan Villa. We were supposed to stop there during our month-long honeymoon, but we changed our minds at the last minute. So, I'm presenting it to you now. For a little recovery time... or maybe you end up liking it and want to stay. Either way."

I close my hand around the key, gripping it and looking her in the eye. "Thank you. As it turns out, I will be needing a new place to stay."

Margot smiles and pats my hand. "Us girls have to look out for each other, don't we?"

Nodding slowly, I give her a pathetic little smile. "Yes, we do."

She takes another sip out of her glass and then pushes herself to her feet, brushing her hands down her hand beaded wedding dress. "You know, we don't know each other very well. Which I hope someday will change. But I do know one thing. Whatever you decide to do, it's the right thing. Stay with Erik. Don't stay with Erik. I just want you to know that either way, you have my enthusiastic backing. That is just automatic."

My eyes fill with tears. Standing up, I walk over and hug her, careful not to cry on her wedding dress. She hugs me tightly, making me realize how small she actually is. She is a tiny person, almost pocket-size.

"Thank you," I whisper.

She beams at me. "That's what sisters-in-law are for. Now if you'll excuse me, I have a wedding party to get back to. Pippa, will you accompany me?"

Pippa rises to her feet, looking graceful. "Coming, Margot." She starts walking towards the rooftop entrance, looking back at me. "Stay in touch, will you?"

I nod and she winks at me. Then she and Margot head downstairs, leaving me and Kal by ourselves. I breathe in a shaky breath and look at my best friend. "So, what now?"

She tips up her glass of champagne, drinking it all down and then looking at me. "Now? Now we dance. Come on."

Standing up, she holds her hand out to me, and I walk over and take it, grasping it gladly. I may not have Erik in my corner, but I will always be cared for.

Taking a deep breath, I head downstairs to the wedding.

35

ERIK

I DRAIN THE LAST FEW DROPS OF EXPENSIVE WHISKEY FROM THE bottle and then chuck the empty vessel off the end of the dock. I'm good and soused… and I feel like absolute hell.

Laying back on the dock, I put my feet into the cool water and stare up at the sky. Nika really did a number on me. And having Stellan kick me out of his own wedding was a humiliation that I wasn't expecting.

Granted, if I kept dating Nika, I would've had to have told him at some point. But I left Copenhagen in a cloud of shame, without either of the people that I claimed to care about.

Nika is nowhere to be found and Stellan is supposedly off on his honeymoon.

And me? I'm renting a house not far from the beach house that the royal family owns. I'm alone and I've been drunk for approximately four days straight. Or is it five days?

I'm not actually sure.

I close my eyes and throw my arm over my face. This is about as bad as I get. I've never moped like this for so long over anyone or anything.

And the kicker is that moping isn't making me feel any better. It's just a little salve on the wound that's sure to bleed me dry soon enough.

I hear footsteps on the dock. Odd, since I don't remember inviting anybody else out to this misery fest. A shadow falls over my face.

I move my arm and find Lars Løve staring me down, lifting his glasses up from his eyes.

"You look like shit." I squint and glance down at what I am wearing. I have on the same T-shirt and shorts that I've had on for three days, black on black. I also notice that I am sunburned beyond reckoning.

I guess that's what I get for getting drunk and falling asleep in this very position for days on end.

I sit up or at least try to. I fall back and laugh a little. "Yeah, well. Apparently, this is what I look like when I've been dumped."

He frowns down at me. "Okay. It's time to get you up and get you sober. Come on." He grabs my hand and hauls me to my feet, helping me down the little dock and up the slanted hill to the magnificent beach house.

I look at Lars, frowning as we walk into the house. "What are you doing here? "Shouldn't you be ignoring me? There's some sort of royal decree against me, I know it."

He grunts. "Shower first. I'll make some coffee. And then we can talk." He wrinkles his nose. "You smell even worse than you look."

I pull a face at him, especially when he walks me into the downstairs bathroom and turns on the taps to the shower. "You're so high and mighty right now. I can't even talk to you."

He just shakes his head and leaves the bathroom, slamming the door as he goes. I take a second to smell myself, inhaling a deep, long pull. I splutter and cough, overwhelmed by my own scent. Lars is right about one thing. I definitely do need a shower.

I strip down and hop in the shower, the warm water doing wonders to sober me up. I'm still a little drunk as I groom myself and get dressed, pulling on a fresh pair of black jeans and a white T-shirt.

When I appear in the kitchen, Lars is just pouring two cups full of coffee. He looks me up and down, judging. "Here." He thrusts the coffee mug in my hand. He points to a seat at the bar. "Sit down and drink this coffee. Then we can really get down to why I am here."

I frown at him, but I move towards the bar, sitting and drinking the fragrant coffee. I realize then that I probably haven't actually eaten anything other than an uncooked cheese sandwich last night. My stomach growls and I try to think what is in the house that I can eat.

"How are you feeling?" Lars asks. "That is to say, are you feeling more sober?"

I squint at him. Now that I am a little less drunk, the world seems harshly lit and missing the buzzy warmth of the world had when I was intoxicated.

I nod at him. "I think I just realized that I'm hungry."

He stands up, padding over to the refrigerator and cracking it open. To my surprise, he has a takeout container filled with a roast chicken and a side of sweet potatoes. He offers it to me with a fork on the side, not saying anything. I give him a questioning look and dig into the food, which is pretty tasty even though it's not brand-new.

After I power through most of the food and two more cups of coffee, I officially have the start of a mean hangover. I beckon to Lars, heading into the cool theater room and lying down. He looks around, completely unimpressed by what he sees, but then again he's an actual Danish prince so…

I cover my face up with my arm again, sighing. "Well, if your goal was to make me more miserable, you have succeeded. Now I'm just suffering from a hell of a headache and some serious dehydration."

He sits across from me, pulling his legs under his body. "Tough shit. I'm here because no one has heard from you in a week. It was actually pretty hard to track you down since you left your cell phone at the palace. So thanks for that, by the way."

I give him a humorless chuckle. "What are you doing here, Lars?"

He goes quiet for a minute. It's long enough to make me look up at him. When I do, I catch his gaze. He looks a little concerned.

"I expected to find you moping about your breakup with Nika. What I didn't expect was that you would be completely tanked. That's not like you." He scowls for a moment. "From what I've heard, it sounds like your father. Is that what you intended?"

Angered by his words, I sit up. But I take it a little too fast and I have vertigo for a moment. Wincing, I rub my temple.

"Are you just here to rub it in more or what? I know that if it was up to your brother, I would be banished from the kingdom altogether. I get that he thinks what I did was wrong."

Lars squints at me. "Leave Stellan out of it. As far as you're concerned, Stellan doesn't even exist right now. What does exist is the rest of the whole entire world. I know that it seems like hiding out here is a good idea, but I came to make sure that you have a better plan than that. Because I think you need one. It seems like you are… floundering a little bit."

I shake my head and shrug. "How am I supposed to just go back to living normally? What am I supposed to do with myself? I can't… I don't know how to do it. Annika won't have me. Stellan can't stand the sight of me. I really screwed up." My eyes mist over, making me more miserable than ever.

No way am I about to fucking cry in front of Lars, friend or not.

"Okay, okay. Let's just slow things down for a minute. What happened with Nika?"

I swallow, looking off into the darkness. "I don't know. I mean… I obviously screwed things up big time with her. She told me…" I pause. "She said some things that indicated that she was getting pretty serious about our relationship.

And I freaked out. I did what I always do, which is push people away. And now I've managed to not only alienate her, but alienate her brother, who is basically like a brother to me."

My voice breaks on the last word. I swallow again and avoid looking at Lars. He sits forward, putting his feet on the floor and bracing his elbows on his knees. "I didn't realize that things had gotten so serious between you two."

I manage a stiff nod. "It went fast. Like, it was so quick that I was just…" I blow out of breath. "I guess I was scared. That's what it comes down to."

I sit back, covering my eyes again. Lars is quiet for a full minute. I'm just sitting here, thinking of all the things I said to Annika that were wrong. If I had any power, I would go back in time and fix every single flaw that I see so well in hindsight.

Lars rises from his seat wordlessly. "Come on."

I groan and follow him into the kitchen, where he grabs several bottles of water from the refrigerator. He turns and sets them down on the counter in front of me. "Get hydrated."

I look at the water, feeling how dry my lips are. I grab a bottle and chug it down, then do the same with another. The third bottle I take more slowly, as the water splashes and sloshes around in my stomach.

Lars leans on the counter, crossing his arms and watching me carefully. "Would you do anything differently if you were given a second chance with Nika?"

I glance up at him, surprised. "Of course. I would do almost everything differently. I would not chase her off by talking about how I don't believe in the idea of having a relationship forever, first of all."

His blue gaze burns into my face. "What about the other thing, the thing where she told you she loved you and you just…" He makes a small explosion noise. "What would you do about that?"

I finish off the third bottle of water, wincing. "I would tell her that I needed a little more time, but that I felt that way too…"

He squares off with me. "Do you love her?"

Looking down at the fourth bottle of water, I slowly nod my head. "Yeah, man. I love her. I can't believe I was stupid enough to run her off like I did."

He studies me for a long second. Then he cocks his head at me. "Would it help if I told you where she was going to be in two days?"

My eyes widen. I look up at him, trying to tell if he is serious or not. "What? How could you know? I thought she was hiding out or whatever."

He rolls his eyes. "My sister is not good at deception. She told Pippa where she is going to be the day after tomorrow. And it just so happens that it's very close. As in three beach houses down, kind of close."

The possibility of being able to talk to Annika again makes my heartbeat speed up. "Are you serious right now? You're not fucking with me?"

He shakes his head. "I'm serious as a heart attack. That's her itinerary, as far as I know. What you do with the information that I just gave you, that's up to you. But this?" He waves his hand over the recycling bin and steps on the latch that pops the lid up. I am embarrassed to say that I'm a responsible drunk and every one of the bottles that I emptied this week is right there, plain to see. My neck heats. He looks at me, dead serious. "This isn't how you deal with bad news. I need you to promise me that you understand that before you try to go win back my little sister."

I swallow, my jaw tensing. "Of course. I mean... Thanks. I don't really know what else to say."

He steps off the latch, looking at me. "Don't say it to me. Say it to Annika. She's the one that you seem to have massively ticked off somehow."

I take a deep breath, sucking it into my lungs. Running a hand over my face, I try to figure out what I could say to her.

"Where do I even start? What does Nika need me to say? Because I will say anything if it means she'll take me back." For keeps this time.

His lips twitch. "I would start with that. And telling her that you love her can never steer you wrong."

He picks up a set of keys from the counter by the fridge, holding them out to me. "It sounds like you have a ton of stuff to work out. I have to head back to the city but I'm glad that you are going to meet Nika at the house."

Bowing my head gratefully, I grab the keys and walk him to the front door. "Thanks man. Really."

We hug briefly and then Lars leaves me alone with a million thoughts crowding in on each other.

36

ANNIKA

As we pull up to the big beach house just north of Copenhagen, I look up at the modern structure with a silent sigh. I don't want to be here. I'm a hundred percent sure that all I will think about the entire time I am at this particular house will be Erik.

How nearly three months ago to the day, I kissed him clumsily for the first time. Little did I know, it would spark something so consuming and burn for so long.

I climb out of the car, pressing my lips into a thin line and shouldering my bag. It's a little cooler outside now then it was that day three months ago. But despite the changing weather, everything else is the same. I glanced up at this cloudless sky and wish like hell that Kal and Pippa had just let me stay in Tuscany.

Kal glances at me, leading the way up to the door. "Are you okay with this?"

I shrug even though my heart aches. "We are here already. There's no point in going back, is there?"

Pippa heads up the end of our little party of three. She just joined me and Kalindi in Copenhagen and she smiles at me carefully, like I'm fragile and going to shatter at any moment.

Granted, I did well up at least twice on the ride here so…

Kal opens the door, standing back to let Pippa and me through. From here, I head straight to the stairs. Pippa stops me with a gentle hand on my elbow.

"Don't you want to check out the downstairs? I think there is some new furniture outside…"

I frown at her. "I just want to go lie down. I'm sorry that I'm not psyched up for this mini vacation. I just feel like I am better off being by myself. You can't make anybody depressed if you don't hang out with them."

Kal comes up behind me, putting her arm around my shoulders. She pushes the bag off my shoulder and gives me a little squeeze. "Come outside. Just for a minute. And then you can go upstairs and hide if you really want to."

I roll my eyes but put my bag to the side near the wall. "Okay, okay. Five minutes. Then I can hang out by myself all I want to. Deal?"

Kal shakes her head at me. "Deal, I guess."

Pippa and Kal put their bags beside mine and we all trail toward the back of the house, making our way to the back door. From here, I can see through the plate glass windows that a white tent has been erected over the whole patio area. I squint at it, seeing a flash of movement inside the tent.

I look suspiciously at Pippa. "What is this? Please tell me that you guys didn't do anything foolish. There isn't a party out there, is there?"

Pivot shoots me a sneaky grin. "Nope. Come on, we want to see your face when you see what is in store for you."

Rolling my eyes like it's going out of style, I open the sliding door and step outside. It's only about forty paces from the back door of the house to the back of the tent. Glancing over my shoulder at Kal, I shake my head and take a deep breath. Then I plunge inside.

My eyes widen. My jaw drops.

I look around at the scene before me, disbelieving. It's noisy in here, lots of electronic beeping sounds. The walls and ceiling are painted to look like an arcade, complete with brick façade and glowing neon electric signs. On the floor around me I see tons of machines, the cabinets of video games, an air hockey table, and a whole bank of nothing but Skee-Ball machines.

At the far end of the tent, there is a whole bar set up, bar taps and everything. Behind it, a whole tower of shelves holding liquor bottles sits, lit by glowing neon lights from beneath each shelf.

I take a few steps forward, looking at a small table that has been placed amongst the machines. It has several kinds of junk food, pizza rolls and popcorn and dishes of sugar free toffees. I look around and realize that there are several such tables sprinkled throughout the machines, all throughout the place.

Everywhere I look, it is bright color and flashing lights. The Skee-Ball machines make a raucous dinging.

I turn to look at Pippa and Kal, extremely surprised. This is my private fantasy, not exactly something that the public knows about. It's a dirty little secret of mine. "How did you guys know that I loved the arcade? I can't ever remember sharing that with either of you..."

Kal steps forward, gently turning me around. "You didn't tell us. You told Erik."

I look up and see Erik himself, wearing dark jeans and a white T-shirt. He has an anxious expression on his face, like he is not sure whether I would want to see him or not.

Instantly, my heartbeat starts pounding in my ears. I catch his eye and swallow, not sure what is happening. I feel Kal and Pippa take couple of steps back, receding into the background.

There is only Erik in this room as far as I am concerned. But do I even want to see him?

He runs his fingers through his hair and swallows. I take a step forward, uncertain. He beckons to me, inviting me to come closer.

Taking a deep breath, I take five steps towards him. When I am close enough almost to touch, I stop and look up at him, licking my lips nervously. "What are you doing here, Erik?"

He smiles at me, a dimple flashing in his cheek. "You said to me once that if you could stay in the arcade forever, you would. So, I thought that bringing the arcade to you wouldn't hurt anything." He reaches out, taking my hand. The feel of his hot fingers against my cool ones makes me shiver.

I gaze up at him, not really understanding what's happening. "That doesn't really answer my question, does it?"

He smiles again and shakes his head. "I was trying to think of the best way to beg you to come back to me. And I figured that using a place that we were so happy once could only help my circumstances." He tugs me closer, using his free hand to brush a lock of my hair back and cup my cheek. My eyes fill with tears as I scan his face. He seems so earnest.

"What about the future?" I whisper.

He pulls me against his big body. I lean my head back, not sure that this is even real. Ever so slowly, he starts talking. "I have realized a few things since you left. I realize I don't have any control over what may happen. I can't predict the future. But one thing I can do is be with you, be whatever you need, for as long as you will let me. And I realized how foolish I've been to push you away for something that's completely out of your control. I'm sorry, Annika."

I bite my lip. "That doesn't really solve any of the things you were really worried about though, does it?"

He laces our fingers together, his eyes burning into mine. "None of that really matters though. Does it? I mean, there is an income disparity between us. There is no denying that. And you are much too young for me. But I can't help the way I feel."

He hesitates. "I love you, Annika. So much that it hurts. And if you are willing to set aside all of these shortcomings that I have, I will promise that you will have me for as long as you want me."

My breath leaves my lungs. It takes a second to get my bearings. "What are you saying, Erik?"

He smiles at me softly, that dimple flashing in his cheek again. "If you're asking whether I brought a ring with me, the answer is yes. I don't know if you want that though." He tilts his head, his gaze dropping to my lips. "I love you, Nika. I'm crazy about you. And I'll do whatever I have to do to have you by my side. Even if that means appearing at public functions as nothing more than your boyfriend."

My brow furrows. "Oh, Erik. I was so destroyed when we broke up. I don't know if I can do that again. I don't know that I will survive."

He meets my eye again, stepping back for a second. Then he pulls a ring box out of his pocket, dropping to one knee. My hands fly up, covering my mouth. My eyes widen. "You're going to do this right now?"

He opens the ring box. I'm expecting a gorgeous, dazzling platinum and diamond ring. But instead of that, the ring he won me at the arcade sits nestled amongst the velvet. I start crying at that, the fact that he managed to keep that ring.

It means more to me than I can say.

"See, Annika? I do know you," he says, grinning. "And I would gladly pledge my life to you rather than see you walk away from me again. Give me your hand."

I hesitate for a moment, wiping my eyes. Then I take a deep breath and extend my shaking hand towards him.

His fingers are warm when he takes my hand.

"Ready?"

I manage a nod. "Yes, Erik. You have to know that my answer is yes."

He grins. "Let me get through my speech, woman."

Shaking my head, I grin. "Okay."

He takes a deep breath. Looking at me, his gaze fears me. "Nika, you are wise and funny and brave and extremely compassionate. I would be lucky to spend my life with you. Will you do me the honor of becoming my bride?"

Tears overwhelm me, making it almost impossible to speak. I nod enthusiastically, forcing out the word. "Yes..."

He slides the ring up my fourth finger, a grin on his lips. "I'm a lucky man."

He stands up and pulls me close, bending me back before kissing me so totally and completely that I am left breathless. I raise my hand to his cheek, cupping his face and feeling so overjoyed that I can't even speak.

That's when Kal and Pippa stepped back into my line of sight, both of them looking pleased as punch. Kal reaches out a hand, touching my arm gently. "We're so happy for you. And I will just assume that you forgive us for our little deception..."

I sniffle. "I think so, this time."

I hug Kal and Pippa, struggling just to breathe. Erik stands back and lets us have a moment. Then he pulls at my hand.

"Come on. I got four Skee-Ball machines. I think that this calls for some champagne and an epic Skee-Ball showdown."

I grin at him, kissing him on the lips. I swear, my heart is so full just from looking at him that I'm on the cusp of crying again. "That sounds perfect."

He grabs me by the waist and lifts me in the air. "I love you, Nika."

Tears gather at the corners of my eyes. "I love you too, Erik."

He squeezes my hand then starts toward the back corner of the tent, a smile on his lips.

37

ERIK

My grip tightens on Nika's waist as I look around the crowded room. She's in her finest, wearing a gown of gold lamé that looks like it was painted on. And I am hovering beside her, an anxious man in a tux. I feel like at any moment, I could be replaced by any decent looking man my age.

Annika reaches over and takes my hand, squeezing it as she looks at me. "We are almost done. Really. This is a pretty fair exchange for stepping away from royal duty."

I look down into her beautiful face and I can't help but smile. "I know. The royal family has to make a big deal over our engagement. I get that. I just… I haven't seen Stellan and I am sort of…" I trail off, shrugging.

My gaze wanders up, taking in everyone in the ballroom again. Nika gets drawn into yet another conversation about her ring. We did the proper thing and went to an actual jeweler, spending a fuck ton of money to nab the perfect princess cut platinum and diamond ring.

She still wears the other ring on a little chain around her neck, refusing to take it off. And I have to say, part of me loves her for that.

I fidget with the coins in my pants pockets, resisting the urge to check my watch for the five millionth time. Nika is right; this is a small price to pay for the relative anonymity that we asked for. In exchange, we've worked out a much stepped down plan with the royal press office. They get her one weekend a month.

The rest of the time, Annika and I can roll around like two happy clams at the royal beach house. Since I purchased the house outright, I will never have to worry about following the royal rules. With the purchase of my second property, my stable of homes has begun to look quite comfortable.

I spot Mr. Earl, his rumpled tux and his graying hair unmistakable. He's one of King Stellan's advisors and he corners me, clapping me on the shoulder and wishing me good luck. "I have to say, we will miss you around here. I know that the rumors about you stealing off with our own Princess Annika are rampant around here… But I still think you are a great fellow."

"Thank you. I have already branched out and started my own venture capital firm. I think Princess Annika and I will be just fine."

Mr. Earl looks puzzled. "Venture capital? Isn't that a little out of your wheelhouse? I would think that you would just apply for a similar position with another high profile person."

I struggle to maintain a blank expression. "Yeah, well. I'm going to miss working at the palace. But I am sure you will be glad to know that I will be working to make the princess happy. And what makes her happy is not being in the spotlight." A little lie, but this is politics, after all. If Mr. Earl were being truthful with me or anyone else here, he would have come out of the closet a long time ago.

Mr. Earl smiles. "So, there's no truth to the fact that you were unceremoniously fired, then?"

I arch a brow. "Nope. I don't know where you heard that."

I see Nika moving away, turning her head back for just a second to make sure that I'm okay. I bow to Mr. Earl, excusing myself.

One of the palace employees manages to step between me and Nika, bringing me up short. I looked down into his dark features with a frown. He smiles nervously.

"If you don't mind, there is a phone call for you, sir."

I take a deep breath and nod. "Lead the way."

I touch Nika shoulder as I go by her, smiling faintly. The employee leads me out of the grand ballroom and across the hall to an empty office. There's nothing in the room except for a desk and an old, gold-plated telephone. I look at the landline, a little surprised. But the palace employee merely bows, letting himself out of the room and closing the door. I sigh, picking up the phone.

"Hello?"

"It's your father."

He coughs loudly, clearing his throat. I narrow my eyes at the phone.

"So... what, now we are in fact related? Because I can definitely give you the name of at least five nurses that will swear up and down that we are not blood relations, according to you."

He coughs again. "You think that you can just get married to one of them royals without even so much as telling your father about it? You're spoiled. That's one of the reasons why I didn't need you or anyone else hanging about my bedside, wringing your hands."

I pinch the bridge of my nose. If I had been told that my father was the one on the phone, I might have just skipped this conversation altogether. "Have you called to wish your son congratulations, then?"

He guffaws. "You think you're so great and so smart. You'll see. You're not any better than me. When the little princess figures out that you are just a haircut in a suit, she will be done with you. And when that happens, don't come crying..."

I grit my teeth. "Shut up! I should've said that to you years ago. Just shut up! If you have anything else to say about Annika or our relationship, about which you know nothing at all, you can just keep it to yourself. You're a hateful old man. And I fully expect an apology the next time that you decide to call me. Otherwise? Don't call me."

I slam the phone down, running my hands down my sleeves and pulling out my cuffs. I'm furious, of course.

But it feels good to have said what I wanted to say for so long to my father. There are some people that just can't change or be helped. I guess my father is just one of them. And I will do my best to do better than he did, if Annika and I ever have kids.

That's years down the road, anyway.

I take a deep, calming breath and center myself. And then I pull the door open, striding out into the hallway.

A tall, dark-haired man dressed in a tuxedo stands by the doorway to the ballroom, looking on quietly. When I get closer, he turns his head and I see that it is Stellan.

I feel like he punches me in the gut just by looking at me. I don't see Margot anywhere. He clenches his fists when he sees me, his gaze narrowing.

My expression hardens. I guess it's going to be one of those days where I get a lot of things off my chest, all at once. So be it.

I stalk up to him, keeping an imperious expression on my face. He watches me warily, holding a hand up to preempt me.

"I come in peace," he says, frowning.

I fold my arms across my chest, unamused. "What are you doing here? I thought you were supposed to be on your honeymoon."

He jerks his head inside the ballroom. I look inside and see a tiny woman with pink hair hugging my fiancée. Margot looks like a pixie, beaming up at Annika. The hard knot in my stomach unclenches just a tiny bit.

Stellan sighs. "I didn't realize that you two were in love," he comments. He looks over at me, pursing his lips. "It seems awfully fast though."

I arch a brow at him. "I think my courtship with Nika actually lasted longer than yours. How long did you and Margot make it before your engagement was announced?"

His lips thin. "Don't."

I just shrug. "I won't apologize for doing exactly what you did."

"The difference is my baby sister. Why did you have to choose her, of all the fucking women in the world?"

My gaze narrows on his face. "It wasn't a choice. You don't fall in love because you want to, in my experience. It just happened. And I'm fucking lucky that I fell for Nika." My lips twitch and my gaze is pulled back to her. "You might not know this, but she's the best person I know. While you guys weren't looking, she was growing one hell of a feisty, funny personality."

Stellan is silent for half a minute. "It's nice to hear someone stick up for her."

I slide him a careful look. "I told you. I love Annika."

He drags in a deep breath, pinning me with that eerie gaze of his. That look wouldn't have been out of place on Nika's face.

"I'm not just going to forgive you."

"Did I ask for your forgiveness?"

He purses his lips. "No."

Brushing the front of my suit jacket off, I give him a look. "As far as I'm concerned, we aren't even friends anymore. You called me garbage. Friends don't do that, especially not when they know that word has been used against me by my father."

Stellan appears taken aback by that. "Ah." He scrunches up his face. "I'm sorry. I was angry."

"You were a douche."

He gives me a flat look. "You slept with my little sister!"

I roll my eyes. "Your friendship has been very important to me, Stellan. When you kicked me out of your wedding and Nika wouldn't talk to me, I realized how much my life and yours were intertwined." I frown a little. "But I think I have to draw a line in the sand. If I have to choose between you or Annika, I choose her. I would choose her a thousand times over."

One corner of his mouth lifts briefly. "As much as it pains me to say this, I understand. If I were put in the same position, I would choose my wife over you." He scrunches up his face. "I don't want to have to choose, though."

"Well, neither do I."

We look at each other for a long moment. Then he glances away.

"We have extended our honeymoon for two more weeks. After we get back, maybe we should talk. We can even talk about you coming back to work for the family."

I hesitate. "I would like to figure things out between us. But… I won't be returning to the palace as an employee. I've devoted my life to you and the royal family. Now it's time to do something different."

Stellan gives me a long look. "You're a part of the royal family now, don't forget."

I smirk. "I have better things to focus on." I nod to the ballroom, where Margot and Annika are making their way over to us. "I have a feeling you do too."

Stellan stretches, putting his arms over his head. "Yeah. I guess I do."

He smiles as Annika comes over, hugging me as she looks at him shyly. I slide my arm around her waist and pull her close.

"Congrats, little sister."

She beams at him. "Thanks, Stellan."

Margot grabs his hand and looks at Nika and me. "We have a plane to catch. But let me just tell you one more time: I couldn't be happier for the both of you."

I look down at Nika, my grip tightening on her waist. "Thanks."

Leaning down, I kiss her lips and smile. Stellan rolls his eyes. "Okay. We're late. But… when we get back, we should all celebrate privately."

I give Annika a squeeze. She smiles at her brother. "That sounds lovely."

Margot and Stellan say their goodbyes. And I can breathe a little easier, knowing that my biological father might be in the wind, but my adopted family still stands strong.

38

ANNIKA

"Ugh," I sigh, dropping the final box I've packed on top of a stack of boxes. Stretching out my back, I look around the living room area of the room I called my own.

Erik comes in, a little sweaty from moving boxes around in my former bedroom. I bite my lip and eye him. He smiles at me, sipping water from a bottle.

"Can you believe we're leaving the palace?" he asks.

I shake my head. "No. I really can't. But at the same time, I'm very excited to go. Now that the seasons are changing, I have a wild hair to go up to a little chalet somewhere. It'll be all cold and snowy. And we can hang out by the fire, just the two of us..."

He arches a brow at me. "Naked, I assume. Because that is how I plan to see you the first four months of us living together."

I bite my lip, smiling. He sets his water down and comes over to give me a hug and pat my butt. I lean my head back and look up at him, offering my mouth up for a kiss.

He brushes his lips over my own but then he pulls back with a sigh. "You are a temptation, that's for sure. But if we don't get on the road soon, we won't make it up to the beach house by dark."

I scrunch up my face. "You need to start calling it *our* house. We own it. And no one else does. It's just a big, beautiful house that happens to be by the beach."

He makes a fake sound of aggravation, a little *grrr*. Then he kisses me on the lips again and starts to head out to the car, picking up a box of my necessities as he goes. He calls over his shoulder. "I'll be right back. When I come back with help, that should speed things along."

I cock my head to the side and watch him walk away, admiring his ass as he goes. Damn. I am still over the moon that I get to see him naked for the rest of my life… What a lucky girl I am.

Sitting down on the pair of couches, I pull out my phone and scroll through my private Instagram. It's mostly pictures of cute animals and feeds from close friends. This way I can still use social media and yet not get overwhelmed by the public.

I see an email from Dr. Baker, my new psychologist. She asks if Tuesday afternoon works for my schedule and I happily reply that I have nothing planned.

That's a weird feeling. Not having to run every single thing by the royal press office is exhilarating.

A knock at the doorway draws my attention up. I look to find Momse standing outside the door, her steel gray skirt suit perfectly complementing her silver updo. When I take too long to invite her in, she narrows her gaze and clears her throat.

"Come in, come in," I say, standing up awkwardly. I probably look like a mess. I've been moving all day and I feel like I look a little squirrely.

Momse walks in, her sharp blue eyes absorbing every detail of the room and my outfit, which is just a pair of black leggings and an old white T-shirt.

"Hello, Annika. I see you have indeed gone through with your little move." One corner of her mouth turns down. "Where is Erik?"

I sweep my hand over the couch, gesturing for her to sit. She perches on it, looking unhappy. Though now that I think about it, when has Momse ever looked happy?

"He's here. He's done almost everything, actually. I've just been directing, mostly."

She crosses her ankles and smooths out her skirts. "Well, that's as it should be. Not only are you the woman of the two of you, you are a princess and he is a commoner. I know you are moving away but there's no cause to forget that."

I repress a sigh. "Are you here to tell me something in particular, Momse? Because I really have a lot left to do today."

That's not true exactly, but it's a coping strategy that Dr. Baker and I came up with.

She tilts her head, looking at me. "Well. Since you are moving out and you will not be under my watch any longer, I thought I would just take a moment to..." She pauses.

My breath catches. For second, as sure that she's about to say something terrible to me. I brace myself for it, blinking my eyes carefully.

But she surprises me.

"I want to say that I was the youngest child in my family. I had seven older brothers and two older sisters. I felt like I spent most of my life being passed over and not made a priority. When I got the chance to marry your grandfather, the king... I jumped at it."

My eyes widen. I lean back, clearing my throat. "Whoa. I didn't know that you came from such a large family."

She gives me a cold little smile. "Yes, well. Family planning wasn't practiced with any regularity back then. Anyway, I wanted to say... I know that being the youngest child can have its disadvantages. And believe it or not, I struggled with being in the public eye when I first married the king."

My brows rise. "Wait, you did? You seem so... poised."

She gives me a smile. "Yes, it would seem that way now. But back in the beginning, my family name was often questioned. It was a lot of strangers, picking over whether my name was good enough for the new king. It was a load of bullshit, if I am perfectly honest about it."

"I had no idea," I tell Momse.

Momse leans closer to me, smiling that cool smile again. "I'm just saying that I have been where you are. Sure, the details are a little different. But I wanted you to know that I do care about you. Things just coincided oddly. Stellan ended up needing so much of my time..." She looks away out the window, frowning. "I suppose I thought that you would be all right here by yourself."

I bite my lip, shifting in my seat uncomfortably. When Momse looks up again, her gaze spears me.

"I'm afraid that I haven't done a very good job with you. Honestly, I don't have the relationship that I would like to have with any of you aside from Stellan. It's… regrettable, to say the least."

If I wasn't working to actively keep my expression straight, my jaw would probably drop. Is this a Momse's way of telling me that she is sorry?

"I… I mean, everything turned out fine." I mumble. "Thanks for coming to me and telling me how you feel, though."

Momse smiles tightly, inhaling deeply. Then she uncrosses her legs and stands up. I hurry to stand up to.

She extends her hand, and I step forward, thinking that we are going to exchange some kind of awkward handshake or something.

Momse surprises me again by pulling me close for a quick, tight hug. Then she steps back, tears in the corners of her eyes. She looks at me.

"Be well, Annika. Please come back to visit regularly."

I open my mouth to answer. She turns, quickly walking out of the room. I stare after her, unsure of what just happened.

Just as Momse leaves, Erik comes through the door. He does a double take, frowning at Momse as she hustles out.

"What was that all about?"

I squint after her. "I think she came in here to apologize. I'm not entirely sure though." I laugh a little, confused.

Erik walks up to me, pulling me down onto the couch again. He seems tired but also, he sounds pretty content. "That's good, I think. We can use all of the royals on our side that we can get."

Burying myself against the wall of his chest, I find comfort in his arms. He kisses the crown of my head absently.

I relax into his hold, feeling like I finally found the person that can make me feel at home.

He picks up my left hand, admiring the engagement ring that sparkles there. "I love you. You know that, right?"

I look up at him, a slow grin spreading across my face. "I do know that. Thanks. And I love you too, if that weren't painfully obvious by now."

He toys with my ring, unable to stop himself from smiling. "It is painfully obvious. But it goes both ways."

I hug him tightly, feeling my heart swell three sizes. I'm not sure what the future holds for either of us, but I know we will face it together.

And with Erik by my side, I could not feel better about the future.

39

PIPPA

I'M STANDING IN MY LITTLE APARTMENT IN COPENHAGEN, staring blankly at the peeling bright yellow paint on the kitchen wall. I reach out and trace my fingertips along a seam above the stove, a silent sigh on my lips.

It was a long day at *Politiken*, the newspaper where I work. I feel like I've been wrung out and all my mental energy has been drained away. Now I'm just waiting for my little microwave burrito to be heated through so I can eat and pass out.

My phone chimes, stirring me. I look at it. Lars's photo pops up, a dark haired devil with a cocksure grin. Lars is the king of Denmark's younger brother, one of family of five. He's actual living, breathing royalty and I...

I am a fool for even thinking about what spending a night in his bed would be like. Being underneath his big body as he growls commands and pulls moans from my lips...

It's forbidden. And yet still, my heart squeezes at the very mention of his name.

I know he's my best friend.

I know I should cherish what we already have.

I know I shouldn't long for him to touch me.

And yet, even getting a text from him excites me beyond reason.

I shiver as I check the text.

I'm coming upstairs.

Goosebumps break out over my skin. I close my eyes and hold my cellphone close to my now rapidly-beating heart.

A few second later, I hear the slide of a key being turned in the lock on the front door. I'm much too tired for any visitors tonight. But Lars has always done exactly what he wanted, exactly when he wants.

This is no exception.

Screwing up my face, I press the pause button on the microwave. Lars walks into my shoddy little apartment, ducking his dark head slightly as he enters. He's so tall that my building's prewar design is really at odds with his height. When he straightens up, he looks at me with his trademark devastating smirk.

I cast a look over his tuxedo, which makes him look ridiculously fetching.

"Hello, Pippa," he purrs.

I swallow, my eyes widening. "Lars." Pushing back several strands of my long, fiery copper hair, I watch as he closes the door behind himself. I spread my hands down the skirt of my gray silk dress, drawing a breath. "It's awfully late. Shouldn't you be on a date with some unnamed mystery blonde?"

His smirk deepens, his aquamarine eyes sparkling. "I was in the middle of a date when I was summoned unceremoniously to the palace."

I fidget. "Why are you here, Lars?"

He wanders toward the living room of my cramped flat, leaving me to follow. He looks around the tiny couch and the ancient television that is stacked atop several light blue milk crates.

Every surface is covered with reading material, books and magazines and newspaper clippings. Piles spill into piles; the television screen is actually blocked by a towering stack of literature. I admit that I'm a bit of a mess and I'm ashamed to say that there is nowhere to sit.

Wrinkling my nose, I automatically start to clear off the sofa, my cheeks burning. I gather an armful of books, but I'm not sure where to put them.

"Let me just find a place for these…" I murmur, casting my gaze around the small space. I find a spot on the very top of another pile of books, biting my lower lip hard as I turn around.

"Pippa, I don't need to sit down," he says, grabbing my hand. His touch is electric. When I glance up at him, his blue gaze sears me through.

I raise an eyebrow. "What do you need?"

He smirks a bit, pulling me a little closer, making me look up into his face. From this distance, a hair's breadth away from our bodies touching, I feel adrenaline coursing through my veins.

"I need a favor."

My forehead creases. My mouth turns down just a bit at the corners. This is what he does, what he has always done. He uses his charm, knowing quite well how smoothly hypnotic his presence can be. I've seen him do it to hundreds of women in the years that I've known him.

Usually he doesn't use it on *me*, though.

I pull out of his grasp, moving back a half step. "What is it?"

His expression grows intense. "I need you to pretend that I have asked you to marry me and you have said yes."

I swear, I don't mean to laugh. But it bubbles up from deep within my chest and bursts out of my lips, a snort of disbelief and a surprised chuckle all at once.

"What?" I ask, the word coming out strangled.

He squints at me. "I slept with the wrong diplomat's daughter."

I fold my arms across my chest, trying to slow my racing heart. "Again? How many times do you have to get caught before someone banishes you from the whole country of Denmark?"

His gaze tightens on my face. "It's really not funny. And now unless I have a really good excuse, I'm going to have to join the navy. Obviously, I don't want that. I mean, have you seen the inside of a submarine? That would seriously cramp my style."

A low throb starts at my temple. I rub it with one hand, staring at Lars. "And this has what to do with me, exactly?"

He steps closer, snagging my free hand and bringing it to rest against the hard wall of his chest. "I need a fake fiancée.

Momse told me today that unless I settle down and get married, I'm going to have to join the military."

I push my cheek out with my tongue. "What is stopping you from finding the right girl?"

Someone royal. Or at least someone without the… let's call them *complications* that my history presents. I know very well the list of reasons why I can't be tied to someone like me.

I'm a fraud.

I'm a fake and a liar.

I'm not who I say I am.

And that's only the *beginning* of my troubles if anyone finds out.

He gives me a wicked little grin. "You're saying I should sign my death warrant, then? Because that is what being told that I have to get married feels like. I don't want to be tied down. I don't want to be smothered. I just want to keep living like I do now."

I shake my head. "Lars, really—"

He slides his hands down my back and pulls my hips against his. My breath catches in my chest as I gaze up into those pretty blue eyes of his.

I'm *this close* to pushing up on my tiptoes and pressing my lips against his.

Arching a brow, he utters the magic word. "I really need this. Please, Pips? Do it for me?"

And just like that, all my defenses melt away.

Of course I will do it for him.

How can I not?

Lars sees the expression of my face change and knows my answer before I even say it.

"Okay," I whisper.

He's already folding his strong arms around me, pulling me into the shelter of his body. "Ahh, thanks, Pips. I knew you would come through."

I sink into the bear hug, my eyes fluttering closed. He's sinfully warm. His smell, pure and clean and masculine, is driving me wild right now.

I inhale of lungful of his scent, feeling like a fool. "That's me. Reliable old Pippa saves the day again."

Lars pulls back. I look up at him with a dreamy-eyed expression and he grins. "Should we wake the jewelers at Tiffany's up right now? Shit, I should've stopped on the way here and gotten you a ring—"

I push him away, eyeing him firmly. "There will have to be rules. A firm time limit, for instance. And... no physical contact."

He gives me a funny look. "It's going to take a little hugging and kissing to convince my family, don't you think?"

I squint at him. "I mean when we are alone."

He rolls his eyes. "Yeah, sure. I will behave like a proper gentleman, if that's what you want."

I shake my head, crossing my arms. "No one has ever thought to call you a proper gentleman, I'm fairly certain."

Lars grins at me, his eyes glittering. "If that's what it takes, I'm willing to try."

I shoot him a look. "I'm regretting this already."

He tilts his head, considering me. "Should we go for a drink to celebrate?"

Stepping closer to him, I turn him around and begin marching him toward the door. "We can figure it all out tomorrow. For now, I want to eat something before I pass out."

He chuckles, opening the front door. He catches my hand and gives me a squeeze. "You really are the best, Pippa. You know that, right?"

The corners of my mouth tighten. "Do me a favor. Don't sleep with anyone, okay? If this little deception is going to work, you'll have to play along and not be your usual man-whore self for a while."

Lars smirks at me. "You got it, love of my life."

For a second, I can't even wrap my head around that. My heartbeat speeds up. If he had any idea of how long I've waited to hear those words…

But then he turns, showing me his black-clad back as he disappears down the hall.

"Goodnight, Pippa…" he calls over his shoulder.

I watch him disappear, slumping against the doorframe when I hear the downstairs front door open and close.

I am in so much trouble.

I know that.

If anyone does the slightest bit of digging, I could be exposed.

My life would cease to be my own at that point.

But I can still feel my heart racing, feel the heat of his body pressed against mine. I can sense the excited energy that follows Lars in his wake, everywhere he goes.

Deep in my soul, I know that I shouldn't have agreed to be his fake fiancée.

Oh god.

What have I gotten myself into?

Turning, I close my door and head back to my sad microwave dinner.

You can pre-order Royal Fake Fiancé here.

40

Thank you for reading His Forbidden Princess! I know if you liked this book, you will LOVE Lars and Pippa's story, Royal Fake Fiancé!

There's a little bit more of Erik and Annika, just waiting for you! Get the bonus chapters — once the beginning of the story — right now when you sign up for Vivian's mailing list! Head to https://BookHip.com/LMWGNK for more info.

Vivian likes to write about troubled, deeply flawed alpha males and the fiery, kick-ass women who bring them to their knees.

Vivian's lasting motto in romance is a quote from a favorite song: "Soulmates never die."

Be sure to follow Vivian through her Instagram or join her email list to keep up with all the awesome giveaways, author videos, ARC opportunities, and more!

VIVIAN'S WORKS

RUINED CASTLE SERIES - PRE-ORDER NOW
Forbidden Billionaire Romance
THE BEAST
THE NANNY

The Caress

Broken Slipper series
Forbidden Billionaire Romance
The Patron
The Dancer
The Embrace
Possessive

Dirty royals
Forbidden Royal Romance
The Royal Rebel
The Wicked Prince
His Forbidden Princess
Royal Fake Fiancé

Lyon Dynasty world
Dark Billionaire Romance
King's Capture
Queen's Sacrifice

Sinfully rich series
Steamy Billionaire Romance
Sinful Fling
Sinful Enemy
Sinful Boss
Sinful Chance
Sinfully Rich

His and Hers series
His Best Friend's Little Sister
Claiming Her Innocence
His To Keep
His Virgin